DO WE NOT BLEED?

DO WE NOT BLEED?

BY

Daniel Taylor

DO WE NOT BLEED?

Slant
An Imprint of Wipf and Stock Publishers
199 W. 8th Ave., Suite 3
Eugene, OR 97401

www.wipfandstock.com

PAPERBACK ISBN: 978-1-4982-9987-9
HARDCOVER ISBN: 978-1-4982-9989-3
EBOOK ISBN: 978-1-4982-9988-6

Cataloguing-in-Publication data:

Names: Taylor, Daniel, 1948–.
Title: Do we not bleed? / Daniel Taylor.
Description: Eugene, OR: Slant, 2017.
Identifiers: ISBN 978-1-4982-9987-9 (paperback) | ISBN 978-1-4982-9989-3 (hardcover) | ISBN 978-1-4982-9988-6 (ebook)
Subjects: LCSH: Fiction.
Classification: PS3570.A92727 D75 2017 (print) | PS3570.A92727 (ebook)

Manufactured in the U.S.A.

For those whom we loved and from whom we learned.

If you prick us, do we not bleed?
if you tickle us, do we not laugh?
if you poison us, do we not die?
    —Shylock, *Merchant of Venice*, Act 3, Scene 1

"Consider the lilies . . ."

ONE

I'M BETTER. THANKS FOR asking.

Not cured of course. What would that mean anyway? Cured of the human condition? There's only one cure for that and few seem eager for it. Some of course have embraced the cure, fled life—the saddest ones among us. May God receive back their souls.

(There I go again, invoking beings I no longer believe exist.)

No, not cured. But better. No more voices—so far. Less mind noise. More purposeful action. (Judy should be proud of me.)

Like working here at the group home for instance. Me and six disciples—each of them wounded, each of them a wonder. Me their patched-together Jesus, they the faithful half dozen, looking to me for the next meal, the next activity, the next tock in answer to this moment's tick.

Actually they don't need me at all. They serve the god Routine and I am just the local priest, one in a long line of Servants of the Schedule. They know What Comes Next much better than I do, but they instinctively grant me a measure of authority, because, after all, I can tell time. I can also count change, use a can opener, and measure out flour—something most of them cannot do at present, though we're working on it.

When I brought my sister Judy back to New Directions last December, after my near-disastrous attempt to take care of her on my own, I had no idea I would be joining the circus myself. I thought I'd just unload her suitcase, kiss her goodbye, and get on with my own deconstruction. But there was this sign in the office offering a part-time job staffing a group home on the campus. And since I felt I was clearly a part-timer in many ways, including metaphysically, I thought maybe the offer was intended for me.

You know—intended, as in fated, as in meant to be. Never mind that there seem to be no certifiable Intenders or Intentions in the universe.

So here I am, hanging out with the . . . what's the word? With the . . . you've got to be careful, because the right word changes regularly, and they're very jumpy around here about getting the right word right. I think I'll just leave it at "hanging out."

So here I am, hanging out with Judy. And Ralph, and Jimmy, and Bonita, and J.P. And with Billy, who lives in Billy World—population: one.

And we're about to start a summer football game.

New Directions is very big on real-life activities for the residents. ("Residents" is a safe term at present, as is "clients." Who knows about tomorrow?) Apparently people in Normal Life play football for fun (I think the Kennedy clan started it), so the activities staff has organized a game of flag football for the enjoyment and social development of all.

Our particular residence, Carlson Group Home, is a big contributor. Ralph is the center, a fitting spot for a fiftyish man of short stature and legendary strength. When I took everyone to the first *Lord of the Rings* movie, Jimmy pointed at Gimli on the screen and yelled, "Hello Ralph!"—much to the delight of the others. Ralph doesn't have a beard, but he is built like a Tolkien dwarf—short, broad, strong, a man of few words. When you talk to him, he has two dominant responses. If you instruct him to do something and he accepts it, he says "Da dooey," turns and goes and does it. If he doesn't accept it, he gives you a dismissive wave of the hand, says "Ah phooey," and turns in the same way and goes about his business. You have as much chance of changing his mind as getting an avalanche to go back uphill.

Jimmy is the running back. He campaigned to be quarterback because he knows that's the position the girls go for and Jimmy is the quintessential ladies' man. He's always campaigning for something. He is the youngster of the group home, maybe twenty-five, with sandy brown hair that he is constantly adjusting with a toss of the head, and very verbal, some would say verbose. Jimmy knows enough of the therapeutic lingo to self-diagnose. He likes to announce to staff and strangers alike, "I'm high functioning," with a sigh and condescending glance toward the other residents, as if to say, "We have quite a load on our hands here, don't we?"

In a shockingly gender-stereotypical move, Judy and Bonita have been informed in advance that they are to be cheerleaders. J.P. as well. This gives them a chance to dress the part. I'm responsible for costuming and the only thing I can think of are sweaters. I'm a severely-lapsed Baptist and a product of the time when cheerleader meant tight sweaters, not cleavage and bare midriffs. Bonita isn't interested much in the sweater, but she is adamant about the accessories: "Get me some pond-ponds, Mote."

Bonita usually calls me by my last name, Mote, unless she wants something. Then she plays the Sweetheart of Sigma Chi, ducks her head shyly and calls me Jon. As in, "Please, Jon, could I have my pop now?" And a quite remarkable head it is, too. About the size of a tennis ball. Okay, maybe a cantaloupe, but noticeably smaller than it should be even in relation to her very slight body. She weighs in at around ninety pounds, stands less than five feet tall, and, with hips substantially wider than her almost non-existent shoulders, gives the general appearance of a bowling pin wearing a fright wig. (Or, for those old enough, a Shmoo.)

By the way, if you happen to say no to her sweet request for the can of pop, you can expect a lightning quick change of tactics: "Damn it, Mote, give me my pop!" So when Bonita says she wants pom-poms (which I take her "pond-ponds" to mean), I make sure to come up with pom-poms (courtesy of the playroom for the youngest residents in the main building).

Judy, as always, tries her best to get along. "Well, Jon, if cheer . . . cheerleaders wear sweaters, then I . . . I should say . . . I will wear a sweater my own self." Now she is standing on the sidelines next to Bonita, putting her little fists in the air, and yelling, "Go . . . go . . . I should say, go team!" J.P. insists on wearing a suit and bow tie. He simply stands there, at attention, cautiously smiling.

Billy seems the least likely of all the participants. I don't know how old Billy is and can't even guess. More than thirty and less than a hundred is the best I can do. Billy is not with us. And never has been. He spends most of his time looking upward, out of squint eyes that dart from side to side, searching the skies (or the ceiling) for God knows what (there I go again). He has dull red hair and spastic motions, jerking his arms, stiff fingers splaying, and twitching his head in obedience to the electrical storm in his brain. I feel a strange kinship. (I know all about storms in the brain.)

The spectators for the game consist primarily of other residents of New Directions, staff, and parents. Cassandra Pettigrew, the executive director, is chatting it up with Mr. and Mrs. Wagner, big-time contributors and parents of Abby Wagner, one of the residents training for independent living. I made a big mistake with Abby when I first started at New Directions six months ago. The first time I saw her, I thought she was on staff. I was sitting on the steps of the group home taking a smoke break when Abby walked by from the main building. I remember watching her and thinking she was good-looking and wondering what her job here might be. I said hello as she passed, and she immediately changed direction and came and sat by me.

I introduced myself and asked her what she did at New Directions. She didn't say anything, but smiled and touched my knee. I jumped up like her hand was a snake. She laughed, stood, and walked away toward the apartments for independent living, turning as she entered the building to give me a little wave.

The facilities manager, Mr. Springer, walks Billy out to his position as a split end. How he would think that Billy could ever see a football coming, much less catch it, is beyond me. But then I decide this too is fitting. Billy, the Lonesome End, like the once-famous Army receiver in the 1950s, stationed out near the boundary, alone, away from his companions in the huddle, and yet one of them. On the team, so to speak, but with an assignment all his own.

Mr. Springer is a model of purposeful bustle, aligning each player on the offense by position. A volunteer father is doing the same for the defense. It takes forever. They put one of the younger residents from the dorms, Ronnie, beside Ralph to play guard. When they turn to place another at tackle, Ronnie walks away toward the sidelines. Mr. Springer runs to get him, but by the time he gets Ronnie back next to Ralph, the tackle has laid down on the ground and started groaning. Ralph tells him to get up and shut up and he immediately does so. Meanwhile Ronnie has started talking with the defender standing across from him. They shake hands and then embrace. The defender points at Ronnie and announces to no one in particular, "He's my buddy." They both beam.

The choice for quarterback strikes me as strange. Jack is a silent teenager from the independent living units. I have never heard him speak, but perhaps he does. What's clear is that he is fast. He is warming up by running full speed in random directions, under the tutelage of Mrs. Francis, the crafts coordinator. He runs with studied intensity, hunched over at the waist but with a long, smooth stride.

Mr. Springer calls Jack over to put him in position so they can start the game. They have decided not to have a kick-off. Why tempt Apep, Discordia, Morgoth, and the other gods of chaos? They will just start at midfield and hope for the best.

Mr. Springer places the ball in front of Ralph and tells him to bend over and then hike it to the quarterback when Jack is ready. Mr. Springer demonstrates. Luckily, Ralph says "Da dooey" instead of "Ah phooey" and bends down and holds on to the ball.

"Now Jack, you come up behind Ralph and put your hands under here, like this, and then say 'hike!' real loud."

But Jack will have none of it. He crosses his arms, putting each hand in his arm pits, and shakes his head. Jimmy, from the running back position, immediately sizes up the situation.

"That's inappropriate touching, Mr. Springer. Ms. Pettigrew says if anyone touches you there, you should tell one of the staff right away. No sir-ree. You shouldn't be telling Jack to put his hands in there. No way, no how."

Jimmy reinforces the speech with vigorous head shaking. And when others see it, they do the same. A moral consensus of shaking heads in a relativistic world.

Mr. Springer is clearly alarmed.

"I only want him to get the damn football, Jimmy. I'm not saying . . . . Well, no problem. We'll use the shotgun formation. That's better for Jack anyway. Jack, you back up three steps."

Jack just looks at him. Jimmy counts out three on his fingers, touching each fingertip with the index finger of his other hand, and flashes them at Jack. High functioning indeed.

Mr. Springer guides Jack back a ways behind Ralph and places Jimmy to his side. He tells everyone to get set, and both the offense and the defense adopt various stances, some very creative. Billy stands out near the side-lines, twitching and gazing at the clouds and humming. Bonita and Judy are trying to yell "Go team" together, but the hitches in Judy's cadence have Bonita flustered. To stay in sync with Judy, she is yelling something like, "Go the hell team."

Mr. Springer backs away and shouts, "hike!" Ralph picks the ball up, turns, and tosses it back to Jack. Jack catches the ball and stares at it in his hands. The others, as dramatically as possible, hold their positions. No one moves.

"Get Jack!" Mr. Springer yells in exasperation.

The command animates everyone and they all, offense and defense alike, start toward Jack. He runs toward the sideline, as though to sweep around the end. It looks like a real football play. Momentarily. Jack runs across the sideline, between Judy and Bonita, knocking a pom-pom out of Bonita's hand.

"Watch where you're going, asshole."

Jack keeps running, football tight under his arm, toward the dorms, never looking back, ignoring everyone calling to him to return. A few members of the defense are in hot pursuit, yelling, "Get Jack!" The others remain on the field giving each other high-fives for a job well done.

There isn't another ball.

Ralph hasn't moved. He surveys the scene, waves his hand in disgust, and walks away.

"Ah phooey."

TWO

JUDY HAS LIVED HERE for nearly thirty years. For most of that time it was run by the Sisters of the Good Shepherd and called by the same name, Good Shepherd. But they had proved themselves unfit in the eyes of government to provide modern standards of care and retreated, with sadness, to the cloister. (An uncommon change of mission for a religious order, but these are not common times.) A large, national, for-profit business, New Directions, had taken over in recent years and was trying to undo the damage the sisters had wrought.

A key part of that campaign involved procedures, guidelines, and models, not to mention action plans, safety plans, medical plans, socializing plans, work plans, and individualized learning plans (ILPs)—none of which the sisters had seemed to care about. The result was multiple shelves of three-ring binders, all in the process of being turned into computer files and databases. Professional care had, like the cavalry, arrived just in time. (I almost said "calvary," further evidence of my misspent youth.)

All that orgasm of organization would have spelled doom for my participation had I really been expected to understand it. The executive director, Ms. Pettigrew, undoubtedly smelled my incompetence when I applied, but with the wages New Directions paid the hands-on workers, she was having trouble staffing the facility with anyone who could speak English. (Not that she would ever be caught suggesting that speaking English was preferable. Lengualism and all that.)

I remember the initial training session very well, sort of like I remember the sex ed talks in junior high and the drill sergeant in boot camp. I had already been working at New Directions for a few weeks. They waited for a quorum of new hires before having the required "Orientation to Working with Those with Special Needs" session.

Cassandra Pettigrew insists on leading these sessions herself. (I call her Cassandra to myself, but Ms. Pettigrew in the outside world.) She could farm them out to staff, but I think she wants both to stamp her authority on the head of every new hire—a sort of corporate 666, you might say—and she enjoys a forum in which she can demonstrate that she knows all the acronyms and you don't. I thought the military had a lot of acronyms, but it doesn't hold a candle to the political-sociological-medical-scientific-academic-bureaucratic-corporate complex. (Eisenhower was a piker with his mere "military-industrial" two-parter. There aren't enough hyphens in existence to describe what's going on in America today.)

I'm guessing Cassandra is in her early forties. She has lost the freshness of youth, but is not yet in serious decline. No longer slim, she is not yet stout. Her brown hair is cut short in a way that says "professional, but still a woman. Find me attractive, but don't trifle."

And she has a boatload of initials behind her name, something that shows up in every memo, staff listing, or newsletter to parents and supporters. She has worked hard to earn those initials and you better not forget them, apparently bonded to her accomplishments like a tick to a dog's ear. She is Executive Director for a reason—and you aren't.

Cassandra made one thing very clear during that initial training session. Loose lips sink ships—and employment opportunities at New Directions.

"Our clients are to be referred to as such—as clients. Because that is what they are. They are the source of our revenue and the raison d'être of our business. We exist to serve them. They are our customers. To an extent, they tell us how to do our business. Not by speaking directly, but by their needs. Their needs are our command.

"One may also call them residents—a term reserved for those who actually live here on the campus. They reside here. This is their home, at least until we can get them out into ILAs—independent living arrangements.

"There is one thing they must not be called. They are not to be called retarded."

You could tell that even saying this word was painful for her. She pursed her lips and wrinkled her nose.

"The use of that word was once commonplace and it is still officially used in parts of the scientific and medical community. Some of our parents even use the word. But that is no excuse for any staff person using it at New Directions. It is demeaning, insulting, and inappropriate. It will not be tolerated. A first documented use of the word will result in a one-week suspension without pay. A second use will result in your termination."

The emphasis she put on the word "termination" made me a little uneasy, but I reminded myself it only meant "fired," which I had experienced before and figured I could deal with again. (After all, Zillah fired me as a husband almost two years ago, though it isn't yet official.) When Judy and I were kids, everybody used the word "retarded"—and thought it perfectly acceptable—but my parents and I had only called her Judy, and so I figured I could avoid the R word as well as anyone.

"If you must use a generic term to refer to a collective medical condition, you should use 'developmentally disabled'—up to the age of twenty-one. Once they are of adult age, 'developmental' is more problematic because an adult is not usually considered to be developing. After twenty-one they can be called 'cognitively disabled' or 'intellectually disabled,' though these terms would not fit everyone of course. All of our clients are cognitively disabled; many also have physical disabilities. All of them also have adaptive or behavioral challenges. And no matter what their needs, they all have their full AAMR rights."

"You can't tell the players without a program," the vendors used to yell at the ballpark. I'm starting to think I need one.

"Some people, of course, wish to use terms like 'differently abled' or a wide variety of 'challenged' constructions. These are acceptable, especially if their use is initiated by a parent or advocate. You may wish to listen to the terminology used by the person you are speaking with and to echo such terminology yourself in conversation with them, as long as the term is acceptable. But it is always appropriate to use the word client, and that is the word I wished used among ourselves as much as possible. Is that clear?"

I nodded vigorously. I learned long ago that the question "Is that clear?" is usually code for "Do this or else." What's clear is that language is a weapons depot of small arms and high explosives, just waiting for a careless spark.

Cassandra then explained the different programs that each resident participated in during the day—day activity centers, sheltered workshops, non-sheltered workshops, work on the New Directions campus, public employment, and the like.

So far I was keeping up okay. But when she got to the federal programs, state programs, local laws and bylaws, industry standards, volunteer organizations, professional organizations, and best practices mandates—all identified by title, letters, and numbers—I was as lost as a lamb in a blizzard. I think maybe she was glad about that. She saw the look on our faces and smiled.

"Don't worry if all this seems like drinking from a fire hose. As with any business, there's a lot to learn. But I am confident you will learn. And I and the rest of the staff are here to help you."

She then turned the training session over to Mr. Springer, the facilities manager, and left the room, the sharp click of her heels fading as she moved down the hall.

Bo Springer, I have since decided, is an example of Hemingway's great American man-child. Zillah would call him a bro. He's in his early thirties, but has not developed emotionally, spiritually, or intellectually since he was seventeen. He went to college, but proved impervious to books, paintings, professors, or any idea that required him to reconfigure his existing understanding of reality. For the bro species that understanding centers on beer, sports, porn, and video games. If he was conscious enough to form a philosophy of life, it would be something like: "I hang out, therefore I am."

How do I know this? I don't. It's simply the conclusion I came to about six minutes into his talk at this training session, the first time I'd ever laid eyes on him. And it's only been reinforced since. Quite judgmental of me, I know, but we make judgments about people that quickly all the time—blink, blink. (You're probably drawing some conclusions about me right now.)

Bo talked to us about safety.

"Safety comes first at New Directions. Well, actually the clients come first as Ms. Pettigrew just made clear. But safety comes second. Or maybe third, since profit comes first or second."

He laughed at the last bit and expected us to laugh as well, but none of the five new hires in the room reacted at all.

"That's a joke of course."

I nodded, though not quite as vigorously as when Ms. Pettigrew asked if everything was clear.

Bo went on to explain some of the safety rules, which were legion, and he gave us a fat notebook that chronicled the top few hundred rules, policies, practices, and procedures. Things like what to do if one of the clients pulled a fire alarm without cause (call the main office), or was reported missing (call the main office), or stabbed one of the staff with a fork (call the main office).

Anyway, that was the training session.

I've since broken a number of the rules I learned in that session, but so far I've gotten in trouble only once. It was when I was trying to teach J.P. how to tell time. They prefer that clients learn to read a traditional clock face. And my job, for thirty minutes each week during my shift, is to help him do so.

J.P. does not look . . . cognitively disabled. Since J.P. is an adult, he is not developmentally disabled, because he is beyond the normal age of development. So he is cognitively disabled, which I've discerned is slightly but measurably more appropriate than intellectually disabled, perhaps because it's slightly more obscure and obscurity is highly prized when one is trying to speak about conditions that are, let's not say undesirable, but certainly not highly sought.

But just between you and me (are you Nobody too?), I've streamlined all this for myself. I've divided the world into Specials (note the honorific capital S) and Normals (capitalized not to honor "normal" but to parallel the capitalization of Specials). I mean, we refer without embarrassment to special education and Special Olympics and special needs, so I've just reduced the wide world of cognitive disability to Specials. It simplifies things for me, and, believe me, I need things simple. I use the word with clean hands—disparaging no one, and with as clear a conscience as a borderline psychopath can muster. (I'm being too hard on myself in self-identifying as a borderline psychopath, of course, but that's something we borderline psychopaths do.) And if you tell anyone I've told you this, I will deny it and call my lawyer. (Not that people like me *have* lawyers, so don't worry about it.)

(You've probably noticed that I interrupt myself a lot. Since I live alone, I have no one to interrupt me, so I have to do it myself. I know it's irritating and I apologize.)

Anyway, J.P. not only looks Normal, he is tall and almost handsome. In his late forties and just starting to gray around the temples, he could pass for a junior senator. I don't know what his story is—they don't usually tell us—but he came to Good Shepherd as a boy and has been here ever since.

J.P. is reticent and painfully polite. He learned early not to arouse disapproval. He wants to make you happy.

So when in teaching him time telling I ask if he can count to twelve, he smiles his small, suppressed smile and counts to twelve. He looks at me expectantly, hoping he has done well.

"Good, J.P. That's right. Now, do you see this clock?"

I hold up a big, round wall clock for him to inspect.

"Um . . . yes, Jon. I see it."

J.P. often starts his sentences with "um" or "mm," a delaying strategy, I think, to allow himself a moment to consider what will please you. And he barely opens his mouth when he talks—or eats, for that matter. I'm not sure why.

"Can you point to the twelve?"

He does so and then looks at me.

"Can you point to the three?"

He does so again without problem. This is not the first time we have done this. It is maybe the fifteenth or fiftieth time (and others have tried before me). He always gets this far.

"Do you know what the hands of a clock are, J.P."

"Yes."

"What two kinds of hands are there on a clock?"

"Um, a big hand and a little hand."

"Excellent. And which is the big hand?"

He points to it.

"And which is the little hand?"

He points to it.

"Now J.P., if I make both hands point to the twelve, like this, what time is it?" I move the clock hands.

"Twelve."

"Twelve what?"

"O'clock, Jon."

"Excellent."

I don't want to ask the next question. I never want to ask the next question. But the individualized learning plan (ILP) says J.P. must be able to tell time—like a Normal Adult—and so I ask the next question.

"If I leave the big hand on the twelve and move the little hand to point at the number one, what time is it then, J.P.?"

He looks at me. He knows this is where he fails. He doesn't want to make me unhappy. So he just smiles and says nothing. I try my best to be nonthreatening.

"Just give it a try, J.P. It's okay if you don't get it right. Try to remember what we said last time about the big hand being on the twelve and the little hand pointing to another number. It's okay if you don't remember, but just try."

He starts to rock a bit but doesn't say anything. He knits his brow to show me that he is thinking hard, that he is trying. I repeat the question.

"If the big hand is on the twelve and the little hand is on the one, what time might that be?"

"Mm, twelve-one o'clock?"

"No, not twelve-one. Try again."

"Um, one-twelve o'clock?"

I have read the articles on teaching time telling to people like J.P. I have tried all the techniques they suggest. They don't work. J.P. does understand time, better than most of the other residents, but he doesn't understand measurement, or clock faces—not traditional ones, not digital ones. He just doesn't understand and a thousand years of instruction will not make him understand.

And I got in trouble for saying so.

Everything at New Directions—from individualized instruction to haircuts—has to be documented. For every minute you spend with the residents, you spend two minutes filling out forms to indicate what happened in that minute. And so when I filled out the form that documented our session that day, I made the mistake of writing that I didn't think J.P. would ever learn to tell time and, even more offensive, that I didn't think he needed to.

Cassandra Pettigrew was not happy with that assessment (who knew that she read them?), as she made clear the next time she saw me.

"It is not your job, Mr. Mote, to evaluate the appropriateness of our ILPs for each of the residents. Those are determined by professionals, including myself. James's CPE tests show that he should be able to master the telling of time. The data are clear on that. Your job is to teach him to do so, not to question the appropriateness of the goal."

"Appropriate" is a favorite word with Cassandra. The world for her is divided into two spheres—appropriate and inappropriate. It is inappropriate that J.P. cannot tell time and it certainly is inappropriate for me to say that he doesn't need to.

"Do you understand, Mr. Mote?"

I didn't say anything, but I gave her a small, suppressed smile. I wanted her to be happy.

THREE

I CLAIMED TO BE better, but I'm thinking that maybe I'm only different. As I say, the voices haven't come back as yet, though they've orbited away before, only to return. But I'm not so much worried about that. It feels like maybe they're gone for good this time. The question is, "What takes their place?" They filled a space that now is simply a void. It does little good to get rid of an evil if you don't replace it with a good. There are plenty of other doubtful things to rush back in. (There I go again, using the exhausted terms of bankrupt ideologies—good and evil, and their siblings true and false, beautiful and ugly. Hopelessly binary. Spray all the herbicide you want, some dandelions keep coming back.)

"More purposeful action," I claimed. (I love quoting myself.) But action for what purpose? Action without purpose is just activity—Brownian motion. And purpose has to be deeper than survival, than outlasting the circling sun of another day. There needs to be at least a baseline purpose for living, on which the merely pragmatic purposes of this minute and that are set. Don't you think? (I'd be a heck of a philosopher if I could just develop the philosophical squint.)

No voices, yes, but silence instead. Is that progress? The big threat now is not Disintegration but Normality. Normal—the usual coupled with the meaningless. Alive but trivial. A brief coalescence of electrified matter, soon dispersed. Coagulated pointlessness. Why hang around?

I depress myself. (Therefore I am?)

I got my first taste of Being with Specials in Public only a few days after starting work at New Directions. In an upscale public space no less. You might say it was in obedience to a government mandate, but that requires a bit of explanation.

Government is a wonderful contraption. I think of it as a vast system of interconnected feeding troughs—as in a stockyard. Every branch, bureau, agency, center, department, headquarters, and office gets a trough. And each trough is presided over by a politician, manager, director, chief, supervisor, administrator, officer, controller, overseer, inspector, examiner, or head. All of whom need assistants, underlings, lackeys, workers, enforcers, advisors, consultants, counselors, subordinates, associates, aides, and, of course, secretaries. Needless to say, every one of these people needs offices, furniture, machines, transportation, security, heat and light, computers, and, not unimportant, wall art. Of course "trough" is too static a metaphor to describe what is more an organism than a contraption. These are neuronic troughs, each one connected synaptically to its next closest trough, like cellular structures in the brain, the whole growing day and night, each one eternal and eternally expanding. In such a system the whole point of existence—for bureaucrats and for citizens—is to get access to one of these troughs. And then to feed.

Which is why the residents and I were heading to the theatre. (Dr. Pratt, my deconstructed grad school mentor and erstwhile life coach, would be proud of me for this brilliant analysis.)

For you see, each of the residents is supported by a program, a title this or a title that. And programs administer troughs and therefore require budgets. And budgets require numbers, including numbers for money spent. So each client is a part of the budget of New Directions, and New Directions has informed Government that dollars X are necessary to spend for the entertainment of resident Y, entertainment being a necessary part of the life of a Special, just as it is for a Normal Human Being. And if that entertainment money (better to call it "programming") is not spent on client Y, it will not be in next year's budget, which is not good for New Directions or for client Y.

So Cassandra said to me a few days after I began, "Ralph's account is getting too big. Buy him something—a new area rug or lamp or radio . . . anything. And take everyone out on an activity. Anything. We've got a report due at the end of the month and we've got to show more spending."

I don't think she really wanted to say it exactly like that. She was thinking out loud. She caught herself and looked at me like we were standing next to a cookie jar and she was holding a macaroon.

"You know what I mean."

Yes, I knew exactly what she meant. Feed at the trough. Keep the slop coming. Oink. Oink.

So we little piggies went to market. High-end market. The Guthrie Theater, in fact. Tyrone's palace across the street from Loring Park and next to the Walker Sculpture Garden. It was December, and at the Guthrie December means *A Christmas Carol*, as it has for something like twenty-five years now. Zillah and I had season tickets for the Guthrie for the first stretch of our time together. It was a nice break from a troubled marriage to go see something like *The Oresteia* or *Who's Afraid of Virginia Woolf?* (This is called irony. I learned it early and it has been my loyal companion lo these many years.)

I've been thinking about Zillah a lot lately. It's easier to keep away from someone physically than to keep them out of your thoughts. I haven't seen her for more than a year, closer to two, but she pays regular visits to all three sections of my Freudian brain—id, ego, and superego. The psych folks have pretty much junked Freud, but I still like the simplicity of the cancer-jawed old geezer. (Did the gods afflict him for telling us lies, or was it just random bad luck?)

How is it that I miss being with a woman with whom I mostly gave and received pain? ("Why should I blame her that she filled my days / With misery?") Maybe it's that the pain did not lessen when we parted, but the sense of being in something significant together did. Or maybe not.

We arrive for our matinee performance. (Specials, with a lifetime of scheduled bedtimes, tend to turn into pumpkins at around 9 p.m., so afternoon activities work better.) It's crowded in the big lobby, which serves both the Guthrie and the Walker Art Center. Dickens's occult, moralistic thriller is the Guthrie's dependable cash cow. Parents love to bring their children to it (moooo!), never mind that it scares the bejesus out of the younger ones and bores the older kids (who consume slasher movies like popcorn).

The residents stick close to each other and to me, the primal herd instinct when danger (read "the unfamiliar") is in the air. Bonita stirs things up a bit.

"Watch out!"

She's points straight up and everyone follows her finger and then crouches down as if death is descending from the sky.

"What the hell is that?"

That, it turns out, is art. An Oldenburg to be specific. A huge, plasticky, leathery, saggy, artsy rendering of an everyday three-way electrical wall plug to be exact. It's the size of a minivan and hangs over the crowd from the ceiling, looking more than a little forlorn.

"It's art," I say.

"*Noah's* ark?" Jimmy asks.

"No, art. With a 't.'"

It's Judy's turn.

"Why, why, I . . . I should say, I like ar . . . art, Jon. It's . . . it's very pretty."

Billy is looking up, but then Billy is always looking up, so I don't take it as a sign that he has suddenly developed an interest in oversized aesthetic wall plugs. Billy is as Special as they get, and he communicates, if at all, with things beyond the ken of Normals and Specials alike.

Ralph, as usual, is unimpressed. He shoots a glance and sums it up for the group with a wave of the hand.

"Ah phooey."

Everyone seems satisfied with that and we move on.

Moving on means getting in line at the Will Call window. I've made reservations but there wasn't time to mail the tickets, so we have to pick them up. It's a long line.

I place myself in the middle of our group, all of us single file. I'd have them wait for me separately but there's no telling where these sheep will go if the good shepherd ain't among 'em. I'm a little self-conscious about having brought them all to the Guthrie. A ballgame or bowling alley is one thing. But a squad of Specials is more than a little unusual at a chic cathedral for the performing arts. (Not that the management wouldn't be thrilled at this unplanned diversity moment. Play it right and we could end up in an ad campaign—"Differently Abled Enjoy a Night at the Theatre.")

I'm looking back toward Judy and Ralph holding hands at the back of our little group when I hear a familiar voice and sounds of commotion in front of me. Bonita has gotten tired of waiting and is suddenly pushing her way through the people ahead of us in line toward the ticket window, Jimmy right behind her.

"Let us through, we're retarded," she yells, her head down like a running back plowing into the scrimmage line, looking for a hole.

People are parting like the Red Sea.

"Let us through, we're retarded!" she repeats.

My God, the R word. In public. And in the mouth of one of my charges. My career with the Specials is hanging by a thread.

"Bonita! Jimmy!" I bark. "Get back here!"

I take a couple of big steps and grab the back of Jimmy's shirt. Bonita continues pushing ahead, delighted with how well things are working out. I am trying to reach for her with my other hand when a purse bounces off the side of my head.

It's an old woman.

"Young man, you leave these people alone! It's wonderful that they are here, and I will not have you bullying them!"

Others nod and shoot me Medusa looks. They all step aside and wave for the rest of us to pass up to the front. I am speechless but caught up in the tidal movement of our group toward the window. When I get there, Bonita is waiting for me with an expression of patient resignation.

"Stick with me, Mote."

We're in the cheap seats, though none of the seats are actually cheap, which I assume Cassandra will be happy about. Oink. Oink. I wasn't able to get us all in the same row, so J.P. is by himself in the row ahead of us, right in front of me, so I can keep an eye on him. We're early and there's no one else in his row at the moment.

All is well. Everyone localized in a seat. Everyone having gone to the toilet before we left the group home. Bonita calm and satisfied after her Pickett's Charge to the Will Call window. Jimmy peering all around, sizing up the possibilities. Ralph and Judy blinking rhythmically. Billy starting to hum.

I see a young woman standing in the aisle at the end of J.P.'s row, looking at her ticket and then at the row number. She's a good twenty seats away from J.P., but hasn't looked up either at him or at the rest of us in the row behind. She starts walking down the row, marking the number on each seat as she passes it, holding her ticket out in front of her. I see J.P. spot her. His eyes get big. A new friend, which, despite his natural reticence, he collects like baseball cards.

She takes a surreptitious glance at J.P. as she sits down in the seat next to him, but then looks straight ahead. J.P. is looking directly at her left ear, a smile on his face that would shame the Cheshire cat. He twists his head around further and looks at me.

"I'm a lucky guy!" he says loudly.

She shoots out of her seat like a pilot ejecting from a burning fighter jet and flees down the row.

"Oh well," says J.P. with a shrug.

"Can't win 'em all, buddy," observes Jimmy the Man-About-Town.

I can't tell whether the residents are understanding anything in the play or not. Judy certainly figures out Scrooge in short order.

"He . . . I should say . . . he is not a very nice man."

And Tiny Tim presents no mystery.

"He's like Don," says Jimmy. Don is a kid on the boy's floor back at New Directions who has cerebral palsy and uses crutches.

"Hello, Don!" Jimmy calls out with a wave. The other residents laugh and Jimmy beams. He's got this trick down and repetition only burnishes it.

But they don't seem to know what to make of the ghosts in the play.

Bonita is suspicious.

"I don't like ghosts," she says under her breath. "Ghosts are dead people and dead people are yuk."

This gets nods and general agreement. I try to get everyone to keep quiet, but they are figuring this out together and ignore me.

"They are not . . . are not ghosts, Bonita Marie. They . . . they are called act . . . actors. They are just pre . . . pretending to be ghosts."

This stumps the group.

"Like on Scooby-Doo," suggests Jimmy.

"That, that's right, Jimmy. Like on . . . on Scooby-Doo."

The troops seem content with that answer and they noticeably relax.

Long before we get to Christmas Future, the residents have lost their zip. After I reject Bonita's call for popcorn all around, she crosses her arms and sulks silently. Ralph is asleep. Jimmy is snapping his fingers and kicking the back of the seat in front of him. J.P. hasn't moved a muscle in an hour, sitting straight, shoulders back, staring at the stage but giving no hint that he is following the action, such as it is.

At intermission we are out of there.

The residents offer their usual post-game analysis. Sometimes they are amazingly perceptive, in their Special Kind of Way. After we watched a rerun of *Rocky* on television one night, J.P. had said, "That was filmed in black and blue." I couldn't tell whether he was confused about a statement of fact or trotting out a sly word play. These guys keep you on your toes.

With *A Christmas Carol*, they seem content to simply catalog the good guys and the bad guys. Maintaining a clear moral order in the universe is important to them, a legacy, no doubt, of the simplified world of the nuns. I got my fill of Sister Brigit quotes when Judy lived with me on the houseboat in St. Paul. Now that I'm working with the older ones at New Directions, I get them in stereo.

As when Jimmy observes thoughtfully, "Sister Brigit would not have let us see that. Christmas is not about ghosts. Christmas is about Jesus."

Van-wide approval. See if I take you guys to the theatre again.

FOUR

THAT WAS LAST WINTER. We've been on many outings since, keeping the spending flowing and the clients occupied. Life for me is approaching that pleasantly killing state (think Roberta Flack) that some call order and some call routine and others call Rut. I'm thinking it might be more dangerous in the long run than heart disease or troubles in the head.

This morning for instance. The end of an eighteen-hour shift that began early yesterday afternoon. Paperwork followed by the return of the residents from their various deployments, followed by meal prep and consummation, followed by work on goals, followed by a group viewing of a rerun of *Life Goes On* (should Specials see themselves depicted?), followed by bedtime. Up at 6:30 this morning, overseeing dressing, preparing and eating breakfast, getting ready to disperse the residents to vehicles for points abroad, after which home to the boat to wait for it all to start again. Eighteen hours of my life allotment, of which eight are spent officially comatose. (I've been comatose much of my life, often while awake, so getting paid for it is an upgrade.)

Only this morning is different. A burp in the cosmic hum. I'm in the upstairs bathroom overseeing J.P. brushing his teeth. He is a master of up and down on the front teeth, but tends to ignore the teeth he cannot see in the mirror. (If molars lack an observer, can they be said to exist? asked Bishop Berkeley skeptically. Yes, answered Dr. Johnson, as you will see when they develop a painful cavity.)

I'm just telling J.P. to move on to the back teeth when I hear Bo Springer calling my name. I stick my head out the bathroom and see him at the bottom of the stairs. He looks severe.

"Abby Wagner is missing. Emergency meeting in thirty minutes."

In the thirty minutes between Bo shouting up the stairwell and the beginning of the emergency meeting, the vans arrive to take the residents to their various places for the day—public work for the high flyers, sheltered workshops for the middle class, and day activity centers for the most special Specials like Billy. A place for everyone and everyone in their place.

The mood at the meeting is grim. Still, Cassandra Pettigrew looks to be embracing the moment. It's a time to put all those degrees and certifications to work.

"Abby Wagner is missing. She spent an evening with her parents last night. They dropped her off at the main building about 10 p.m. In keeping with her long-range plan for independent living, they did not walk her to her independent living apartment. She has made that transfer on her own at night many times, as she will need to do when she is living independently in the community."

I believe we've established the independent part.

"However, she was not in her apartment this morning when her supervisor checked on her. And she appears not to have slept in her bed last night. A preliminary search of the apartment building was conducted, but there was no sign of her and none of the other clients reported seeing her last night or this morning."

She pauses, then addresses the staff like a field general before battle, laying out plans and going over strategies.

"This is officially a level three alert. We will be following contingency plan 22-C, which you will find in the handbook that you all have."

All have? I remember getting a binder of something at that first orientation meeting, but I haven't looked at it since and have no idea where it is, most likely in the trunk of my car or back on the boat. I'm hoping for more details about 22-C and the executive director obliges.

"In compliance with the contingency plan, we will bring all clients still on campus to the gymnasium. Ms. Francis and two staff people from the children's dorms will supervise the clients while all remaining staff will conduct a search of the buildings and the grounds. Mr. Springer, as director of security as well as facilities, will organize the search. I will continue to be in contact with the police, who will send over additional personnel if our initial search is not successful. I have just spoken to Abby Wagner's parents. They will be here shortly."

Cassandra's voice tightens a bit when she mentions Abby's parents. This has the potential to be a worst-case scenario for New Directions and a career-ender for her. Stuart Wagner is the head of a powerful local clan. In fact he has some crooked Roman numerals behind his name, an indication that he comes in a long line of powerful (and, it goes without saying, wealthy) Stuart Wagners that stretches back into the nineteenth century. His family initially made their money in railroads and timber, then in banks, and now in everything. And he is not a man you want to disappoint. All things I learned a few weeks ago over coffee with Mrs. Francis before a staff meeting.

Abby is the daughter of Stuart Wagner's old age. And of his trophy wife, Wendy. The first Mrs. Wagner succumbed to the temptations of prosperity and alcohol—the first figuratively, the second literally. The next Mrs. Wagner avoided the latter and better managed the former. And she produced a daughter—Abby—twenty-five years ago, when Mr. Wagner was fifty. The first Mrs. Wagner had produced a son, adorned with the next Roman numeral and now groomed to take over the family empire when and if the reigning Stuart Wagner relinquished his death grip on it. Sort of like an aging English prince waiting for the aged monarch to move aside (yes, think Charles, the wrinkling Prince of Wales).

The executive director then turns the meeting over to Bo. He hands out a list with the heading "Search Teams." There is a team for every building and two teams for different areas of the grounds.

"You can see what team you're on. The first name listed with each team is the captain. When we finish here, please find your captain and gather in this room. Then proceed to your assigned building or area. Search every room, closet, or other space in every building. Then search the area immediately around your building. Your team captain will immediately fill out a written report on your findings and give that report to me. I will collate them and give them to Ms. Pettigrew, who will have them available when she meets with the parents and the police."

I look on the list and see that I am not on the team to search my own group home. Instead I am partnered with Sam Raven to search the grounds along the front of the New Directions property between the buildings and the highway. Sam Raven is the old groundskeeper. He looks to be either black mixed with something else or something else mixed with black. I know enough not to ask.

Sam and Mrs. Francis are the only holdovers from the Nuns Era. I've talked to him before about the Medieval Period, when the nuns were in charge. I use the term respectfully, quite sure that the current Enlightenment regime thinks of that time as the Dark Ages. Sam doesn't. He liked the nuns better than the technocrats. He is especially reverent toward the memory of Sister Brigit, as was clear when we once talked about her.

"She were a wise woman. She understood things. She kept things right, if you know what I mean. She knew the people here and they knew her. She knew where they come from. Back then, none of them had last names. Families didn't want anyone to know they had people here. Most of them never had a visitor. The sisters were their mothers and fathers and the other people like themselves were their sisters and brothers. Sister Brigit—she was tough with them but she loved them and that's how it ought to be. You know what I'm saying?"

I think of that conversation now as I'm looking at the list. Sam and I are assigned the front of the property, Bo is taking the playing field and the back of the property, and everyone else is searching a building. I see that Sam's name is listed first, so I look around the room for the captain of my two-man team. He is standing at the back, not looking at his sheet, which, it occurs to me, he may not be able to read.

I walk up to him.

"Well Sam, looks like we're on the same team. I guess we're supposed to search the area between the buildings and the highway."

Sam nods and heads outside, me trailing.

Actually, there's not a lot to search. It's only about a hundred feet from the entrance to the main building to a frontage road, and the highway is just beyond that. There are some trees here and there, and some landscaping shrubs that should be looked through, but it's mostly open space and easily surveyed.

I ask Sam what he knows about Abby Wagner.

"She came here when the nuns were still in charge. Near the end of their time. She was a teenager I think. Her brain got messed up in an accident. That's all I know. She looks regular, but she ain't regular. She's got problems."

Don't we all. But he's right about her looking Normal. I recall the hand on the knee the first time I saw her and thank the Big Bang that it didn't get me in trouble.

Sam and I don't find anything. Neither does anyone else. I fill out our report in two sentences and hand it to Sam who hands it in. We are told to go back to our Normal Routine. We will be updated As More Information

Becomes Available. Since my work is done for the day, I head for my car. As I open the door, I see the Stuart Wagners pulling up in front of the main entrance, with two police cars not far behind. I'm glad not to be an executive director of anything.

FIVE

MY BRAIN AND I are glad to be going to what I euphemistically call home. Home is where the snacks are. Where your finger automatically goes to all the right buttons on the remote control. Where the ratty easy chair is more desirable than any throne. Where you scratch any place that itches. And the common denominator to all this is familiarity. Not health, not wholeness, not peace—just the familiar. The devil you know and all that.

Funny how "broken" feels right when you're used to it. We talk about comfortable shoes being "broken in," which actually is just an intermediate step toward "worn out." I think it's the same with lives. We make a thousand little choices that collectively give our lives a certain shape. For some of us, too many of those thousand choices are little cracks in how things ought to be. (The "broken" in "broken in," perhaps.) They're small distortions that add up to a misshapen life, like how gaining a pound a month will eventually give you a belly the size of the Hindenburg. ("Oh, the humanity!") Just as you get used to each new pound as it finds its place on your globe of a gut, so you strike up a friendship with each new distortion in your increasingly defective but familiar life.

When I say my brain wants to go home, I also mean it misses its old broken self. It's not comfortable, not "at home," with my recently improved mental state. It's not that my brain wants the voices back; they were nasty to live with and hopefully gone for good. It's just that pathology can be a kind of friend, an old buddy, a soft pair of slippers.

Not that I'm now a poster boy for mental health. I got yanked back from the precipice, but I can still see the pit edge from here, not all that far away. I'm like an alcoholic who's been dry for some months, maybe even a year or two. I'm 100% cured right up until the moment I'm 100% relapsed. I'm just one little stimulus away from a free-fall response. My brain knows it, and some of its lobes are nostalgic.

But why do I say "my brain and I" instead of just sticking with "I"? I mean, who's the "I" asking "Who am I?"—the dusty old question, beloved of writers and thinkers and commuters staring out windows. Am I my brain or am I my mind? Or my consciousness? Is consciousness the same as mind? Are both mind and consciousness wholly produced by brain? Is my foot part of my "I" or is this "I" of mine just a mind jockey riding this old nag called the body? And how do you get something as seemingly immaterial as consciousness out of something as unconscious as pure matter? And if you say consciousness *is* material, then explain to me how a molecule can store a memory of Zillah's perfume. Pretty soon you'll be blowing smoke. Pile up enough quarks and you get a tiny closet for a memory to live in? How charming. How unconvincing. The gap between micro and macro is as wide as the cosmos.

And don't even talk to me about soul. That's an eye-rolling word among Those Who Know. In the same forgotten parking lot for mothballed ideas as astrology, bloodletting, and slavery. The soul—titter, titter—how quaint. Next thing you know you'll be believing in resurrections.

(I once believed in resurrections. I found the idea very encouraging. When Judy and I lost track of our mom and dad, I was ravenous for resurrection—or at least for afterlife. If not resurrection, at least reunion. But like most of the hopes of childhood, it faded. I haven't found a way back to believing it since. Not that I don't see the attraction.)

Anyway, I'm okay with ditching soul. Having one didn't do me much good all those years, so let's deal the deck with no soul card in it and see how the game turns out. But I would certainly appreciate an "I" card, and it seems like it's next to go. If "I" am just my brain, and my brain is just neurons firing in strict obedience to their underlying chemistry, and that chemistry is nothing but configurations of molecules, and molecules are just the combination of atoms that started flying with the Primordial Pop (and so on into the dark), then how can Zee blame me for wanting to watch football instead of talking to her about her cousin Irene? I mean, who or what is left to blame—or to feel guilt—whether I turn on the TV or I cut off someone's head? ("It wasn't me, Your Honor; it was the Big Bang.")

So do I freely choose to turn on the TV or am I required to do so by the inexorable logic of the distribution of matter when time began? What is freedom, anyway, in a Big-Bang-is-the-only-Bang universe?

But then some Seriously Scientific People, much to the consternation of Other Seriously Scientific People, allow that there is something besides the brain. Let's call it mind. The mind is bigger than the brain even if you wouldn't have mind without the brain. Pain talks to the brain, they say, whereas suffering dialogues with the mind.

I mean, how do I explain feeling terrible when my dog Blue died when I was kid? Why should the brain care? What in the Great Explosion inscribed suffering into the passing of a mutt? And what adaptive value does it have? Maybe something about reinforcing social ties that increase survival rates, I suppose. But how circular is that? Seems more adaptive to immediately forget a dead loved one and start looking for someone else with whom to pass on your genes. Isn't that what it's supposed to be all about? (Or are the All-Confident socio-biologists not talking to the All-Confident physicists?)

I suffer, therefore I am. Is that the mind's mantra? (A lot of whiner writers apparently think so.) Brains don't suffer. Brains register the stimulus we label "pain," but they don't give a damn about it. They don't even care about their own continued existence. All those molecules will just reconstitute themselves as something else, something not bothered by questions of brain and mind and soul. Something loamy, perhaps, or tree-like. They will just float out into space with the ejecta from the next asteroid that punches the earth in the nose. No hurry, no worry.

Then again, maybe suffering is evidence for the existence of God. Not pain—that requires only neurons. But suffering seems to imply values and oughts—because it lives in the gap between how things are and how they ought to be. And values and oughts create a possible space for God. Something that transcends. (I hear the materialists screaming.) Genuine values, that is. Real oughts, real shoulds and shouldn'ts. Not just pragmatism ("things will operate more efficiently if"), not just power ("we will punish you if"), not just arbitrariness ("the big end of the egg is good, and the small end of the egg is evil"). No, I want real right and real wrong and real should and shouldn't or I won't play this game anymore.

And my brain says, "So quit playing. Who cares? You're boring me."

And I *am* boring. I know it. I bore myself. But these are the kinds of ruts my brain-mind-consciousness is heir to. These are the worn tracks that feel most familiar to me. Ideas and emotions and physical sensations pinballing inside, colliding with each other and with the rubber bumpers that make up my inner space, flung out in seemingly random directions to collide and combine and re-collide and re-combine, creating the "I" that is me at this moment but not-me at the next. Mixed as my metaphors.

And my dirty little secret is that I like pinball. It's what I'm used to. The bells and flashing lights and whirling scoreboard are what I've known. And now the noise and flash is muted, though not far away. Do I want them back? I can't win the game with them, but do I even want to play the game without them? Should I put another quarter in the slot? Just one more turn? Like I said, what's the advantage of silencing the voices if the result is simply . . . well . . . silence? If overly full is replaced by completely empty, how is that an improvement?

And what does any of this have to do with the fact that I'm supposed to be back at work tomorrow morning?

SIX

LIFE DOES NOT STOP just because someone goes missing. Someone going missing, in fact, is the very stuff of life. It happens about 150,000 times a day. If it touches us personally, we sometimes call it tragedy, but that word means less and less in a world that does not believe there is anything to fall from or fall to. If everything just is, then "missing" is just another is.

(There I go trying to figure things out again and be clever at the same time. It's a bad habit.)

Anyway, the Schedule says today, only a couple days after Abby's disappearance, is a special day. Every day is a special day for some of our Specials, but no day is more special than Special Olympics day. It's the day some Specials realize for the first time how entirely Special they are. It's four hours of hugs, medals, high-fives, hugs, food, doing your best, everyone a winner, hugs, self-esteem, more medals, thumbs-ups, more food, laughter, hugs, and cheering. Did I mention hugs?

New Directions has a big field, and so the local Special Olympics folks have chosen it for a preliminary competition in preparation for the state-wide competition next year. The nuns had used the field to raise vegetables for the dinner table, provide work for the residents, and raise a few cows. But New Directions plowed it all under and turned it into a big, grassy recreation field. *Mens sana in corpore sano*. Well, not exactly.

We have a number of Special Olympic immortals in our own group home. Jimmy is a bowling force—and bowling is part of the expanded field of Special Olympic events. He is more about style than pin count. He likes to dry his hand on the air blower for an inordinately long time—both hands in fact—holding the ball first in the crook of one arm and then the other, peering into the distance with chin held high, a look as resolute as Napoleon's before Waterloo. He then finds his pre-established mark, a piece of tape on the floor, places both feet together as instructed, tosses his hair into place, puts the ball under his chin, and stares down the lane at the pins, his mortal enemies. Waiting patiently for the synapse to fire that says "bowl," he sometimes holds this pose interminably, deaf to the occasional outburst from Bonita: "Bowl the damn ball, for Christ's sake!"

He eventually shuffles purposefully toward the line and swings the ball gracefully, releasing it with an upward motion of his arm that he holds overhead, like a Greek statue frozen in time. He invariably releases the ball late, causing it to arc to the floor, bouncing once or twice on the lane before settling into a roll. About half the time, that roll leads to the gutter, sometimes immediately, but this is of no concern to Jimmy. He pivots back toward the onlookers—proud, solemn, regal—and returns to the bench, collecting high-fives and other tributes along the way.

There will be no bowling today. This is a field day—all running, jumping, and throwing, with some lifting and tossing along the way. The tossing is bocce ball (that famous Olympic sport) and Bonita and Judy are both competing—Judy in singles and Bonita in what they call a "unified" event that pairs her with a Normal.

One of those explosive words—normal. Seems innocent enough, but for some it reeks of elitism, condescension, insensitivity, Otherism, and who knows what. Start with the idea of norms—how things ought to be— and you end up with firing squads. Cassandra seems to think "as normal as possible" is the goal for our clients, but the whole concept calls out the "who are you to say?" types that reject all generalizations about anything so "totalizing" (or whatever the word of the day might be). And nothing, apparently, is more totalizing or generalizing—or abusive—than the notion of normal. (I thought I left this stuff behind when I fled the academy, but I've found that snow is general all over Ireland.)

But I have to say, I think the anti-Normalizing crowd has a point. I mean, if they themselves are normal, who would want to be like them? Or me? If normal is measured by Western, productivity-obsessed, make-money-don't-cost-money, be successful or be gone, self-actualized individualism, then Lord make me a Special. As I guess he has.

Anyway, Judy is in the bocce ball singles division and Bonita is paired with, let's just say, a non-Special. They should, of course, have had it the other way round. Bonita—irascible as a wild boar—should have been in the singles, and Judy—mender of the world—should have been someone's partner. But perhaps pairing up was seen as a growth opportunity for Bonita, and so the die is cast.

I've been asked to keep an eye on my residents, especially Bonita, and so I watch as the bocce competition proceeds. Her partner is a quite large, middle-aged woman with a constant smile on her face. She is wearing tight stretch pants that no woman would inhabit in public who had a full, three-dimensional understanding of the consequences. Her name is Flo.

Bonita's bocce style betrays something about her upbringing before she arrived at Good Shepherd as a teenager. She holds the ball in her hands, bends low, kisses it and says things like "talk to me baby" or "go fetch," then snaps off a line-drive throw in the general direction of the object ball. She actually is pretty good, and on the occasions when the ball bounces off course, she has a ready explanation—"Damn gophers." Or something equally exculpatory.

Bonita and Flo make it to the finals. That's when the wheels come off. It looks like they're about to pick up two points at a crucial moment in the championship match when one of their opponents—a Special from a facility in the next suburb—puts a toss within six inches of the object ball. He lets out a whoop of delight, which gets Bonita's engine running.

"Keep it down, retard."

There is a gasp from the onlookers, some of whom stare at me as though I had said it—or, just as bad, created an environment where she was allowed to demean herself by saying it. (Some folks are big on the "creating an environment" thesis.) This is Bonita's second offense, which makes it my second offense. If this gets back to Cassandra, I'm cooked. We clearly have a situation on our hands—and I have a lifelong aversion to situations.

Flo tries to help. She shouldn't have.

"Now Bonita. We ought not use that word."

"What word?"

"Well, you know what word. It's not appropriate and it's mean."

Bonita is not a woman to be lectured.

"No, mean would be calling you a lard ass. I'm not calling you a lard ass, even though you are one, so I'm being nice. But he *is* a retard. Just look at him. He's like me. I know a retard when I see one."

This is too much. The person running the competition, a slight man with a now deeply mournful expression, intervenes.

"I'm calling a time out here. Let's take a break and we'll resume the finals in fifteen minutes."

Bonita isn't having it. Her eyes narrow and she starts gesturing dramatically with her arms.

"I want my medal! You're trying to cheat me out of my medal! That's not fair! You bastards, I'll see you burn in hell if I don't get my medal!"

Not—definitely not—the Olympic spirit.

I move in to hustle Bonita away, but she's already moving back toward the group home on her own, spouting as she goes, me trying to catch up.

"I know my rights. They can't treat me this way. I'm going to tell Miss Pettigrew." (Bonita has never mastered the "miss/ms." distinction and I'm not going to be the one to correct her.) "She'll fix their asses. They won't get pop for a year! Ten years! Things are going to change around here or somebody's going to hear from me!"

I've heard it all from Bonita myself any number of times. It's her standard rant against the universe. Losing your pop privileges is the ultimate expression of the problem of evil—and the ultimate grounds for revenge.

Halfway back to the house we run into Bo Springer. He's familiar enough with Bonita to know not to ask any questions when she has that carnivorous look. I have to get back to the field to help monitor things, so I enlist his help.

"Bo, can you take Bonita here and get her some pop? Then bring her back to the field after she's cooled off a bit?"

"Sure. No problem. Come on Bonita. Let's get some pop."

Bonita brightens and heads off with Bo. I head back to the field.

Coming down the hill, I see they are about to run a heat of the fifty-yard dash. Ronnie, the young kid from the football game, is in lane three, wearing a cape. He looks to be about twelve—physical age of course—and I call him the Black Proteus. I call him that because, well, he's black—which is to say, African American—and because, like Proteus of Greek myth, he is a shape-changer. One day he presents himself as a superhero, the next as a movie star, the third as a sports icon. He fully inhabits the character of the day (or month) and expects you to respond to him as such. I once greeted him outside the main building with a "How are you doing, President Lincoln?"—the character he had been for weeks before. He looked at me solemnly and stuck out his hand for a shake, "Cash is the name. Johnny Cash."

Mrs. Francis, the crafts teacher, is watching the race from a distance. I walk up to her and ask, "What's up with Ronnie's cape? Superman?"

She laughs.

"Oh no. Wonder Woman."

"Wonder Woman doesn't have a cape."

"She does in Ronnie's version. And you don't mess with Ronnie's version of anything."

Good for you, Ronnie, I think—gender-bender, all-inclusive, be-whatever-you-want-to-be, All-American boy.

The race starter claps two big wooden blocks together and they're off. (No starter pistols allowed in Minnesota Special Olympics. Another blow against militarism and the NRA.) Off, yes, but at greatly different speeds. Three actually run at a pretty good clip, heads back, eyeing the finish line ahead. A couple more, bent at the waist and staring at the ground as they move, are mostly stamping the grass, a lot of energy going up and down with the legs, not so much going forward with the body. And then there is one fellow, a teenager, for whom the concept of "race" seems rather obscure. He is on a stroll, waving to the crowd, smiling, wandering back and forth across two or three lanes, but heading roughly toward the finish line—a crowd favorite.

Ronnie is in the first group. He knows how to run and he is leading the race until he starts to notice his cape flapping behind him. He tries to look at it and run at the same time, quite conscious of the profound effect the cape must be making, perhaps wondering if he is going to fly. Looking slows down running, and he is passed near the tape. But no one really cares, including Ronnie. Because each runner is engulfed by a hugger as he or she crosses the line. There hasn't been this much public excitement since the moon landing. Whoops and hollers and hugs and high-fives all around, for the stroller as much as for the winner. And this was just the first of many heats. Six new huggers wait in the wings for heat number two. If we had more huggers—say at the United Nations, for instance— the world would be a happier place.

I look over and see that Bo is back, sans Bonita. He is talking to Cassandra, whose anxiety is evident even from a distance. This is a big day for New Directions—lots of donors, parents and grandparents, local media, the entire board, heads of local government agencies, corporate sponsors, a celebrity athlete or two, and, of course, clients galore from various organizations. Abby's disappearance has cast a pall over the event for New Directions folks, but most of the people here haven't even heard about it yet. Bo puts his hand on Cassandra's shoulder in a gesture of support, but she sort of pulls away and goes to talk to a couple of parents with their client-child.

I decide to check in on Ralph. They've set up the lifting events in the center of the field. His event—the deadlift—is almost over by the time I get there. The deadlift is the most cognitively straightforward activity imaginable: here is something on the ground, pick it up, then put it down. Take turns. Keep picking it up and putting it down until someone tells you to stop. Right up Ralph's alley. Rarely does life match need with gift so perfectly. God should have made *me* a deadlifter. (Maybe he did.)

By the time I get there, the ninety-pound weaklings have been eliminated (weaklings being a seriously inappropriate word that I would never utter aloud). It's just Ralph and one enormous black kid about eighteen years old. (Should I have noticed that he's black? If so, should I have said it to you? It's a tough call. Let's just pretend I didn't bring it up.)

Anyway, this kid is huge and he looks like he could deadlift the Great Sphinx of Giza. I think that for once Ralph has come across someone who is stronger than he is, and I don't know how he'll handle it. He's pretty much as silent as that Sphinx most of the time and not one to tune in to any particular emotion, but he does have his pride and losing here might chip it some.

What I didn't figure in were their respective amygdalas—you know, the part of the brain they say deals with aggression and competitiveness. It's not how you were raised that determines what pisses you off or how much you want to win; it's electricity moving through that particular neighborhood of the brain. (Bonita must have constant thunderheads in that huge amygdala of hers!) Ralph is not aggressive at all in the usual sense, but apparently he doesn't mind a little competition.

So they both struggle pretty hard to lift the barbell with three big plates on each end. But when they add two smaller plates for the next round, the kid waves his hand.

"No way. That's enough for me."

So they ask Ralph if he wants to try it. He chuckles his contentedness chirp and walks up to the bar. Jimmy and Billy are in the crowd watching (if you can describe Billy as ever genuinely watching anything) and Jimmy shouts out encouragement.

"Go gettem, Ralph. You're the best! Pick that sucker up!"

Ralph bends down and grabs the bar, bends his knees and keeps his back straight, just like Bo taught him. "Da dooey!" he yells as he pulls the bar up and arches his back, legs shaking. The small crowd erupts in applause.

Da dooey power!

That's when the trouble starts. They come trooping down the hill with their signs and placards, singing "We Shall Overcome." The activists have arrived.

Their signs are professionally printed and come in rainbow colors of earnest aggrievement. One reads "Ableism=Racism=Sexism=Homophobia." I think there would have been a longer list but there wasn't room.

Another says "Keep Your Attitudes Off Our Genes!" I like that one. And then there's "If We Can't Do It, It Doesn't Need Doing" and "Rights for the Neurodivergent." The last one is a head scratcher for me, but then I'm new to the disability branch of the Euphemisms R Us industry.

There are about fifteen activists altogether. They march onto the running lanes marked out on the grass and stop. None of them looks disabled, but what do I know? The leader has a bullhorn and he leads them in a chant.

"Oh no, we won't go, / we are here come rain or snow. / Stop your running, stop the schism, / stop your ugly ableism!" (Schism and ableism—a rhyme never contemplated by Shakespeare or Poe.) They repeat it a half dozen times while people gather round—some puzzled, some angry.

The activists lock arms in an outward-facing circle around the man with the bullhorn, like mother elephants around their calves when predators threaten.

I am highly perplexed, one of my default states. I've been too obtuse to realize that the Special Olympics are a bastion of oppression. The guy with the bullhorn enlightens me.

"Ladies and gentlemen and beloved victims. We are here to put a stop to this charade of misplaced compassion and pseudo-acceptance."

His pronunciation of charade catches my ear—this "shah-rod" he says, with a strong emphasis on the second syllable, "this shah-rod of misplaced compassion." I am a word collector and I start wondering where that pronunciation comes from—shah-rod—and whether it signifies anything. So I miss the next couple of sentences of his critique. Then I pick him up again.

"Your hearts are in the right place, but you are actually abusing the people you want to help. You are infantilizing them. All these hugs, all this mindless cheering. These people are, for the most part, adults, and you are treating them as though they are little children. This is not normalizing. This is not treating them as equals. We do not have huggers at the end of the races in the 'non-special' Olympics"—he flashes air quotes—"so why here? No one hugs you at the end of the day at the office, so why here?

"And these sponsors—Wells Fargo and Medtronic and Cargill." He gestures toward their corporate signs around the field. "It's all public relations. It's feel-good propaganda. Do you think they hire these contestants? Will you find the people competing here—faux-competing I should say—behind the bank window at Wells Fargo or in a business meeting at Medtronic? I don't think so. These are giant, soulless corporations—international conglomerates—and they eat up and spit out real people like pistachios."

Some people start giving him pushback.

"That's not fair." "We're having a good time here. Why are you trying to wreck things?" "Go save some other part of the world!"

The guy with the bullhorn seems glad for the interruption. It gives him new material to work with.

"Having a good time here? Is that what you said? Having a good time? Well, let's see if everyone is having a good time. I have someone here who does not seem to be having a good time at all. Because oppression never creates a good time for the oppressed. Let's see what she has to say about your good time."

The ring of protestors opens at one point and who is led into the circle and up to bullhorn man but Bonita. How he has managed to recruit her between the parking lot and the center of the field only God knows.

"What is your name, please."

"My name is Bonita Marie Anderson."

"And where do you live, Bonita?"

"I live right here at Good Shepherd."

He looks confused.

"Right over there." And she points to our group home.

"And are you having a good time here today, Bonita?"

"No, I am not. They are trying to cheat me out of my medal, the bastards."

More people start yelling and even pushing against the security circle.

"Now who's the abuser, fella? You're exploiting that woman."

Bonita doesn't know what exploiting means but she doesn't like being interrupted.

"Pipe down, asshole. I'm talking here and I know when I'm being cheated."

This is not exactly how bullhorn man wants the interview to go, so he tries to end it and move on to other issues.

"Well, thank you, Bonita, for helping us see through the 'just having fun' shah-rod."

But Bonita is not one to be cut off so easily, shah-rod or no shah-rod. Activist boy keeps the bullhorn away from her, but she just starts yelling instead.

"I'm not finished yet. They didn't give me my medal and Mote promised me a pop and I didn't get that either. And I'm not going anywhere until I do."

Then activist boy makes a big mistake. He puts his hand on Bonita's back and tries to direct her out toward the opening in the circle.

No one pushes around Bonita Marie Anderson. She pivots away from him and turns back into his face.

"Take your hands off me you dirty pervert! You can't touch me there! You can't touch me anywhere!"

He looks stricken—and then he is stricken. Bonita kicks him in the shin. He drops his bullhorn and howls in pain, holding his injured leg while pogo sticking on the other.

Now the crowd, most of which can't see what's going on, is angry. They start breaking through the security cordon.

"Where's he touching her?" "Somebody stop him!" "Get him!"

Things are turning ugly, but then people at the back of the crowd start looking behind them. A young boy is running toward us, coming from the reed marsh beyond the athletic field. He's yelling something as he runs, but I can't tell what. Some people start running toward the reeds as he enters the center ring of the crowd.

"There's a body out there! I found a body! Call the police! There's a body!"

SEVEN

THIS IS WHAT EVERYONE feared but no one would speak. It was the worst possible for Abby and her family, of course, but it was also extremely bad news for Cassandra Pettigrew and New Directions. We live in an age dominated by lawyers, commentators, activists, gossipmongers, frightened politicians, and perpetually offended people. All of them need to feed, and this promised to be a feast.

Suddenly no one cares about ableism or inappropriate touching. Some head for the marsh, others for the parking lot. I start looking for my Specials, knowing that a couple will want to lead the charge to the marsh and others will be frozen in place.

I've gotten everyone together except Billy when Bo Springer rushes up to me. He's hyperventilating and looks like he's about to cry.

"Get your residents to the group home. I'm calling a code four. We're going into lockdown mode. Cassie is upset big time. This is bad. Real bad."

I tell him that I am, in fact, in the process of gathering my folks, but he isn't listening.

"And whatever you do, don't talk to the media."

Yes, there are a few reporters around, even a television film crew or two. Special Olympics makes good filler on the six o'clock news if there aren't enough car accidents or house fires that day. It would be an assignment for the junior varsity journalists to be sure, but now they find themselves, serendipitously, on the scene of a major story.

Sure enough, as we approach the door of the group home, a man comes up holding a pad of paper and a pen. He walks past me and up to J.P., which gives me mixed emotions, mostly positive.

"Would you be willing to answer some questions, sir?"

J.P. is his usual model of cooperation.

"Um, um, I will try my hardest."

"Did you know the deceased?"

"Yes, I know Denise. She's on the girl's floor. I have her picture."

The reporter is confused, but clearly intrigued.

"So her name is Denise?"

As he's writing that down, I make a move to intervene, but Jimmy beats me to it.

"What's going on? What's the scoop? Do you know Jimmy Olsen?"

It's clear the residents don't quite understand what has happened. Judy is trying to piece things together.

"I . . . I heard someone say it is . . . Abby? Is she okay?"

The reporter is the source of news rather than the collector.

"If you're talking about the young woman who they just found, no, she's not okay. She's dead. Do any of you know what happened to her?"

I jump in before Jimmy creates a story that he himself will believe as soon as he hears it from his own lips.

"These folks don't know anything about what happened."

"Well, what about you? May I ask your name?"

"My name is Kit Carson, Johnny's brother."

Why did I say that?

"Well, Mr. Carson, do you know anything about what happened to that woman? I'm told someone has been missing from here. Is that right?"

I am too stunned by my own stupidity to answer coherently.

"I've got to get these people inside."

Luckily, most of them are already going in on their own. Only Jimmy seems to want more action. He addresses the reporter.

"Did you ever watch Columbo? He used to go like this."

Jimmy puts the fingertips of his right hand to his temple and tries to look like he's thinking real hard. I grab him by the arm and get him into the house. The news guy doesn't try to follow. He knows a dead end when he sees one.

"Nice job, Mr. Carson."

Bonita is looking at me with her hands on her hips. I pretend not to hear her and tell everyone to gather in the living room. It's a glum group, except for Billy, who seems a stranger to emotions. I don't know if any of them knew Abby well, but it has sunk in that she's dead, and each in one way or another feels the loss.

"Well, I'm sorry to say that Abby has died. We are supposed to stay in the house for a while." Of course, I'm not certain the body is Abby's, but there are quite a number of things in life you can be sure of without being certain. We'll know soon enough.

I try to think what Zee would do here.

"Does anyone have anything they want to say?"

Jimmy doesn't need any prompting.

"She was a peach of a girl. We're all going to miss her. She's gone to a better place."

Bonita corrects him.

"The only place she's gone, numb nuts, is down the toilet. I need a pop."

Judy is still processing what Jimmy has said and misses Bonita's comforting response. But she has formulated one of her own.

"Yes, Jimmy. You are . . . are right. We are going to miss . . . I should say . . . miss her very much. I think we should pray to Jesus for our . . . our friend Abby."

I start to nip this in the bud, but before I can suggest that each person remember Abby in his or her own way, Judy follows up thought with deed.

"Dear Jesus, son of the . . . the Most High, and of our mother, Mary. This is Judy. I am with my . . . my friends here—Ralph, Jimmy, J.P., Bonita, Billy, and my brother of mine, Jon. We are sad. We are . . . I should say . . . we are sad about Abby. Abby has died. She is in . . . in heaven now with . . . with you. Maybe you can say hello to her for us—her friends here in the Carlson Group Home, Wayzata, Min . . . Min . . . Minnesota. Tell Abby that we miss her very, very much and we hope . . . we hope that she is happy in her . . . her new place. Amen."

This gets echoing amens all around, a da dooey from Ralph, and a low hum from Billy.

We spend the next couple of hours with our thoughts, not the kind of company that has been rewarding for me in the past. Then there's a knock on the front door. I open it and find a tallish man in his fifties with graying hair, wearing a fedora. He flips open a badge in his hand.

"I'm Detective Strauss, Minneapolis Police Department. Are you in charge of this unit?"

What an idea. Me "in charge" of something. The phrase implies so much that is so far from my experience—competence, command, confidence, responsibility, authority. But I figure he's using the term loosely.

"Yes, I'm on duty this afternoon."

"And your name?"

"Jon Mote."

His eyes narrow and he studies my face.

"How many people live here, Mr. Mote?"

"There are six residents, plus whichever staff person is on duty."

"Are these their names?"

He shows me a list of everyone living on the New Directions campus, broken down by where they live.

"Yes, they're all here in the living room if you want to talk with them."

He looks over my shoulder.

"No, not today. I just came to say I will be interviewing each one in the next few days. I'll arrange with the executive director what day that will be, and she'll let you know. In the meantime, please avoid talking about the case among yourselves. I want each one telling their own story. Do you understand?"

"Yes, I understand."

Detective Strauss looks closely at me again.

"Sergeant Wilson at headquarters recognized your name on the staff list we got a couple days ago when the young woman went missing. He told me about you and that case with the U of M professor. He says you weren't helpful. In fact, he said you were a pain in the ass. He says I should tell you not to try playing detective again. He was quite clear about that. So that's what I'm telling you."

"Message received."

It's not pleasant to be widely considered a pain in the ass. I mean, everybody rubs somebody the wrong way, but to have it be a consensus— "This guy's life is best summed up as 'a pain in the ass'"—is sort of hard to take. I know Uncle Lester thought of me that way, and more than one officer in the army, and Zillah came to that conclusion, and now it's the semi-official position of the Minneapolis Police Department: Citizen Jon Mote—Pain in the Ass.

About the only people who have held a different view are my mom and dad—God bless their departed souls—and my Not Quite Up to Speed sister Judy. And Judy would no doubt add Jesus to my list of defenders. "Jesus, lover of my soul" we used to sing. But who believes in either Jesus or souls these days?

Frankenstein (Mary Shelley's, not Boris Karloff's) was a fairly sweet guy until they rejected him one too many times (evil, evil society say the Romantics, past and present). Then he decided to be exactly what everyone said he was—a monster.

I don't have the energy for that myself. Evil on a big scale is tiring, and after a while, perhaps a bit boring too. I think I'll just settle for being a small pain in the ass, eating of my bitter heart. I like it because it is bitter. And because it is my heart.

EIGHT

"That . . . that's right, Jon. Mzzz Petti . . . Pettigrew says that Ralph and I should go on a . . . I should say . . . a date."

That was a few weeks ago.

Oh my goodness, I thought at the time. The Normalizing drum is beating again. It isn't good enough that Judy and Ralph like each other, are even fond of each other, sometimes go out of their way to sit next to each other (and oftentimes don't), and even, when spirits are high, occasionally hold hands. Now it's been decided that Normal means they need to go out on a Date. Which of course is only the camel's nose under the tent.

And the rest of the camel has a name—sex. It's the hot new question in the world of Specials. Sex is an old question in the rest of the world, but it's new with Specials because for so long the answer to it was obvious—no, none, nada, nein, nyet, not a good thing (for all involved). But now the goal for many is Normal, and if there's one thing that's pretty Normal among Normals, it's sex.

So what about sex for highly dependent people with highly varied problems (from messed up genetics to messed up frontal lobes) and with very poor prospects for taking care of the consequences of being Normal in this way? (I can be a master of indirection.)

I quickly found out that it often breaks down into a battle between parents and professionals. Parents are likely to dislike the idea a lot and professionals are likely to think it worth discussing. Parents think the professionals are playing "The Progressive Social Experiment Game" with their children, and professionals often think parents are playing the "Keep Them Children Game" when their loved ones are adults and capable of functioning in most areas as adults.

And how useful are terms like "child" and "adult" anyway when mental age and physical age grow increasingly apart? Judy is in some ways as

44

young as a preschooler and in other ways as old as Methuselah. And thinking about Judy and this request for a date makes me suddenly realize that my instinct is all on the nada side. I feel a little rush of protectiveness. This is my sister. This is Judy. Shaped by the Baptists and polished by the nuns. She is, in fact, the Virgin Judy (that pervert Uncle Lester not withstanding). Who's this Ralph guy anyway? How much do I know about him? What are his intentions? What are his prospects?

All this came over me in a wave, and I realized that I'd been standing there thinking these things for some time and that Judy was waiting for a response. Fortunately, waiting is one of Judy's gifts.

"A date, huh."

"Yes, Jon, a . . . a . . . I should say . . . a date."

"You and Ralph?"

This time she just blinked.

"Well, I would need to talk to some people. To see if it's okay."

She was only asking for a simple date. She wasn't announcing plans to buy a house downtown by Lake Harriet and start a family. Why did this feel like the sound of one big boot dropping? I was definitely overreacting, and it was all instinctual. (But given all the messes that people have carefully *reasoned* their way into, I'm not going to bad-mouth instinct.)

And it wasn't as though there weren't something going on between Judy and Ralph. After all, Ralph plays the bones for her—or at least it seems it's for her. The bones are actually four polished ebony sticks a little bigger than pork ribs that Ralph holds between his fingers on both hands and clacks together with quick flicks of his wrists, beating out a rhythm that would be the envy of a Calypso drummer. No one knows the hour of his appearing from his room with his bones a-clacking and a proud smile on his face, but Judy is delighted every time, certain, I think, that she is being wooed.

And so I did talk to people, to confirm that the idea actually did originate with Cassandra Pettigrew. I was told "of course" it's a good idea, and that I simply needed to arrange the time, get some money from their accounts, reserve a vehicle, and find someone to drive them. Even the progressives on the staff, however, are not averse to a chaperone in this particular case, though I am advised the chaperone should keep a distance. "It should be as normal as possible," I'm informed. Ah yes.

I had an extensive discussion of possibilities for the event with Judy and Ralph. Judy had one answer for every suggestion: "Why, why . . . that sounds good." And Ralph had no answer for every suggestion. Neither a "da dooey" nor an "aw phooey." I'm not at all sure that he even understood what we were discussing. He is taken on outings all the time, but does he understand that this time it's specifically with Judy, and that this time it is—ta da—a Date?

Since Judy was up for anything and Ralph was mute, I decided to please myself. First, I decided that *I* will be the chaperone—not one of these other staffers who have who-knows-what kind of morals. And second, I decided that the date will consist of a boat ride on Lake Minnetonka with a treat dockside in Excelsior.

And today's the day. I pick up Judy and Ralph at the group home after breakfast on a Sunday morning. The other residents give them a sendoff like it's the start of a honeymoon. Bonita hugs Judy and gives her a kiss on the cheek. Jimmy yells out some timeless advice for Ralph.

"Don't do anything I wouldn't do, buddy." Accompanied by the obligatory two thumbs up.

Even Billy is humming louder than usual.

We take the short drive down Wayzata Boulevard to Superior Street and down the hill to the lake front. It's all blue water on the left and the leftovers of small-town business on the right, waiting patiently for gentrification. (If charm is present, can development be far behind?)

The dock where the boat takes off is right behind the old train depot. James J. Hill himself, the placard announces, declared it the best depot in the whole of the Great Northern Railway when he opened it in 1906, replacing an older depot which had itself replaced the original. We look around it while we wait to get on the boat, and it shouts "charming" at the top of its lungs—light tan, half-timbered stucco with a steep wood-shingled roof. The trains last stopped here in 1971 when I was eleven, nineteenth-century technology giving way to twentieth-century reality. And now a twenty-first century is beginning. (When is that Big Reunion in the Sky going to happen anyway? Norman G. is waiting and the Big Fella is badly overdue.)

I've booked us on the steamboat *Minnehaha*. The Dakota Sioux first got pushed out of the area by the Chippewa, who got pushed out by Progress. (I have no idea who the Dakota may have pushed out, but it seems white men did not invent empire, though they became very good at it.) The

46

railroad came to Lake Minnetonka in the 1860s to serve the small towns that had grown up, and crowds from the city soon followed. They needed excursion boats, and the *Minnehaha* was one in a long line. After the fad was over, it was scuttled off Big Island in the 1920s but then raised and restored in the 1990s and now again runs tours around the lake. Judy is suitably impressed.

"Why, why . . . it looks like a boat from . . . from a fairy tale."

Well, I don't know about a fairy tale, but the boat is narrow and long and bright yellow, with a smokestack in the middle and lots of windows. And it is atmospheric in a kitschy kind of way. Most important, it has "Date" written all over it, and even Ralph gives his approval as we survey it from the dock.

"Da dooey."

I'm impressed myself to be riding on a boat that spent decades on the bottom of the lake and is now sailing again. I probe its metaphorical potential. I mean, human beings have long created myths and metaphors that reflect our wish for a life after life. The Phoenix rises from its ashes, the Isis statue is buried in the mud and then sprouts, the seed "dies" before it germinates into life, the caterpillar goes into its tomb-like cocoon and comes out a butterfly. We have this unquenchable thirst to believe there's more for us than three score and ten, and all the logical positivists in the kingdom can't make it go away. I know the thirst hasn't gone away for me, no matter how much post-superstition water I drink.

Today there are maybe ten customers all together. We pull out into Wayzata Bay, heading for Excelsior a few miles across the lake. After some minutes we pass small Spirit Island on our right and then move into the biggest part of Lake Minnetonka. The lake is about twenty-four miles long but with all its bays and inlets has hundreds of miles of shoreline. And more than a few of those miles are dotted with the homes of people to whom capitalism has been unusually kind—some for generations. The private docks reach out from Robinson Bay and Gibson Point like teeth on a comb. Makes me think of that "single green light, minute and far away" that Nick sees out east in the novel, but which F. Scott might have first seen here on Lake Minnetonka.

Just beyond Gibson Point I spot Deephaven Beach tucked into a small bay on the left, a place with some fleeting resonance for me. I once dated a girl who was a lifeguard there. She was cute and bright, but a little too religious for me at the time. That was long after my own farewell to baptisms and Bible studies and "bring it all to Jesus" babble. She wasn't pushy, but when she let it slip that she was "praying about our relationship," I knew it was time to pull anchor. I wanted my dating life to be a "god-free zone." The rest of my life too, for that matter.

Wanting to shake such memories, I check out Judy and Ralph in the row in front of me. They are sitting like an old married couple, upright, hands in their laps, looking vaguely out the window and not saying a word. I wonder whether I should perform an intervention, maybe try to get a conversation going between them. But then it occurs to me that perhaps that would be an offense to Normal. There are other couples sitting silently. Inserting myself might violate some Star Trek directive about not interfering in other worlds?

I decide to risk it.

"How do like this, guys. Pretty nice, huh?"

"Why it is . . . I should say . . . it is very nice indeed, Jon. It reminds me of our very own Como Lake, it does."

Judy's ability to connect things has always amazed me. For a Special that is. We had, in fact, grown up near Como Lake, just north of St. Paul. Before our parents died in the car wreck, they would take us out on foot-powered paddleboats on the small lake. Dad and I would race mom and Judy. Dad made sure it was always a tie, much to my disappointment. I mean, if you can't beat two girls, I thought, who can you beat?

It takes us about an hour to get to Excelsior on the south side of the lake. They give us ninety minutes to explore the little town and have a snack before the trip back. I spot a yellow, faux streetcar sitting next to the docks that is selling hot dogs and ice cream out a side window. Perfect. Skirting the complexities of choice, I reduce the multitude of ice cream offerings to three for Ralph and Judy's consideration—vanilla, chocolate, or strawberry.

Benches line a walkway along the lake that leads to a waterfront park on a small hill. We choose one and sit down to enjoy our cones on our tripartite date. That's when we experience a visitation as stunning to me as anything recounted in a sacred text. I see it on Judy's face before I see it with my own eyes. She stops in mid-lick, her tongue still on the ice cream but her eyes widening and her eyebrows arcing dramatically. I follow her gaze to the source and see an attractive woman walking alone toward us with a large dog on a leash. I first focus on the dog and then on the woman.

It's Zillah.

The Virgin Mary coming down from the clouds wouldn't have had any greater impact on me. It's going on two years since we separated. She has become a mythical figure in that time, as mythical *as* the Virgin Mary. She is the only woman I've ever loved and the only woman I've ever tried to please and the only woman to ever leave me. She is a symbol of my failure as a husband and as a human being, and, shockingly, I'm thrilled to see her. Sort of.

The expression on Zillah's face when she recognizes me is somewhere between startled and petrified. Or maybe that's the look on my face. I'm not sure. When her eyes shift to Judy, she softens and smiles.

"Hello, Jon. Hello, Judy."

For her part, Judy is the Personification of Delight.

"Why, why . . . look what the dog drug in." This is an expression straight from our father, used liberally whenever unexpected company showed up at our door, and quite literal in this case. It creates a small twinge in me to hear it. Pain mixed with longing.

"Please . . . I should say . . . please join us, Zi . . . Zillah. We can have a . . . a catch-up chat."

If I had issued the invitation, I am sure Zillah would have politely declined and moved on after a few sentences. But there is something irresistible about Judy. She draws people to her the way a large celestial body bends light. The invitation seems freighted with significance, as though coming from another place. Like a solemn invitation to a royal wedding.

"Well, all right. I have a few minutes. And it would be good to catch up, as you say, Judy."

Zillah sits on the far end of the bench next to Judy, who is next to Ralph, who is next to me. This requires me to sit on the front edge of the bench and turn toward them if I am to avoid talking to the lake instead of to Zillah.

I can't stop staring at her. The cut of her short blonde hair is unchanged. Her eyes are the same icy blue, her cheekbones as high and architectural as before. But in some strange way it is as though I am looking at her for the first time. She looks . . . not older, not quite sadder, but, I don't know, more experienced or something. More weighted by life. Maybe I look the same.

Judy clears her throat for something she does very well: introductions.

"This is my . . . my boyfriend, Ralph. We are on . . . a date our own-selves. Ralph, this is Zi . . . Zi . . . Zillah, the wife of my brother of mine, Jon."

Ralph makes brief eye contact but keeps working on his cone. I find myself suddenly nervous as heck.

"It's good to see you, Zillah."

I am surprised to discover that this is actually true. It does feel good to see her. It's been a long time and seems longer. (Calendar time versus psychological time and all that.) Some lonely months on the houseboat under the Wabasha Bridge after she left, then some months there with Judy before I returned her to the group home, now some months alone again, working part-time at New Directions. A lot of alone even for a man who courts it.

Zillah just smiles. I search my data banks for a good follow-up and come up with a null set.

"What have you been up to?"

Yikes. How flippant does that sound? My wife leaves me, her attorney eventually sends me divorce papers, I ignore same (stacking them together with mail order catalogs and unread copies of *Sports Illustrated*), we have no other contact, and when, by chance, I encounter her on a bench by a lake, I ask, "What have you been up to?" I may be less haunted than I was before, but I am no more suave.

"Just living, mostly. How about you?"

An answer worthy of the question.

"Oh, the same. Mostly. I'm working some at Judy's place."

I decide there's no reason to say anything about Judy living with me for a while on the boat, or about me working on Dr. Pratt's case, or about what happened or didn't happen in that storefront church by the river, or about my getting a haircut last week. Turns out I don't need to. Judy becomes a veritable diary of my life since Zillah left it.

"Jon and me lived . . . I should say . . . lived on the boat in the river. And he took me to Co . . . Como Zoo where we saw Brianna Jones and her boyfriend but it was really her bro . . . brother of hers. And we went to Memphis and saw a . . . a very nice lady, who was very sad. But we did not see Mr. El . . . Elvis Presley, who has, as you may . . . as you may know, has tragically passed away his own self. But Jon was not doing so good. So I . . . I prayed to Jesus and Jesus . . . I should say . . . Jesus made him better. And now I am back with my . . . with my friends, and we are all doing very, very well, thank you very much."

Judy smiles and claps her hands and swings her feet, delighted with her performance.

"Sounds like an interesting time, Judy."

"Oh yes, most very interesting, Zi . . . Zillah."

Then something comes out of my mouth without permission or precognition.

"I've missed you, Zillah."

I don't know whether to cover it up with a laugh or simply pretend I haven't said it at all and scurry away with Judy and Ralph in tow. Instead I default to paralysis—a state of mine with which Zillah has abundant experience. She seems a bit paralyzed herself, a small smile fronting a deeper pain.

Judy is the only one with moving parts.

"Yes, that is right . . . Jon. We both miss you very, very much, Z . . . Zillah. You should come . . . come by more often. You and Jon should . . . should see a movie to . . . together."

Great. Judy is on the first date of her life and now she's the Patron Saint of Dating.

"Maybe *The Wizard* . . . I should say . . . *The Wizard of Oz.*"

The Wizard of Oz is the archetypal movie for Judy (never mind that the Munchkins are an abomination to cultivated sensibilities these days). Our parents loved it, and we saw it many times in the sixties when it came on television, a big annual event, like *Gone with the Wind*, the other movie permanently etched in Judy's mind. Our father used to make a big deal out of Judy Garland sharing the same first name with our Judy. "Two beautiful young ladies with the same name," he used to say, "both on their way to see the Wizard." I was never sure who the Wizard was in *our* Judy's life, but she and my father seemed to know, and she laughed every time he said it, often jumping up, putting her hands on her hips, and clicking her heels together while my dad beamed.

Judy's suggestion unfreezes Zillah and she rises.

"Yes, perhaps we should, Judy. That would be fun." She looks at me and puts out her hand as I awkwardly stand. "Perhaps we should."

I take her hand and give a slight bow, like I'm taking leave of the Queen or something.

"Good to see you, Zillah. All the best."

"You too, Jon."

And then she is gone—down the path, down time's tunnel, back to "mostly living." Same with me.

The boat ride back from Excelsior to Wayzata is a blank. All I can think about is seeing Zillah. The Baptist residue in me says nothing in life is accidental. The modern me says everything in life is accidental. At the moment, the Baptist side is winning. It's not until the boat bumps the dock in Wayzata that I return to the world in front of me and notice that Ralph has his arm around Judy's shoulder and they both wear contented smiles.

NINE

BECAUSE THERE ARE SO many people the police want to interview at New Directions, they set up shop in the main building and have staff and residents pass through in waves over a few days' time. The Carlson Group Home is scheduled for a Thursday morning, five days after Abby's body was discovered. Everyone is kept back from the workshops and activity centers. It's big news among the residents. Jimmy is particularly excited.

"They're going to want to know where I was on the night of the crime. They're going to see if I have an ali baba."

Bonita is confused and suspicious.

"What's an ali baba?"

"It's like an excuse. Like, say, somebody kills Jon."

Oh thanks a lot.

"And the coppers ask me, 'Where were you on the night of the crime?' And I say, 'I was bowling.' And the coppers say, 'Was anyone there bowling with you, Jimmy?' And I say, 'Yes, my friends were there bowling with me, copper.' And that would be my ali baba."

Judy considers this carefully.

"Where . . . where . . . I should say, where do I get an ali baba for my own self, Jimmy? I . . . I do not bowl."

This seems to stump them all, so I, with my superior intelligence, step in.

"Don't worry about ali babas, guys. All you have to do is answer the policeman's questions the best you can. He knows that none of you hurt Abby. He just wants to know if you heard or saw anything that might help him find out who did."

"I saw plenty," Bonita asserts confidently. "But I'm not saying nothin' unless they give me a pop."

"Bonita, this is not about pop. And you didn't see anything."

"How do you know what I saw, Mote?"

"I know that you were here in this house and that you went to sleep in your bed that night like everyone else, because I was on duty."

She crosses her arms and finishes me off.

"Well, I know what I know and that's all that I know."

Jimmy mops up.

"She's Popeye the sailor man."

Jimmy and I apparently have similar tastes in cartoons.

When the time comes, I take everyone over to the main building. We sit ourselves in the lounge, waiting our turn. There's a woman from a state agency who will join the residents for their interviews, but I'm on my own. I appreciate the distinction being made, but am not sure I deserve it.

After a time, Detective Strauss appears in the doorway of the conference room off the lounge and calls my name first. As I rise and walk toward the room, I am supported by an unwelcome chorus of encouragement.

"Good luck, Jon."

"Tell the truth, now."

"I will pray . . . pray for you, I will."

I am expecting Detective Strauss to read me my Miranda rights—the right to remain silent, anything you say can be used against you, and all that—but that just shows I watch too much television. (Why didn't they Miranda us on our wedding day? Could have saved both Zillah and me a lot of pain.)

I considered bringing a lawyer for this interview just to be safe. I do know a few, a legacy of my work for some of them back in the day, but I also know what they charge. I did a quick calculation of their likely hourly fee divided by my known hourly wage and figure that even minimal representation would cost me at least two weeks' pay. So I decided to go toe to toe with The Law with my bare hands. (Which sounds like something Jimmy would say.)

When I see the camera I think maybe I've made a mistake. It has been set up on a tripod and I can't help but stare at the tiny red "on" light. I'm suddenly very nervous. My record in one-on-one conversations is not good. Ask Zillah. Ask God.

Besides, I have promised not be a pain in the ass and I'm not sure I can live up to it.

"Where were you on the evening of Wednesday, June 27th, the night Abby Wagner disappeared?"

"I was working that night at the group home. I sleep there two nights a week and that was one of them."

"What is the group home?"

"The Carlson home, a house for the adult residents who aren't yet placed in community group homes and aren't in training to live independently. It's right here on the campus."

"Why are they not in training to live independently?"

"They are not considered sufficiently high functioning to do so."

"How do you define high functioning?"

I don't know whether Strauss is just warming me up with dummy questions or whether he is unsure of what kind of people he will be dealing with and trying to get some help. Either way, I'm not the person to be answering. I'm basically a caretaker who specializes in reading clocks and making change. I have mastered neither the lingo nor the required sensitivities for this job. But I have a history of rushing in ahead of the angels.

"Well, I think it has to do with IQ and life skills, or something like that."

Actually, I haven't a clue as to how to define high functioning. I am not very high functioning myself. I mean, I misplaced my parents, I fled the army, I dropped out of grad school (just when I was in danger of succeeding at something), I botched my marriage, and I eked out a narrow (and perhaps temporary) victory over my inner voices. Who am I to say who's high functioning and who isn't?

"IQ?"

"Well, they tell me that 70 was once the cut-off point for one thing or other."

This rings a bell for Strauss.

"Yes, I remember something about that in a Mississippi case. Seems you couldn't execute someone with an IQ under 70 and this guy was at 67, so they retested him and he improved up past 70 and right on to death row. Poor sucker was too stupid to stay stupid, you might say."

Well, I'm thinking I wouldn't say that and I would suggest you not say that around here either. But I don't say so.

"So what about life skills? What does that refer to?"

"Oh, just the things you need to able to do to get through a normal day."

I can't help wondering about my own life skills. Dressing, driving, ordering off a menu: I'm a superstar. Making myself understood, keeping my mind going in one direction, knowing what I'm here for—pretty much a bust. No, my life skills definitely need work.

I mean, can you say you have good life skills if you aren't happy? Isn't that the most crucial life skill of all? Just plain old ordinary contentment? Like the cow with its muzzle in the hay, swishing its tail, being what it was made to be? Why can't I even get that far? Judy can. Most of these Specials can. They aren't nearly as unhappy about their . . . what? . . . condition . . . as we are unhappy *for* them. We ask ourselves how we would feel to be that disabled, differently abled, cognitively diverse—hell, you pick the term—and we think "I wouldn't want to live that way" and then conclude that they don't want to live that way either. Or live at all. And we make policies accordingly. What's so important about telling time or making change any-way? Screw the quid pro quo of the marketplace. Jesus, my sister is happy and I'm not, and yet I'm the one who gets to go back to my houseboat every night and pretend I'm Normal. Maybe I *am* Normal, but if being lost in the cosmos is Normal, then I'll sign up for Plan B.

"Like what kind of things to get through the day?"

"Like dressing, eating, telling time."

"And the people in your house can't do that?"

"Well, they're fine on two out of three. But not so good on some of the other things people need to be out there on their own in the world."

I pause for a moment.

"And, truth be told, maybe they don't hanker so much to live indepen-dently. Maybe they actually prefer to live together—and maybe with me."

I'm hoping that last thought doesn't get back to Cassandra Pettigrew. It would earn me a serious reprimand. Normal people want to live on their own, making their own decisions, and to suggest that being independent is anything less than a sacred goal is like handing out matches while you're tied to the stake.

The detective is reading his notes. I'm thinking maybe we're done. We're not. He looks up at me with a new intensity.

"Are any of the people in your place dangerous, Mr. Mote?"

"Dangerous?"

"Dangerous."

I want to say, "Define dangerous," but decide against it. I actually had never thought about that. Ralph could break you in pieces. Just last week he showed up at the door of the group home holding a dead gopher by the tail. He and Sam Raven trap them for fun. (Don't tell Cassandra.) Ralph was smiling broadly, displaying it to me like an excited hunting dog displays a retrieved bird to the master. "Broke his little neck," he announced with a beaverish chuckle. I'm thinking he could break most anyone's little neck if he wanted to, but I've never seen anything more violent from him than a dismissive wave of the hand. So I don't mention it to Strauss.

J.P. and Judy are as dangerous as marshmallows. Jimmy is a danger to all the good-looking women in the world, but only in his own mind. Bonita kicked the activist in the shins and is maybe capable of punching you in the gut, but with arms the size of pipe cleaners, you wouldn't be at great risk.

"No, not dangerous. Not violent. Any resident who would be a serious threat for violence is sent elsewhere."

"Where?"

"St. Peter. To the Security Hospital."

Come to think of it, I'm probably the most dangerous one of the group. To Judy, for instance, when she came to live with me on the houseboat while I was melting down. And to myself, with my voices cooing about how peaceful and inviting the water looked that winter night on the bridge. I'm in no position to assess how dangerous anyone is.

"Can you be sure that none of them is dangerous?"

"Well, they've been assessed for that."

Cassandra would be proud of me.

"And would you vouch for the accuracy of those assessments?"

"I don't do those myself. That's above my pay grade. I leave that to the experts. I just supervise the group home when it's my shift."

Detective Strauss pauses again. I'm hoping he's played out this vein of questioning.

"What were you doing between 9 and 11 p.m. the night the victim disappeared?'

"I watched television with the residents until 9:30 or so and then we all went to bed."

"Did everyone watch television?"

"Everyone except Billy. No one knows what Billy is watching, but it isn't television. He was in his room."

"Are you sure he was in his room?"

"Yes, I said good night to him around 9:45 when I checked to see that everyone was in their rooms."

"And after that? Could he have left the house after that?"

"I suppose so. Anyone can leave the house at any time. It's locked to the outside but not to the inside."

"That would include you as well. Correct?"

"Yes, I can leave too. Anytime."

After all, I'm a Normal.

"That's all for now. I may want to talk with you again."

When I come back into the lounge, the residents all perk up. Jimmy speaks first.

"How did you do, Jon? Did you give them your ali baba?"

"I did fine, Jimmy. Thanks for your concern."

TEN

ABBY'S FUNERAL TAKES PLACE on Saturday, two days after the interviews. Cassandra makes clear that she expects the staff to be there.

"You cannot be required to attend, of course, but as part of your professional capacity you are expected to attend, and I know that many of you want to attend as a reflection of your personal relationship with the deceased—that is, with Abby Wagner."

My folks certainly want to go. They don't understand lots of things, but they understand loss, and they know that death is loss for everyone, I don't care what the "gone to a better place" people say. Even Judy is sad, who thinks death just initiates a high-speed elevator ride to paradise (if, I should say, you love Jesus).

"Abby was our . . . our friend. We will miss her . . . very, very much."

Even Bonita, whose capacity for empathy is cramped, seems reflective and as genuinely sad as the rest.

The funeral takes place at the Unitarian church on Rice Street. The notice in the newspaper indicated that the Wagners were founding members when the church moved to Wayzata in the 1960s.

I can tell when we drive up that the Unitarians bought this place from a previous church rather than building it themselves. The main window is the shape of a stylized three-leaf clover, a muted symbol of the Trinity (see St. Patrick), not something that universalists are eager to push. And the roofline points too obviously toward heaven. Unitarians lean toward flat roofs, symbolizing, I'm thinking, their primary interest in the horizontal things of this world: social justice, the environment, neighborliness. Less interested, you might say, in Jesus' footprints in Galilee than in their own carbon footprints in Minnesota.

Of course, I'm beyond my depth—but when have I ever let that stop me.

The steps up to the entry door are steep, a bit of a challenge for some of our folks.

The pastor greets us, appropriately long-faced, at the door. But I can tell he's thrilled. Having so many Specials at his church at one time gives him the feeling of being one of the good people, a feeling for which liberals are ravenous. (We Baptists, on the other hand, prided ourselves on how sinful we knew ourselves to be, even while knowing everyone else was a lot more sinful than we were—and not forgiven.)

I'm keeping an eye on each of my residents when I have the misfortune to overhear two sixty-something women talking in the vestibule. They are smiling sweetly at my crew when one says to the other, "It's a mercy that their diminishment protects them from grief."

I want to say back to them something equally foolish, but hold back. Then I think, "If you're ever going to get well, Mote, you have to start saying what you think." And so I do, looking the woman in the eye but not breaking stride.

"Yes, and it is a mercy that your vanity protects you from seeing how wrinkled your face has become."

I hear a gasp as I keep walking. I feel crappy for having said it.

Bonita has heard both comments, though I doubt she understands either one. Still, she knows something snarky has taken place and she reaches out to me for a fist bump.

"You tell 'em, Mote."

As we find our seats, I notice the New Directions brain trust in the row just behind the ones reserved for the family. Cassandra, the board chair, what looks to be a home office bigwig, Dr. Kirkoven the facility physician, and various other staff members. The only one missing is Bo. Must be a big game on television this morning.

The organ music stops and everything goes silent. Abby's closed coffin is wheeled slowly down the center aisle followed by her family. Their faces are a study in responses to death—the mother's is limned in grief, the father's in anger, the brother's in blankness. None of them seems aware of anyone or anything else—each staring down into the dark cellar that death has opened for them. Aunts and uncles and cousins trail behind.

We sing a nondescript song that is vaguely transcendent, in a psychological kind of way. Something about bringing your spirit to the sea and then to the trees and then feeling peace from your inner flame, or something like that. I look at the family—none of them seems comforted.

I'm not sure we should even try to comfort people in times like this. I mean, what the hell, feel the loss, feel the pain, drink the cup to the lees as some Romantic poet or other said. Screw the "better place" talk—especially if the dead one is way too young to be taking her leave. Climb the birch tree if you must, but accept that it's going to bend when you get near the top and set you back to earth again.

After our collective shot at singing, a soloist shows us how it's done. Believe it or not, she starts belting out "The Impossible Dream." I'm thinking this must be a joke of some kind. Don Quixote at a Unitarian funeral? Ralph Waldo must be turning in his grave. Even the blank brother seems aware of the incongruity. He looks up at the soloist with a knitted brow. It must have been Abby's favorite song at some point in her life. I guess we are to picture her reaching even now for the unreachable star.

It's no surprise that the pastor follows the solo with a spread of warm bromides. He hits all the right notes—a celebration of Abby's life, a loving girl, dear to all who knew her, taken too soon and yet never to be forgotten, always in our hearts, a kind of immortality. He throws in a story about Abby as a little girl bringing an offering, a tithe of her weekly allowance, to be given to help children who were less fortunate.

This story brings convulsions to the shoulders of Mrs. Wagner and a change in color to the face of Mr. Wagner, who does not comfort her. The preacher should have stuck with the bromides. Perhaps their banality makes them soothing. They certainly don't require anyone to think. I find myself desperate for this to be over. It's Kabuki theatre, every movement choreographed, and I feel the need for air.

But why am I being such a tough guy? Didn't I cry my eyes out for months when my parents were yanked untimely from this world? Didn't Judy and I sit in dark places and hold each other and talk about our mom and dad and how we missed them? And didn't Judy try to comfort me with words and beliefs—about heaven, about Jesus, about some day and some how? And didn't I grab that comfort with both hands, even as it slipped away between my fingers?

So let them sing about the sea and trees and inner flames, and preach about never to be forgotten, and even reach for the unreachable star. I will just pray—if I can remember how—that the words will comfort Mr. and Mrs. Wagner and Abby's brother and all the aunts and uncles and cousins. And my Specials too. After all, it's what we humans do. When one of us falls, we stop for a moment, we take note, we say a few words, touch, and then we move on, awaiting our own turn. Maybe that's the best we can do.

ELEVEN

APPARENTLY HAVING INITIALS IN your name is not Normal. So says Cassandra Pettigrew. It was revealed at a staff meeting yesterday, part of a long list of micro-directives announced by the Executive Director of Micro-Directives.

"Finally, James McCloskey will no longer be referred to as J.P. His name is James Paul, and from now on all staff and clients will call him James."

Cassandra seemed to assume everyone understood immediately the rightness of this—perhaps as Stalin expected everyone to understand the rightness of rounding up Jewish doctors—and she started to close the meeting. But, slow learner that I am, I spoke up.

"Just so I understand, why is it that J.P. should no longer be J.P.?"

Cassandra stiffened but then perhaps decided this was a teaching moment for those with no initials following their names. (Initials before a last name—bad; initials after a last name—good.)

"The use of initials instead of one's actual name is associated with childhood. It is appropriate for a child. But for an adult, the use of initials is diminutive and therefore demeaning. James is an adult and James is his name and so James it will be. Does that make it clearer, Mr. Mote?"

I was too busy making a list in my head to answer: T.S. Eliot, W.H. Auden, P.D. James, even J.P. Morgan for heaven's sake. But Ms. Pettigrew took my silence as consent and brought the meeting to a close.

How were we going to get the residents of the group home to refer to J.P. as James Paul when for decades they have known him—and he has known himself—as J.P.? (Explain "diminutive" and "demeaning" to Ralph and wait for the "Ah phooey.")

Unfortunately, Cassandra has an answer—behavior mod. This morning a memo appeared in everyone's box that documented the previously announced directive and explained the technique that would be used to bring it about. A rubber band was to be placed around J.P.'s wrist. He was to be asked from time to time during the day—by any staff member—what his name is. If he says "J.P." the staff person is to take his hand and snap the rubber band on his wrist. If he says "James" the staff person is to smile and say, "Yes, James. That's right." In a very short time, the memo declared confidently, J.P. will realize he is really James and all will be appropriate with the world.

And I, as the one on duty at the group home this morning, am to be the person to explain to J.P. that he is no longer J.P. and to put the rubber band on his wrist and, if necessary, to administer the first snap. Conveniently, a rubber band is sitting in my box along with the memo. (Can waterboarding be far behind?)

I hate this. It calls up all kinds of ghosts—and I've got plenty of them. The big one is Uncle Lester—God damn him. (There I go again, invoking a Punisher I do not believe exists in order to invoke a punishment I also do not believe exists but at times devoutly wish.) Uncle Lester used to withhold food when he sensed there was too much of the devil in me. Like forgetting to take my shoes off when I came in the house in Duluth, apparently a divine expectation that didn't make it into the Bible but every good person knew anyway. (Not being a good person, I didn't know—or couldn't remember. Or maybe subconsciously I kept my shoes on to give the finger to Uncle Lester. Freud would know.) So I'd walk in out of the snow with my shoes on and Uncle Lester would say, "Nice work, Jon. You just lost your supper." To which one of the voices in my head would sometimes say, "We're getting bigger every day."

I re-read Cassandra's memo and hold the rubber band in my hand as I walk from the main building to the group home. I try telling myself I'm just following orders, but a sign of metal script pops into my head: "Arbeit Macht Frei." Ridiculous comparison, I say to myself. It's only a rubber band.

I find J.P. in his bedroom after breakfast. His room is decorated in what you might call "Early Truck." Truck photos everywhere. Big semis. What the Brits, in their inimitable way, call articulated lorries. Big trucks of all kinds—including a lot of old ones. I don't know why. But they seem important to J.P. They're part of his mental world. The other morning I asked him if he slept okay.

"Um, not so good, Jon. Those trucks make a lot of noise when you're sleeping. When I woke up this morning, I had gravel all over my bed."

He looked at me hopefully, as though wondering whether this was an appropriate comment. Appropriate be damned, I thought; beats the things I dream about.

Anyway, this morning J.P. is sitting on his bed holding a binder or album of some kind in his hands. I don't know what it is.

"What you got there, J.P.?"

"Oh, just my friends."

"What do you mean?"

He turns it around and shows it to me. It's an old photo album with rows and rows of mostly individual portrait photos—headshots—like they take in school.

"My friends. I've got a lot."

"Nice," I say, but then notice something that gives me a start. They are mostly photos of young girls, maybe eight to twelve years old. And some boys of the same age.

"Where did you get these photos, J.P.?"

"Oh, I ask people for them. People I like. Sometimes people I know and sometimes people I don't know. But once they give me a picture, then I know 'em."

I'm thinking, "When is J.P. with kids this age that gives him the chance to ask for their pictures?" I look at them more closely. Some of them are clearly Specials. I recognize a few from the children's dorms and the independent living units. But there are quite a few Normals too. You can tell that a lot of them are from years ago.

"How long have you been collecting these, J.P.?"

My bad. I've asked a time question. He knits his brow.

"Mm, maybe since twelve o'clock?" he says with a rise in his voice, glancing at me out of the corner of his eye to see if this is the kind of answer the question calls for. With a nod, I pretend that it is.

"Where do you keep this album?"

"Under my bed. Sometimes I sleep on it at night."

"Sleep on it? You mean over it, under your bed?"

"No, like this." He opens the album to a middle page, sets the whole thing on his pillow, then lies down on the bed, the back of his head resting on the album.

"Um, I do this so I can dream about my friends."

"Dream about them?"

"Yes, I dream about my friends. We have a good time. If I want to dream about someone, I open to their page and then I sleep on their picture and dream about them."

It is starting to sound logical, which is a bit worrying.

I know I'm stalling anyway, so I cut to the chase.

"Well, J.P., do you know what your name is?"

He looks wary, like maybe this is a trick question. Perhaps he's thinking "big hands" and "little hands."

"I mean, do you know what your real name is, what J. and P. stand for?"

He decides to risk an answer.

"Um, J. means J. and P. means P. and I think my real name is J.P. Is that right?"

He is hopeful.

"Well, yes and no, J.P. J. stands for James and P. stands for Paul, and your real name is James Paul McCloskey."

This seems to awaken a distant memory.

"That's right. James Paul McCloskey. J.P. That's my name—J.P."

He's not getting it. It's time for the rubber band.

"So, Ms. Pettigrew and the staff believe that you should be called by your real name, J.P. So they want you to call yourself James from now on. And they want me and everyone else to call you James, not J.P. Do you understand that?"

He doesn't understand that. Neither do I.

"Did I do something wrong, Jon?"

"No, J.P. . . . James. You didn't do anything wrong. Nothing at all. Nobody is mad at you. They just think you should go by your real name."

"Um, J.P. is not real?"

"Well, it's real, but I guess it's not . . . I don't know, appropriate. It's not what adults are called."

"Am I an adult?"

"Yes, James, you are."

"What is an adult anyway, Jon?"

This is a stumper. J.P. senses my confusion and reassures me with a pat on the shoulder.

"That's okay, Jon. I don't know either. Don't let it bother you."

I decide I'm not going to bring out the rubber band. Not now anyway. They're not going to make a collaborator out of me. I'm taking a stand.

Maybe later.

TWELVE

THERE'S BEEN A MURDER. Everyone's upset. And—until the murderer is found—afraid. But that doesn't suspend the need to attend to everyday things. Like Auden's poem about the Breughel painting. Icarus falls to his death from the sky, but the ploughman keeps plowing and the ship keeps sailing and the dog goes on with its doggy life. Maybe one guy notices, in the corner lower right, but mostly it's a nonevent to the universe. It's not right, but it's necessary. Only a sliver of us at a time can afford to stop to note the disappearance of an Icarus here or an Abby there—not to mention tens of thousands every day with names we don't know at all. Mourning is a luxury. Frost, McCartney, and Tupac all agree—life goes on.

And so does my own doggy life. I mean, where am I now, where have I been, and where am I going? Nothing in my life is pointing anywhere. Instead, everything is a response to this moment's stimulus, like a fly-trap closing on its prey. No organization to my life, no telos, no story. Not long ago I was staring down at dark, icy waters and finding them inviting. Now I'm spending my days with Specials and my nights alone on a boat—sometimes the other way round. Enough food, enough shelter, enough air—but not enough plot, not enough theme, not enough prospect of happily ever after. I call it a doggy life, but truthfully, I'd give a lot to be as happy as the average pooch.

And life goes on at New Directions, too. The Schedule says to take Billy over to the main building to be seen by Dr. Kirkoven. The doc comes in twice a week for low-level medical issues and checkups. If something is more serious, the client is sent to his clinic. He's almost officially an old man, in his seventies, and he's been seeing some of these people all their lives. He's a no-nonsense, these-are-the-facts kind of guy—a throwback to when docs were somewhere between divinity and plumbers (they made house calls) rather than mere technicians dancing to the tune of corporate bureaucrats.

As we walk over for the appointment, Billy jerks along beside me—stiff-legged and fingers splaying, head cocking first to one side and then the other. I ask him a question—for his sake and mine.

"What are you thinking about these days, Billy?"

Of course it's like asking a tree if it wants to dance, but I do it anyway. Some might think it's mean, but I don't. I want to give him a chance. Maybe someday he'll shock us all and say, "Thank you for asking, Jon. I'm thinking about how beautiful the sky looks today, a veritable medley of variegated blues."

Okay, not that. Very likely not anything—ever. But how do we know that just because he doesn't speak he's not processing anything in there. He can pass a bowl of potatoes. He responds to his name, or seems to. When I took him by the elbow just now and said we were going to see the doc, he headed toward the door without complaint. Maybe he enjoys being talked to even if he doesn't understand most of what we're saying and never answers back. And so I continue.

"What about those Twins, Billy? Think Torii is going to have a good year? How about Ortiz? I say get rid of him. He'll never amount to a hill of beans."

I mention the Twins because Billy seems to actually enjoy watching baseball on television—if you can call it watching, and if you can call it enjoy. Who knows whether "enjoy" is a mental category for Billy. (Does a bird enjoy its food?) He does rock and hum while the game's on. Then again, he rocks and hums during the pregame, postgame, and commercials. Life is one big rock and hum for Billy. Which is more than I can say for a lot of people.

Dr. Kirkoven does the usual ears, mouth, and chest thing. Billy doesn't open his mouth when commanded, but the doc jabs a tongue depressor in there anyway and expertly pries it open. The doc also keeps up a steady monologue, not really talking to me but talking aloud to the air for me to do with as I wish.

"I've been seeing Billy here since he was a tyke. When the nuns got him, he'd already been at three or four other places. Nobody knew what to do with a case like him. Most of them died in the first year or two, especially if they were taken away from their mothers right away, like they almost always were. It's a limbic brain phenomenon. The limbic brain controls nurture and bonding. They're as crucial to a child as breast milk. More crucial, because you can replace a breast with a bottle but you can't replace a mother's love with a crib in a big room in an institution and expect the child to survive. They just shrivel. Failure to thrive we call it. You can feed them all you want. They lose weight and die."

Dr. Kirkoven is serving up these observations against a practice wall. He isn't looking for me to hit the ball back, and so I don't.

"Which in cases like Billy is for the best. The shame is that it ever gets to this point. Thank God we have ways of detecting these things now, before it's too late. Because once they're born it *is* too late. You have to take care of them. It's an instinct. I've seen them left to die in a closed room after birth, but that's more than I can stomach myself. The doctor in me wants to save them, even if I know rationally that there's nothing there worth saving."

Billy has stopped humming, but he's still rocking, sitting stiffly on the examination table. Kirkoven is tapping on his knees.

"We can detect a lot of things prenatally these days. And within ten or twenty years we'll be able to detect most everything. There won't be any excuse for bringing the Billys into the world. At least not in developed countries."

An interesting word that—"developed." As in "further along," "more advanced," "more sophisticated," or "on a higher plane." Progress, I think, is the umbrella concept. Once we were in the dark, now we are in the light. Light, lightness, perhaps an unbearable lightness.

"Don't get me wrong. I love the retarded. I've worked with them my whole career. That's why I think we should do what we can to prevent people from having to live with these afflictions. They shouldn't have to suffer and the rest of us shouldn't have to watch them suffer."

Be careful when someone is doing something for you—or to you—for your own good, especially if they're not asking your opinion.

"Not to mention the waste of resources."

I'm my safety-first, mum self, but the doc knows he's let off a stink bomb and smoothly opens the rhetorical window.

"I use the word 'retarded' without hesitation. It's the scientific word. The scientific term has been 'mental retardation' for decades. It's a factual, neutral word. I believe in facts. If some people use the word pejoratively, then we should educate those people, not get rid of a scientifically accurate, useful word. I understand there are people, including our current executive director, who do not like the term. But we cannot progress if we keep changing scientific terminology to fit the fickle whims of nonscientists. I use retarded because these people *are* retarded—they are delayed, usually permanently, in their development—and it does no one any good to pretend they aren't. A rose by any other name and all that."

Do you get the feeling he thinks the word retarded is quite scientific—scientifically speaking? (I do, but wisely keep this ironic observation to myself.) The problem is that not everyone is a scientist, and not even every scientist believes science is the only legitimate way to think about things. I tried being scientific with Zillah from time to time when we were together. I'd say something like, "Can't we just talk about this factually, without all the emotional baggage?" and she'd say, "Baggage to you, buddy, but factual to me—and you better get used to it!"

I never did get used to it. Hence these days with the Specials and nights alone on a boat.

"Ah, what's this?"

Dr. Kirkoven has pulled down Billy's underwear and he does not like what he's seeing on his butt.

"He has a decubitus ulceration here. Fairly advanced. Has he been spending an inordinate amount of time in bed of late?"

"Nothing unusual."

"Has he been bathing regularly?"

"Three times a week."

"Well, he'll need to bathe every day for the next two weeks. Supervised. I'll prescribe an ointment. You will need to apply the ointment to the sore after each bath and then apply a bandage."

Great. A daily appointment with Billy's butt. And imagine, Uncle Lester thought I'd never amount to anything.

THIRTEEN

LATER IN THE WEEK following Abby's funeral, everybody has returned home in the afternoon from their various places and the general mood is grim. At least I'm attributing grimness to them. I don't have access to their inner state any more than I had access to Zillah's. For that matter, I don't always have access even to my own inner state. It's a sometimes foreign land that often speaks a language I do not understand.

Jimmy is sitting at the dining room table, head on hand, drumming his fingers. Bonita is stewing about something, walking between rooms muttering. J.P. is studying his rubber band, put on by Cassandra herself the day before. (I'm sure there is an entry now in my file noting my failure to do so myself. Bad soldier.)

I decide we all need a diversion. There's just time for a short trip before dinner. So I sign out a van and we head for the Ridgedale Mall, just across the highway from New Directions. Somebody always needs something, so I figure I can make the trip look necessary on the excursion report I'll have to file (form 12-B in case you're interested).

We're walking toward the main building on the way to the vans when Bo comes out the door. He stands there as we walk past and then calls out.

"Hey J.P., what's up?"

J.P. doesn't appear to understand the phrase "what's up" and after a glance skyward he simply says, "Hello, Mr. Springer."

Bo smiles and walks over to him.

"Sorry, James. You're not supposed to respond to J.P. anymore. Have to give you a little reminder."

With that he takes J.P.'s hand and snaps the rubber band on his wrist.

"Keep working on it, buddy."

J.P. looks at his wrist.

"Mm, okay Mr. Springer."

Bonita gives Bo a scowl and Billy makes a strange hissing noise that I've never heard from him before.

You'd think that going with the residents to the mall to shop would be like leading cats through a tuna cannery—temptations at every turn to wander away to this delight or another. Not so. More like leading frightened kids through a haunted house at Halloween, everyone staying close together for fear of something reaching out from the dark. For the mall, you see, is a "not" place—not the group home, not the workshop, not the main building, not the handful of places they are used to and know how to behave in. They have all been to the mall before, just a few weeks ago in fact, to buy J.P. some red tennis shoes, but it seems to feel like the big ocean after the snug harbor of the familiar.

There are, for one thing, the looks. You should hear that in capitals—The Looks. Walk with one Special through a public place and you won't draw much attention. Walk through with a half dozen or more and you become the new center of the universe. You are one giant black hole of Public Attention—sucking in eyes from every corner, stopping people in their tracks, causing mothers to reach instinctively for their children's hands.

Actually, I'm not sure the residents even notice. But I do. I am the one leading the Specials and I find myself doing little things to let people know that I'm not a Special myself. I call out commands in a slightly raised voice to show that I am the one in charge of these people, not a member of the tribe. I'm a Normal, just like the rest of the Lookers.

I've ascertained before leaving the group home that Ralph needs boxer shorts. The former President may wear briefs, but Ralph is a boxer shorts guy. And boxer shorts means Penney's. Actually, pretty much all clothes mean Penney's—for all the residents and for myself. I was raised on Penney's. Growing up, Penney's fit our socioeconomic class, our taste, and our theology. We thought specialty stores were for Episcopalians, Marshall Field's was for Presbyterians, Sears was for Lutherans, Penney's was for Baptists, and Kmart was for Pentecostals. Atheists got to shop anywhere they wanted.

(I've heard similar analyses for the types of cars in the church parking lot and for the way the women wear their hair—the more filled with the Spirit, the bigger the hair.)

On the way to the men's department, we pass through women's underwear. Most of the group averts their eyes, but Jimmy's are bugged and his head is on a swivel.

"Whoa, look at this. Pretty hot stuff, eh Jon?"

I pretend not to hear. Two or three shoppers have turned around and are taking in our passing. I try to keep us passing, but Jimmy stops at a bargain bin and grabs a pair of lacy underwear, holding them up for all to admire.

"I'm getting some of these for my girlfriend."

Bonita corrects him.

"You don't have a girlfriend, dog breath."

The insult is random, but it's an insult, and that's all Bonita needs to know.

"I will have if I start handing out these!"

I pivot back, using my I'm-Not-One-of-Them voice.

"Put those back now, Jimmy, and move it."

Bonita lowers the hammer.

"No pop for him tonight, right Mote?"

I ignore the Enforcer and shepherd everyone onward.

We manage to get Ralph a couple of packages of boxer shorts. He refuses to engage the process, expressing neither approval nor disapproval of the patterns Judy picks out for him. But everyone else agrees they are a fine choice and so the deal is done.

I'm feeling expansive, having lopped the Hydra heads of lingerie and boxer shorts. So as we walk out of Penney's and into the atrium on the upper level, I am about to propose treats. It's a cheap trick: win approval of those you lead by promising them things—at no expense to yourself. Politicians have been doing it for millennia, so why not me?

But before I can get it out, I notice we are one short. Billy is not with us. Literally.

"Where's Billy?"

Judy turns slowly and looks back into the store.

"Well, I think Billy . . . That is, I saw Billy . . . I should say . . . go off back there by his own self."

"Great. You guys stay right here. Don't anyone move. Bonita, you're in charge."

It may seem like making Mrs. O'Leary the fire marshal, but I know that, except for Ralph, they are all afraid of Bonita and I know she will enjoy making them toe the line.

"Got it, Mote. Take your time."

I hurry back into Penney's and spot Billy right away. He's standing staring up at a nude, female mannequin on a pedestal with no arms. He's humming a happy tune. One Special to another, neither a waster of words. Perhaps he's finally discovered someone who understands him.

Having found the lost one, I bring Billy back out to the ninety and nine in the atrium. The residents are gathered at the railing, looking down at the floor below. They seem worried. Jimmy is speaking.

"Looks like trouble, ladies and gentlemen. Give me some time to think."

"Think about what, Jimmy?" I ask.

"The waterfall," says J.P.

"Waterfall? What are you talking about?"

Bonita points to the escalator descending from our floor to the floor beneath us.

"That right there, Mote. No way you're getting me on that sonovabitch."

I start looking around for an elevator, but then remember that Billy absolutely will not go into an elevator. There must be stairs somewhere.

Then it occurs to me that I can make this one of those famous teaching moments. If we master the escalator, I can put it into the excursion report and claim it as meeting an adaptation objective. It's as Normalizing as all get out. What could be more Normal than riding an escalator at the mall?

"Why not, Bonita? A stupid escalator is easy for a woman of your magnitude. And if everyone makes it to the bottom, I'll buy us all treats!"

I say this is my most enthusiastic, This-Is-Going-to-Be-Great voice, the one I use whenever I'm planning something that has all the earmarks of disaster. It creates a sea change in attitudes.

"Well, why didn't you say so before? But I'm not going first. That's for sure."

"Amen," says Jimmy, crossing himself.

Judy is silent. J.P. just stares and Billy fixates on the massive chandelier hanging over the vast space from the ceiling high above.

The troops study the enemy as we move along the railing toward its all-consuming maw. It swallows one person after another, moving them down its throat like chunks of unchewed meat. Bonita is finding even the promise of treats an inadequate incentive.

"What happens if we fall off?"

"You won't fall off."

"But if we do?"

Jimmy offers his help.

"Then you'd hit the floor like a big water balloon, Bonita. Splat. And they mop you up and throw away the keys."

He was doing pretty well until the keys part.

"You aren't going to fall, Bonita. We're going to go one at a time, and we're going to be very careful, and I am here to help."

You had to be a Special to believe that someone like me was going to be much help at anything. But these people *are* Special, and I'm starting to figure out that they trust me.

Luckily no one else is coming to ride the sinister Descent Monster as we approach. I have to decide whether it's better for me to go first and wait at the bottom, a sort of Escalator Moses leading the people to the Promised Land, or to go last, making sure everyone actually boards. I decide to be the captain on this sinking ship.

"So who gets to go first?"

I congratulate myself on the phrase "gets to." They don't fall for it. There's lots of jostling and backing up.

"How about you, J.P.?"

He reaches nervously for the rubber band on his wrist and ever so slightly shakes his head.

Finally Judy steps up.

"Well, if somebody has to be first, it . . . it might as well be me."

Score one for the Mote family.

Judy edges up to where the steps glide out, like little ice floes. She studies them for a few seconds and then her head starts gently bobbing to the rhythm of their appearance, like she is timing a skip rope before entering the vortex. With a whispered "now," she jumps with both feet and lands on the newest step just before it starts to descend. The other residents erupt in praise and hope.

"Way to go, Judy!"

"You did it, Judy! You're the best!"

Judy herself is holding tightly to both handrails, hunched over like a ski jumper sliding down the fifty meter hill. I try to keep the momentum going.

"Okay, see how easy it is? Who's next?"

Ralph figures if Judy can do it, so can he. We gives an "ah phooey" wave to any lingering fear and steps confidently on the next step. Down he goes, pronouncing "da dooey!" to the universe.

Bonita doesn't look impressed. It's still Russian roulette to her. Two people have made it safely, increasing the odds that the next person will be the water balloon. But now Jimmy is eager to jump on the competence bandwagon. He presents himself at the top of the steps like Caesar appearing before his subjects at the Forum. He sets his jaw, looking out and up at things mere mortals cannot hope to see.

Then he suddenly sits down on the floor and scoots himself onto the moving steps before I can grab him. But it works out fine. He waves from his sitting position to the others who have dismounted below and they wave back. I'm yelling for him to stand up, lest he end up with a serrated butt, or worse, and when he is almost to the bottom he does so, gathering high-fives from his admirers as he emerges like said Caesar returning from the Gallic Wars.

That's when I notice that a crowd has gathered. People stand in small bunches around the lower atrium watching the show, others are leaning over the rail on the second floor, pointing and talking to each other. Some are smiling, some are frowning, but all of them have decided this spectacle is more compelling for the moment than anything offered in the stores. And it's free.

When I look back, I find that J.P. has already gotten on. He is standing tall, arms stiffly to his side, like this is something he does every day of his life.

That leaves Bonita and Billy and me. I figure Billy and I need to be last.

"Okay, Bonita. Hop on. Let's get us some pop!"

The word "pop" is like a cattle prod. She jerks to the head of the moving steps. She eyes them, then eyes me, then eyes the people who are eyeing us all.

"What ya looking at, ya bastards."

She then reaches her trembling right foot and places it on the moving rectangle. But she's only willing to risk one foot. Which means, regrettably, that the right leg moves inexorably away from her left leg and her more circumspect self still planted at the top. As she's stretching into an ever widening drafting compass she falls back against one side of the escalator, until finally the laws of physics have their way and her anchor foot joins the descent. Her short legs span three steps as she continues down, frozen, legs splayed, back against the glass side, arms stretching up and down the railing. The other residents position themselves at the bottom, arms out, ready to catch her when she arrives.

I've had more than enough and grab Billy by the upper arm and guide him onto the steps. As usual, he's looking up, not at the steps, which perhaps makes it easier for him than for anyone else. He and I share the same step, descending, as it were, out of the clouds like demigods to the earth below.

We are greeted at the bottom by a group of happy Specials. Handshakes, backslaps, and hugs all around. Bonita looks shaken but is recovering fast.

"Now how about those treats, Mote."

We walk away to a smattering of applause from the Lookers.

FOURTEEN

THERE'S SOMETHING ABOUT DEATH that gets our attention. When it's close—in the family or shared by the community—it sends us back to our most basic understanding of things. Back to our presuppositions you might say. Death requires of us an explanation. Some invoke the periodic table, some the human condition, and some go back to church—at least for a while.

I don't know for certain that Abby's passing—a nice euphemism that—has prompted it, but there seems to be a groundswell of sentiment in the group home for going to church.

Judy started it.

"Well, Jon, we have . . . I should say . . . we have not been to church in a very long time. I would like . . . like very much my . . . my own self to hear about Jesus."

I would point out that we were in church just last week, but I know a funeral doesn't really count.

She has proselytized among her companions. Even Bonita is up for it.

"Yeah, Mote. What about we get our butts to church?"

Jimmy chimes in.

"We aren't getting any younger. Right J.P.?"

J.P. just smiles and fingers his rubber band. I haven't told any of the other residents about his name change yet, and they haven't asked any questions. (Maybe they think the rubber band is a stylish accessory.)

New Directions is not big on church, but since going to church is Semi-Normal in America, Cassandra tries more to ignore it than ban it. If volunteers want to take willing clients to church, then fine, but she's not going to waste staff time on such things. When I ask her about us going, she plays the diversity card.

"We cannot favor one religion over another. And we must, I repeat, must respect the rights of the nonreligious. And clients must not be manipulated into religious participation when they have not expressly chosen it."

In other words, the way to protect the clients' religious freedom is to have no religion at all. In the name of fairness, of course.

While Cassandra is temporizing over my residents' revival fever, I decide to play on her ignorance of all things ecclesiastical.

"It's All Saints' Day this Sunday."

This is a counter play to her diversity card. I continue.

"That means it's ecumenical. Everybody is included."

The word "All" does the trick.

"Well, in that case, I of course approve. Maybe it will relieve some of their stress over Abby Wagner's death."

Religion as comforting illusion. It's the best she can do and I am fine with it.

I don't have the foggiest idea when All Saints' Day is, of course, or even if it still *is* for that matter, but I know I've heard of it. We Baptists didn't believe in any special days beyond Christmas and Easter—except tithe-pledging Sunday when everybody made up a number for how much money they were going to give to the church over the next year. We liked our religion plain and simple—God was our God and we were His people. Many of us didn't even know that the Jews said it first. (Why waste time with the Old Testament when the New one had all the good stuff?)

So we're going to church. But which church? Americans like choice in their churches, as in their snack foods. We favor designer churches and a God designed to fit our tastes. We even start sentences with "My God is" followed by a descriptor, as though we each get to create the kind of god we want from a checklist of qualities that please us: loving (check), reasonable (check), favors my causes (double check).

I decide to honor the nuns who started the place and go to a Catholic church. Since all the folks in this group home did time under the nuns, I figure it's the kind of church most likely to seem familiar to them. After talking with my residents, I decide on St. Bartholomew's on Wayzata Boulevard. Judy fills me in.

"Why . . . why . . . Sister Illuminata used to take us to St. . . . . St. Bart's, she did. I . . . I like it very much."

As we pull in, I can't help thinking what a contrast it is to be with the Catholics on Sunday after being with the Unitarians the week before. One a celebration of the Great Chain of Being—one big hierarchy from protozoa up to God—the other an "I'm okay, you're okay" progressive debating society, everybody equal and god whatever we want god (no pronouns, please) to be (or not be). It really is a smorgasbord world.

It's been a long time since I've been in a church in back-to-back weeks. When I was a kid I'd punch my dance card four times just on a single Sunday: two meetings for us young people and two with the adults, morning and evening. I'm thinking it was designed to tire Satan out—having to be all over the world tempting people and distracting them from the gospel day and night must have been exhausting. No wonder he was always pissed.

I've never been in a Catholic church except as a tourist, but this one more or less lives up to the image formed in my childhood—lots of statues and candles and high ceilings. "Bells and smells" is how one of my Sunday School teachers summed up Catholicism. And they don't much believe in the Resurrection he said, pointing out that the Protestant depiction of the cross mostly shows it empty, but, with the Catholics, Christ is always hanging there—end of the road. I'm pretty sure Catholics believe in the Resurrection, but then I haven't done a lot of deep theological reflection since I tried to figure out as a kid how God decides which team to let win in major league baseball games. ("Help the Dodgers, God. Please help the Dodgers to win.")

The big cross high on the wall behind the altar fits what my Sunday School teacher said, but in an unusual way. Instead of Jesus slouched down, hanging from his nailed hands, this Jesus looks like he's jumping off the cross. His hands are nailed at waist level, his torso raised up and leaning out, as though diving into eternity, impatient to get to Easter morning.

The interior is a modern interpretation of a Gothic cathedral—with understated pillars and a clerestory that bathes the interior in light. A giant organ of steel and copper pipes, ranked in mirroring rows of ascending and descending size, fills the back wall of the sanctuary, a reflection of a faith in the intricate order of the universe, perhaps. (I suppose if people want to find order, they do. Or create it themselves.)

Just inside the middle entrance doors at the back is a big baptismal font, maybe six feet across, with steps into the water. Not big enough for a proper Baptist baptism, but made of dark marble and more inviting than anything I'd seen in the aesthetically-starved churches of my childhood.

Bonita comments.

"If they're going to have a swimming pool, they could do better than that."

Bonita has not spent a lot of time studying church architecture.

I want us to sit in the back row, figuring the more one stays on the borders of sacred spaces, the better. I remember from my childhood the story of the priest who reached out to steady the Ark of the Covenant when it was being moved on a rocking wagon and how he got struck dead for it. I don't believe in God anymore, but I don't see any reason to tempt the universe. I've been wrong before.

But while I'm eyeing the back row, Bonita is heading down the aisle deeper into the kingdom, and the others are following. I catch up as quickly as I can and divert them into an empty row about halfway to the altar.

After a few minutes the organ kicks in and everyone stands. I notice the priests and altar boys and the like coming in a side door not far from us. Jimmy is impressed.

"Nice threads. I got to get me one of those hats. Where do they get those hats? And the cape things? Those are cool."

J.P. helps out.

"I think they make them in crafts with Mrs. Francis. Don't you think so, Jon?"

"I don't think so, J.P. We need to be quiet guys. Just watch."

The priest and his crew assemble up around the table in front.

In the name of the Father, and of the Son, and of the Holy Spirit.

Everyone around us makes the sign of the cross. Jimmy tries to mimic it, touching his nose, chin, and left elbow. J.P. throws both hands straight up in the air, as though signaling a touchdown. Then they give each other a fist bump and nod.

. . . and the love of God and the fellowship of the Holy Spirit be with you all.

And also with you.

Coming together as God's family, with confidence let us ask the Father's forgiveness, for he is full of gentleness and compassion.

Well that's something that rings a bell. Catholics and Baptists agree, apparently, that we have screwed up and need forgiveness. Like we're children who have broken the rules and have to apologize to papa or we don't get dessert. Really. When is religion going to treat us as adults?

I confess to almighty God,
and to you, my brothers and sisters,
that I have sinned through my own fault . . .

Though I guess it wasn't really all that different with me and Zillah. I'd mess up, she'd get pissed, and there wouldn't be any dessert for weeks at a time.

and in what I have failed to do . . .

Does God get pissed? Is he mad when you break a rule? Or just sad? Or mad-sad? Or objective about the whole thing—the Unmoved Mover and all that?

Kyrie, eleison.

And why am I asking questions about an imaginary being? When am *I* going to finally grow up?

Christe, eleison.

God's like a bad itch. Smart people say don't scratch it and it will go away. But scratch or not, it doesn't go away. Not for me. Not for a lot of people it seems.

Kyrie, eleison.

And who are Carrie and Christy Ellison, anyway?

I look down the row to see how we're doing. Jimmy is all attention, soaking it in. Bonita is bored. Tired of standing, she is resting her head on her hand, elbow on top of the pew in front of her. This is not good. When Bonita gets bored, she starts plotting. J.P. stands erect, looking formal and properly serious. Judy, next to me, has her usual look of mild puzzlement, trying her best to figure out what is expected of her so that she can do the right thing. And Billy, at the far end of the line is, of course, staring up to the ceiling, twitching and jerking, but with a cracked smile that would suggest he is quite content to be God's puppet. ("Pull the string, and I'll wink at you.") (Ralph has stayed home with an "Ah phooey.")

Lord God, Lamb of God,
you take away the sin of the world: have mercy on us

After a bit more of this and that we all sit, with a loud "Finally" from Bonita. Then they read to us from the Good Book. I always thought that was a strange phrase, even when I believed it was good. I mean, if this is the good book, I thought as a kid, there must be a bad book. Who wrote the bad book and what's in it? And then more than a few sermons in my time suggested that *all* the other books were bad. You only needed the one book, the good one. Every other book was wood, hay, and stubble. In fact, most everything was wood, hay, and stubble, which made me feel a bit guilty about the pleasure I took in my baseball card collection.

. . . when I saw, coming on the clouds of heaven, as it were a son of man . . .

All the fun stuff in life, apparently, was wood, hay, and stubble. Which is why my pagan friend in junior high said he wanted to go to hell when he died.

. . . which will never pass away, and his kingship will never come to an end.

I was shocked. "Why would you want to go to hell?" I asked, frightened for him for having said something so awful out loud. "Because that's where the roller coasters and all the fun stuff will be," he replied. He knew I was a church kid and he liked to stick it to me every once in a while. I didn't know if he was right or not, but I figured he would eventually find out. They had *Playboy* magazines at his house. Enough said.

. . . we were not slavishly repeating cleverly invented myths; no, we had seen his majesty with our own eyes . . .

Then again, he didn't seem that interested in the magazines himself, and I was transfixed.

. . . you will be right to pay attention to it as to a lamp for lighting a way through the dark . . .

Maybe I was the one who was going to find out whether hell had roller coasters.

Thanks be to God.

Then we were back on our feet. Except for Bonita, who sat there picking her nose and inspecting byproducts.

Alleluia!

Then some more reading. Something about a high mountain.

Then back to sitting for what I assume will be the main event. The homily, they call it in the bulletin, but I know right away it's the sermon. I haven't heard a sermon in a long, long time. Well, I guess I heard one down by the river that night, all about the man in the cemetery and the pigs in the deep, but that was more a happening than a church service. Though I still don't know exactly what did happen.

The priest starts with one of the passages from the readings we've just heard, but pretty soon he's talking Latin. (And they wonder why no one comes to church anymore.) *Imago dei*, he says. The image of God. We're all made in the image of God.

"Not just the rich are made in the image of God, my brothers and sisters. Not just the intelligent. And not just the successful. And not just the productive and the confident and the independent and the good-looking."

Blah, blah, blah. Here the world is crying out for practical solutions to practical problems and religion is giving us theological trivia. Image of God, image of God—if you look in the mirror and see God, I say it only proves you've got serious mental problems.

". . . and not just the healthy either. You are God's image in sickness and in health, when awake and when in a coma, in the womb and in the hospice."

Can "right to life" be far behind? I'm glad Zillah's not hearing this; she'd go ballistic.

"It says in Genesis that God looked at his creation and pronounced it good."

He should have taken better care of it.

"And in so doing he pronounced you good."

Or maybe that was our job.

"And he pronounces that about you, about all of us, even now, even after we are no longer good. No, in the moral sense we are no longer good, but we are still in God's image; we are still immensely valuable; we are still loved of God, perhaps more so than ever, if that is possible."

A strange love this.

"And so accept the love of God. And return the love of the one who loves you so much that he came to suffer as we have suffered."

More of that cross stuff. The world is hot after roller coasters and all the church wants to talk about is crucifixion. What a downer.

"And pass on that love to everyone you meet. Everyone! Amen."

All in all a disappointment. Ten minutes max. They call that a sermon? It shows they aren't really serious. It really is all bells and smells.

Then we're standing again. A creed of some kind. And they shoehorn the whole story into just a few sentences—alpha to omega.

God from God, Light from Light, true God from true God,
Begotten, not made . . .

Tell it to Augustine. I myself can't make heads nor tails of it. And if I can't, what good does it do Judy or Jimmy or, God knows, Billy the Skywatcher?

I think we must be about done, as we would be in the churches I grew up in, but this has just been an appetizer before the main course. I forgot about communion. When I was a kid it was just once a month at most and took about ten minutes if the ushers were efficient. Pass out the bread, pass out the grape juice in the tiny plastic cups, recite the Reader's Digest version of the story about the night he was betrayed, stick the cups in the rack on the back of the pew in front of you, and then home to football.

But no Express Eucharist for the Catholics. This, it would appear, is why we were in church in the first place. Lots of "blessed be" and "pray for" and "truly right." At least we get to sit down again. No, hold that, we're kneeling this time. Cartwheels next?

Let us proclaim the mystery of faith:
Christ has died, Christ is risen, Christ will come again.

They got the mystery part right, at least—no shortage of mystery in this religion. Including why people are still looking up for a return, two thousand years after the hero exited, stage up. Face it, folks, he's just not coming back. Put away the good china and turn on the television.

. . . and so we have the courage to say:
Our Father, who art in heaven, hallowed be thy name . . .

Okay, there's something I recognize, and, I must admit, seriously wish were true. Heaven. Not the place, not streets of gold, not the singing. But the people. Mom and Dad, extinguished by that drunk driver so many years ago, setting Judy and me adrift, drifting still in my case. Who wouldn't invent a place for them, a place of continued existence, a rendezvous point? I'd gladly die right now in order to meet up with them if I thought it were real. And who wouldn't invent a hell, a place for Lester the Molester, a place where everything evens out and the bad guys get what they have coming. Sigmund didn't have to work very hard to see both of those as wish fulfillment, did he? But who can believe it?

Well, Judy can, I guess. And the nuns who once took care of her. And I guess these people now standing around me mostly do. But what good does their belief do me? If you could buy ten pounds of belief, I'd buy. But you can't create it out of nothing, and, at present, nothing is what I got.

. . . but deliver us from evil.
Amen.

Then things start to fall apart.

The Peace of the Lord be with you always.

And also with you.

That's when people turn and start shaking hands, the only thing the Catholics will admit to having learned from the Evangelicals. Jimmy comes alive, lighting up like a politician at a baby shower, pumping hands and making small talk.

"Hello, my name's Jimmy. I'm from Good Shepherd. I live there with my friends. What's your name? Where do you live? Do you come here often? Did you ever see *Lord of the Rings*? Me and my friends saw *Lord of the Rings*. I think it's from the Bible. Do you know about the Bible?"

Bonita is less outgoing. A woman offers her a hand to shake and Bonita folds her arms.

"We don't talk to strangers."

J.P. is shaking hands and smiling his small smile, but saying nothing.

Judy is used to church. She knows what to do.

"Hello, how, how . . . I should say, how do you do?"

No one is brave enough to try breaking through to Billy, which I'm sure is fine with him. He's starting to hum, busily exploring the Mystery.

I'm so occupied monitoring my disciples that I pay no attention to offers of instant American friendship directed toward me. They're probably trying to figure out whether I'm one of the inmates or their guard, a distinction that feels increasingly problematic the longer I'm with them. I certainly have as many "Special Needs."

It's all over in an instant, everyone back into their personal space and mental cubicle.

Lamb of God, you take away the sins of the world: have mercy on us.

Bonita is suddenly all attention. She sees people ahead of us sliding out of their pews and walking down the center aisle.

"They're handing out treats up there. Let's go."

I realize I haven't planned for this. It's not just the priests who are having communion—the faithful are streaming forward. I'm pretty sure it's not open house. I call down the row in a loud whisper.

"Stay where you are. It's not for us."

But Bonita is in charge now.

"Bullshit, Mote. This is for everybody! I'm going!"

If I had been at the end of the row on the center aisle, I could have blocked the path, but I am the caboose instead.

"Move it Jimmy," says Bonita.

And, verily, Jimmy moves it.

Before I can say anything else, they are all down the aisle to the end of the communion line. I have the choice of either letting them go on their own or joining them. I find myself joining them. Someone has to shepherd the sheep, good shepherd or bad.

I have only a few seconds to figure out what to do. I go to the head of our group, much to Bonita's displeasure.

"Hey, Mote. No budging!"

I fight fire with fire.

"Can it, Bonita."

I consider telling the priest that we're mostly a bunch of renegade Protestants and to please just give us a pat on the head and we'll be on our way, but I know Bonita will make a scene if she thinks she's being aced out.

This is the Lamb of God who takes away the sins of the world. Happy are those who are called to his supper.

Lord, I am not worthy to receive you, but only say the word and I shall be healed.

What are the consequences, I think, of paying tribute unworthily to a nonexistent being? I'm a kid again. Does God know that we know that he isn't real? Of such is modern theological speculation.

I decide to fake it. I see that the people ahead of us are holding out their hands and receiving a wafer from the priest. I turn to our crew.

"Just hold out your hands. Don't say anything. Just hold out your hands and take what he gives you."

Everyone except Billy immediately sticks out their arms stiffly in front of them, palms up.

We're now at the head of the line. I stand aside to monitor each one as they receive the wafer. Bonita is first. The priest doesn't look concerned. He's seen it all. He places the wafer in her hand.

The body of Christ.

Bonita looks at it without moving.

"Is this it?"

"That's it," he replies, with an emphasis on *it*, and smiles.

I tell Bonita to wait by the statues in the corner nearby and then I watch as the rest get their reward. Billy is last. He doesn't put out his hand.

He is humming and seems to be looking at the leaping Christ on the crucifix over the priest's shoulder. The priest does not hand him a wafer but puts his hand on his head.

"Bless you, my son. May Jesus our Lord be with you and in you."

I turn to lead Billy to the group gathered by the four statues, next to the burning candles.

"And you, my son?"

"What? Me?"

"Yes, you," he answers with a smile.

I'm flustered but want to end things as quickly as possible. So I stick out my hand.

"Sure, why not?"

"The body of Christ."

"Right. Thanks."

I pop the wafer into my mouth and lead the humming Billy over to the others.

"Not much of a treat," Bonita says. "And no pop." But she is resigned, not belligerent.

I quickly guide everyone up the outside aisle and out a side door, nipping like a border collie at their heels.

"Keep going, guys. Out the door. It's all over, thank God."

Go in peace to love and serve the Lord.

FIFTEEN

Everything about Abby Wagner's murder is disturbing, and the surrounding community is more than a little disturbed. Rumors and innuendos are flying, followed closely by accusations and threats. Even here and now, the safest time in human history, it takes very little to make people feel unsafe. And murder in the neighborhood is more than enough to raise primitive emotions.

So Cassandra, in consultation with the board and the police, decides to call a public meeting.

"Knowledge is power," she says. "And information is a form of knowledge."

Not exactly pithy, but everyone agrees a public meeting is necessary. It takes place at Wayzata City Hall. The terraced room is crowded, maybe 125 people or so. At the front is a dais with a long table, a microphone, and chairs. A uniformed security guard stands by each of the two entry doors at the back. I sit in the last row on the extreme right—keeping everybody in front of me, as usual. Tension floats in the air like a layer of smog and there isn't much talking.

A camera crew from a Twin City television station is set up in the left aisle near the front. I am surprised to see that the reporter is Buffy Love. Buffy is something of a local celebrity. She covers stories that hover between news and gossip, if there's any difference between the two any longer. In an interview, she can change from purring to spewing in a blink, whatever it takes to "get the story." She's in her mid-thirties, has bottle blonde hair, and wears the familiar pink lipstick of aggressive young woman television journalists who understand that news is entertainment before it's anything else. She's going places and this story is another chance to get there.

Right at starting time, a door opens to the back left of the dais, and in walk the lambs for slaughter. They have their game faces on. Everyone knows how these things work. For the next hour or so they are required to be professionally courteous, patient, apologetic, and deferential, even to a world-class idiot. (I apologize for using the term idiot, but we both know it fits some people perfectly, regardless of their IQ.) Cassandra leads the way, followed by Detective Strauss, the chair of the board of directors, and Bo.

After all are seated, the board chair slides the mike in front of himself and begins.

"I want to thank you all for coming this evening. I also want to thank our panelists, who I will introduce. On your far left is Detective Strauss of the Minneapolis Police Department, who is heading the criminal investigation into the matter for which we are gathered. Next is Ms. Cassandra Pettigrew, the executive director of New Directions, a facility for the developmentally disabled and the cognitively challenged. My name is Thomas Beck and I am chairman of the board of the local franchise of New Directions. Next to me is Mr. Bo Springer, who is our facilities manager and, thereby, in charge of security at the campus."

The cameraman zooms in on each face in turn. Bo raises his eyebrows and nods his head, like he's just been introduced as the starting quarterback at a college football game.

I look over the audience as these introductions are made. The dominant body language is folded arms, tilted heads, and pursed lips—as in, "All right, we see the Christians, now what about some lions?"

"I want to begin by acknowledging our genuine grief at the death of Abby Wagner. We know this is a tragedy for the Wagner family and it is a tragedy for us as well, though not, of course, to the degree that it is a tragedy for them. No, not to that degree. But still a very real tragedy for both the staff and the clients of New Directions. We have never had anything remotely like this happen before and we are devastated by it."

Someone needs to tell him he's said enough.

"We've had problems before, of course, but nothing like this. Never a loss of life. Never a real crime."

Cassandra jumps in.

"I think Mr. Beck would agree that we need to move on to some short presentations from each of us before we open the floor to questions."

The chairman nods and looks relieved.

"Yes, that's right. We will start with Detective Strauss."

Strauss seems less happy to be here even than the others.

"I will simply say a few words about the state of the investigation. Of course, I cannot give many details so as not to compromise the case against the perpetrator, who I am confident we will find."

A voice from the audience calls out, "I should hope so."

"Most of what I will tell you has already been in the media, but I want to establish the facts as known at present. Abby Wagner was dropped off by her father in front of the main building at New Directions at approximately 10 p.m. on 27 June, the night of the crime. The expectation was that she would walk to her apartment, as she had done many times before. However, she apparently never arrived at her apartment. This was not discovered until the following morning. A search of the buildings and grounds was organized—to no effect. On the morning of 30 June, her body was found in the reeds behind the property. The cause of death was a broken neck. Criminal sexual conduct is suspected."

Though this is not new information for anyone following the news, there are gasps and murmurs in the audience.

"In the time since the discovery of the body, we have continued to conduct interviews and have done extensive lab work. I am not at liberty to discuss the results of that part of the investigation, but I can say that it has been fruitful. At present we have no suspects."

Then it is Cassandra's turn. She looks into the camera rather than at the audience.

"As Mr. Beck indicated, I am Cassandra Pettigrew, the executive director at New Directions. New Directions is a national corporation providing the highest levels of care across the country for the developmentally and cognitively disabled. As executive director of the Wayzata facility, I oversee all its operations, including its programs—both on and off campus. I want you to know that I have ordered a complete and exhaustive review of every aspect of the organization, with a special emphasis on security and public safety, so that no stone goes unturned to ensure that nothing like this tragedy ever happens again."

Another voice comes from the audience. "Closing the barn door after the horse has left."

Cassandra ignores the comment.

"I will be glad in a moment to answer questions about any aspect of our work at New Directions."

Now it's Bo's turn, but he seems not to realize it. He is smiling at the audience—a vacant smile, but a smile nonetheless—drumming his fingers lightly on the table. He appears not to have heard what anyone else has said. The others at the table look down at him, while he looks out.

"Mr. Springer?" says the chairman.

Bo jumps a bit and then quickly starts talking.

"My name is Bo Springer. I'm in charge of facilities. The buildings, and the operation of the buildings. That's what I do. And campus security, which is part of being in charge of the buildings. We have some first-rate security policies in place, I want to insure you of that. First-rate. And we're currently reviewing those policies to make them even more first-rate, you can bet your life on that."

An unfortunate choice of words. Mr. Beck moves things on.

"We will now open the floor for questions and comments. We want to do everything we can to give you all the information we have—consistent with privacy rules and the needs of the investigation. There are microphones in both aisles. If you want to come to a microphone we will alternate between them."

There are already people standing at each of the mikes. Mr. Beck points first to his right to a woman who looks familiar to me but I can't quite place. She is well dressed, maybe forty-five or so. And she is holding a three-by-five card.

"My name is Mrs. Rose Rissota. I just want to say that I think New Directions is a wonderful organization. They provide a great service to our community and have done so for many, many years. This incident truly is a tragedy, but it would also be a tragedy if anyone should try to use it to diminish or hamper their great work. That's just what I wanted to say."

Obviously a plant. Mr. Beck smiles broadly.

"Thank you, Mrs. Rissota. We appreciate that very much. Yes, we have been here more than fifty years—counting the earlier administration of course. And we like to think we have met a genuine need in an exemplary way."

The next speaker, an old guy in a blue work shirt, is less charitable. Every assertion is marked with a jabbing finger toward the panel members.

"I want to know when you are finally going to close this place down. We have had these people living among us for way too long. They are dangerous and you know it! And if you don't know it, then you are incompetent, which is even worse."

Cassandra and Mr. Beck stiffen. Bo retains his queer smile. Only Detective Strauss seems unfazed. Buffy is smiling and making hand motions to the cameraman. She is mouthing the words, "close-up, close-up." Mr. Beck speaks.

"Your name please, sir?"

"My name is irrelevant, but it's Jason, and I live about a hundred yards from where that young woman's body was discovered, and I think it's pretty obvious that she was killed by one of the other inmates that live there, and all this 'We're looking into it' and 'We're reviewing our world-class security policies' is just a bunch of bullshit."

The reference to animal droppings gives Mr. Beck the opening he needs.

"All right. That kind of language is inappropriate. Next speaker, please."

But Jason is just warming up.

"Inappropriate? Inappropriate? You trying to shut me up with inappropriate? I'll tell you what's inappropriate. Having buildings full of defectives—with no fences and no guards and regular field trips to the outside world—*that's* what's inappropriate. Why should we and our children be put at risk just because a bunch of bleeding hearts want to pretend that these people are just like the rest of us?"

Buffy is giving the cameraman a thumbs-up. Mr. Beck has nodded to one of the guards, and the guard walks slowly but overtly down the aisle. Jason spots him and finishes his harangue.

"Ok, you're calling in the muscle. That's fine. But don't think I'm the only one who sees it this way. I've talked to my neighbors. They're just as mad as I am."

With that he sits back down and crosses his arms.

I can't help picking up on his describing himself and his neighbors as mad. It's a reflex of mine—investigating words. Mad. "Mad house." Mad as a synonym for insane. "Mad as a hatter"—from the eighteenth- and nineteenth-century chemical poisoning of hat makers. Morphing into a synonym for angry. "Mad as a hornet." But retaining the link to loss of mental control, loss of stability. So the self-described mad man is upset about being forced to live contiguously with, well, his fellow mad folks, most people not distinguishing between insanity and mental handicap. Sort of like a bee complaining about the other bees cramping its space.

Then I notice another man, around forty and dark-skinned, standing patiently at the first mike.

"My name is Amid Abed and I just want to speak up for the people who live at New Directions. I am a small business owner. I own the Dairy

Queen in Wayzata and over the years I have employed a number of people from Good Shepherd—now New Directions. J.P. currently washes dishes for me."

Apparently he didn't get the memo on J.P.'s name change.

"He is a hard worker who shows up on time and does his job well. He is also polite and a pleasure to be around, which is more than I can say about some of the so-called normal people I've hired. About a month ago I had a customer come in and tell me that she had tripped and fallen because of a pothole in the parking lot and that J.P., who was heading home from his shift, helped her up. She wanted me to know. That act of kindness probably saved me a lawsuit, and I, for one, hope these folks are here for a long time to come. Their minds are in heaven and they are favored."

There is a smattering of applause, and then this response from a woman in her thirties back at the other microphone who is holding the hand of her young daughter.

"Well that's a swell endorsement, but this is a numbers game. I'm sure the majority of these people are perfectly sweet and harmless, but the fact is that *some* of them are not and *none* of them are confined. So even if there's only *one* bad apple—which I doubt—we are all at risk unless they are *all* under tighter constraints."

I'm thinking, so how is that different from the random Bad Apple among the Normals you live and work among?

Cassandra has heard enough.

"I would like to address that point—and the earlier assertion about the supposed danger posed by our clients. Every client at New Directions has undergone a rigorous screening—including the SADA protocol. They have been certified as nonviolent and not a danger, either to themselves or to others. If they were so, they would be at the Minnesota Security Hospital at St. Peter or elsewhere. We have never had a major incidence of violence and furthermore, in this instance, we know that one of our clients was a victim of a heinous crime, but we have as yet no evidence that another of our clients committed the crime."

A few people wave their hands dismissively and Jason hoots.

Some others say their piece and the panelists answer a few questions, but things wind down and no one else seems inclined to continue. As Mr. Beck is inhaling to bring the meeting to a close, someone calls out, "I want to hear what Sister Brigit has to say."

It's a little bombshell. Cassandra looks startled. Several folks in the front half of the audience swing around to look at the back half. There's a hitch in my own breath. I search the back of the room and there, sure enough, sits Sister Brigit in the corner opposite mine. She is wearing a long dark coat and a scarf over her head. I have talked to her more than once over the years because of Judy being at Good Shepherd, but I doubt she'd remember me. She does not move or acknowledge the searching looks.

Mr. Beck breaks the silence.

"Welcome, Sister. I apologize for not having noticed you in the audience. If you would like to make some remarks, we would be very glad to hear them."

Sister Brigit still hasn't moved. It's clear she is not eager to participate. But finally she rises. She does not go to a microphone but speaks forcefully enough from where she stands so that no word is lost.

"It was not my intention, nor is it my desire, to speak. I came here tonight to hear what the people of the community have to say about my friends. It has been instructive. I have heard some hard words about them and also some compliments. Both have merit. You are right, Mr. Thompson—Jason—that these people are dangerous. As are we all. They are not little saints. Diminished abilities do not automatically confer a sweet temperament. But I believe Ms. Pettigrew is right to say they are not a significantly greater danger to the community than the rest of us. And I would remind you, Jason, that when your young son was lost in, what was it, 1963 or so, that we organized a search party that included some of the residents and that one of them found your son alive in the drain pipe. I think that deserves mentioning."

Jason is looking down at his shoes.

"And yes, they are capable of hard work, especially if it is repetitive and rewards their frequent yearning for order. But some of them are lazy, too. And some are devious. And some are whiners and some are leaders and encouragers and others are some mix of all these and more. Just like you and me."

The camera is now squarely in front of Sister Brigit's face, and she doesn't like it.

"Young man, would you please keep a respectful distance with that camera."

He backs up but I can see that he extends the lens to keep her in a tight shot.

"I was not the first director of Good Shepherd. There were others before me who did good work. And I believe those who have followed us"— she nods toward the panelists—"are trying to do good work too.

"What kind of work is this? What is the point of it? I think the main point of this work is to make things more how they ought to be. Perhaps that's the goal of all work for that matter.

"And one part of how things ought to be is understanding that everyone is valuable. I say they are valuable because their being made by God guarantees their value, but if you can get to valuing everyone by another way, that's okay with me. The world is better for their being here, and they make us better if they bring out what's good in us. Of course, they can bring out what is bad in us, too."

Some people in the room seem happy with the way this is going. Others not so much.

"Abby came to us not long before our time was over—and it's clear our time *is* over. I did not have the opportunity to know her well, but I know that God loved her and that he loves her still and I am confident that he welcomed her back to himself."

She pauses for a moment.

"I don't expect everyone to believe that. But I do hope for us all to rise to our better selves. We have lost one of God's creatures, at the hands of another of God's creatures. This is as old as Cain and Abel. We must give Abby justice—and both parties the dignity of being moral beings—by finding who did this to her and holding that person accountable. But mindlessly blaming her friends, without evidence or proof, is not justice. Nor does it make us more secure. Our only true security lies in doing what is right. And that's all I've got to say."

Sister Brigit sits down and Mr. Beck eagerly wraps things up.

"Thank you, Sister Brigit. Those are good words. And a fitting close to this public meeting. We thank you all for coming and assure you that New Directions and the police will do everything possible to bring this sad event to a just conclusion."

Buffy Love springs into action. She heads straight for Jason Thompson, signaling the cameraman to join her, and I do the same, giving my best impression of being a potted plant. I want to see Buffy at work. She grabs Jason by the arm and turns to the camera.

"We've just concluded a tumultuous and emotion-packed public meeting here this evening that centered on the brutal sexual assault and murder earlier this month of young Abby Wagner. Tempers were raw tonight and for good reason. I have one local citizen who expressed his view very forcefully. Mr. Jason Thompson, could you tell our viewers how you feel about the recent killing?"

Jason looks a bit deflated. The fire has gone out of him. He leans away from the microphone Buffy is waving in his face.

"Well, I just wanted to tell folks that a lot of us are worried about what happened. And that we want a thorough investigation of this tragic death."

Buffy is not satisfied.

"Well, Mr. Thompson, I think you called for closing the facility down, did you not? And you spoke of the danger of what you called 'defectives' living in the local community. Can you speak more to how you feel about that?"

But Jason is no longer a willing spokesman and turns away.

"I've got to go. Sorry."

Buffy drops the mike to her side and speaks to the cameraman.

"Okay, we won't be able to use that. But you got his original comments during the meeting, right? We'll make that the lead to the piece."

An assistant asks, "Do you want to try to get any more comments from the nun?"

"No, that was dull as dirt. Nuns don't create buzz unless they can fly. I think we'll lead with Mr. Thompson's rant and then balance it with the positive comments from the small-business guy, then close with a few crime scene photos, if we can get them past the candy-heart censors at the station, and wrap up with a short summary of the state of the investigation. We only get forty-five seconds for this piece as it is, what with the coverage they're giving to the big storm that's coming. Let's get out of here."

I turn to look for Sister Brigit, but she is nowhere to be found.

SIXTEEN

STUART WAGNER, TO SAY the very least, is not a happy man. He wasn't happy before his daughter was murdered and now he is exponentially more unhappy. Unhappy people prefer having a good reason for their unhappiness. It isn't really necessary, but it helps them focus. And now he has one.

One way Mr. Wagner has expressed his unhappiness is by hiring a private investigator. The police have assured the public, and presumably him, that they are making good progress on the case. Nevertheless, Mr. Wagner is a person used to having people report directly to him, the kind to want all available information and to want it now. If he can find the killer before the police do, so much the better.

Hence the phone call I get from Mr. Daniel Randle. He identifies himself as a private investigator who has been hired by Stuart Wagner to look into the death of his daughter. He asks if I'd be willing to speak to him. I don't have to legally, of course, but I have a kind of professional interest in the work he does. I played Private I for Mrs. Pratt without knowing what I was doing. It might be interesting to see how a real one works. (Private I, Private Eye, a word play for the solipsistic—"Detective Monad speaking.")

Who knows, maybe there's a career option there for me. Most people have something going by my age, but I'm thinking PIs probably start off as something else and then find their way into investigation later on. After all, no one majors in sleuthing in college. ("Hello, Miss Coed. I'm a senior Private I major. I've done some background work on you and discovered that your moral boundaries are, shall we say, fluid. Would you perhaps be interested in a date this weekend?")

I meet Mr. Randle at the Starbucks on the water at Lake Street after work. He's at least as nonconforming as any of the residents I'm working with. He's maybe fifty. Tall and skinny. Mostly bald with a head that bulges behind like a pterodactyl. (I can hear the playground chant of his boyhood: "Daniel Randle, his head is shaped like an anvil.")

He's an encyclopedia of tics. Every few seconds he either bugs his eyes, stretches his neck, or clears his throat. Billy is an ice sculpture of repose compared to him.

He gets us started.

"So what's it like working with . . . those people."

He bugs his eyes.

I know this is a rapport-building question—put the interviewee at ease and all that—but he's lucky I'm terminally phlegmatic. "Those people" would get you a rhetorical poke in the eye from a hair-trigger activist, and might even be a conversation stopper. I toy with making him squirm a bit by being faux offended, but decide to cut him some slack, something I'm often desperate for myself. Besides, faux shock takes more energy than I can muster.

"Oh, it's a job. Good days, bad days. Same with the residents."

I can tell he's relieved to have gotten off easy. He quickly moves on to the "what have you told the cops" stage.

"I assume you've talked with the police."

"Yes."

"Do you mind sharing what you told them? It would be helpful."

He stretches his neck.

"Mostly general stuff. Detective Strauss wanted to know where I was at the time of the murder, some background on the residents—whether any of them is dangerous—things like that."

"And where were you?"

"For the interview?"

"At the time of the crime."

"Oh. I was in my bedroom at the group home. Reading in bed actually."

"What were you reading?"

I want to say, "The Murders in the Rue Morgue," just to get a rise out of him. But I decide not to dig any holes for myself.

"I'm not sure. *Cosmos* maybe."

"*Cosmo* the women's magazine?"

He both stretches his neck and clear his throat. He looks surprised, not a way PIs are supposed to look during interviews, I don't think.

"No, *Cosmos* the science book—with an 's.' You know, the TV series."

He doesn't know, but also doesn't care—a potent combination of forces among the masses. I should know.

"Do you have witnesses?"

"Can't say as I do. I sleep alone these days."

He clears his throat and consults his notes.

"Yes, separated from your wife Zillah, if I'm not mistaken."

"You're not mistaken."

I don't like this. What else does he know about me? That I was ushered out of the army after a breakdown? That I more or less flunked out of grad school? That my head used to be crowded and perhaps will be again? That I prefer waffles to pancakes? I guess these are things a PI is supposed to find out, but it irritates me.

Mr. Randle moves smoothly from me to the residents. He's been studying my face closely in the last few minutes, and I'm guessing he's not seriously considering me a suspect. Which is a little disappointing. I wouldn't mind being considered a bit dangerous. It would make me more interesting.

"What can you tell me about Ralph?"

I know Cassandra has refused him permission to interview the residents—protecting their privacy and all that. But there's nothing to prevent Mr. Randle from asking me questions about them. It suddenly occurs to me, however, that this guy is looking for perpetrators and the last thing I want to give him is anything that will make life hard for my folks. So I exercise my considerable powers for blandness and give him a series of handleless answers.

"Ralph has been at the place since he was eight or so. He was born in Nebraska."

I don't mention that Ralph once told me, with a smile on his face, that "back in the home"—I don't know whether his own home or a previous institution—they used to put him in stocks in a dark attic when he was bad. Might be used to construct an implicating scenario.

"Where was Ralph at 10 p.m. on the night of the murder?"

"He was in his room?"

"Do you know that for sure?"

I want to say, "Of course I don't know that for sure. This is the beginning of the twenty-first century, buddy—who knows anything for sure? 'For sure' is for accountants and mathematicians and suspicious wives. Everyone else is guessing, about everything. Good God, I don't know for sure that

. . . well, that there is a Good God. Or that there isn't. I don't know for sure who or why I am. I don't know for sure that a free society is really free, nor that it's better than an authoritarian one. I don't know if baseball is a slow waltz or just boring." In short, Dr. Pratt is alive and well inside my head.

Instead, I say, "Well, I have no reason to think he wasn't in his room."

Mr. Randle bugs, clears, and stretches, then asks a few more questions about Ralph. And I give a few more unhelpful answers. Then he moves to Jimmy.

"I understand that Jimmy is quite a ladies' man."

"Only in his own mind."

"Well, most crimes start in the mind, don't they, Mr. Mote?"

"Yes, I guess they do."

"Can you tell me more about Jimmy?"

So I describe Jimmy as best I can—confident, high-energy (even manic at times), well-stocked with clichés (both verbal and conceptual), many of them supplied since New Directions took over, with its surplus of "you can do it," "you can be anything you want to be," "shoot for the stars," "stand up for your rights," "don't let anyone put you down," self-actualizing American individualized rah rah. These residents don't know Nietzsche from Parcheesi but the younger ones especially have been raised on a steady diet of Übermensch, and Jimmy has fattened his self-esteem on it. Judy sometimes tries to rein him in with a little Calvinist self-abasement, but Jimmy will have none of it. He's Special and he knows it and it doesn't bother him one bit.

None of which, I make clear to Mr. Randle, makes him a candidate for murder. He talks about girls all the time, but someone like Abby scares him to death.

So we move on to Billy. I don't mention Billy's ulcerated butt, even though I've just put salve on it for the first time and found it a not altogether uplifting experience.

"Have you ever seen Billy?" I ask.

He says he hasn't. So I describe Billy the Skywatcher in terms that make him seem as likely to attack a woman as Mae West to enter a convent. He doesn't get the Mae West reference, so I think about invoking Madonna (not *the* Madonna) but decide to let it pass. I choose to go high style instead.

"Billy is the last guy on earth to attack a woman with carnal intentions. He has neither the inclination, nor the strength, nor the organizational ability, nor the contact with earth, nor, for that matter, the fully functioning equipment to execute such an assault."

I say this with breezy confidence, but the truth is that Billy has been known to go AWOL at night. He's been found more than once wandering the grounds in the dark, humming and jerking and staring at the stars. A red-headed E.T., looking, perhaps, for his heavenly friends. ("Phone home, Billy. Phone home.") I decide not to mention it. It's true he conceivably could have been out that night, but it's not a useful truth.

Mr. Randle is taking notes, which only encourages rhetorical flourishes on my part, frustrated word-lover that I am. He pauses, bugs, and asks a delicate question.

"And what if it didn't require an 'assault'?"

"What do you mean?"

He chooses his words carefully.

"Well, what if he were encouraged by the victim?"

I flash back to Abby's hand on my knee the first time I saw her and took her for a staff member.

"You mean, what if she were promiscuous?"

"I mean what if she were vulnerable."

"Well, it wouldn't matter. Billy can be led from place to place, but he maintains a strict distance between his reality and everyone else's. He would be totally unseduceable."

Mr. Randle seems to take my word for it.

"And James Paul?"

"In his room; no, can't prove it; no, wouldn't do it; yes, I'm sure."

"Okay, I can see you've had enough of this. Don't blame you. Just something I need to do as part of my job."

Mr. Randle rises as he says this and performs a final clearing of his throat.

"I appreciate your help, Mr. Mote. I know we all want to find out who killed Abby, and eliminating suspects is an important part of that. I'll report to Mr. Wagner what I've found and we'll keep looking."

We both walk out into the parking lot of the coffee shop. Mr. Randle turns to me.

"It's clear to me that none of your clients were involved. Do you know of anything, however small, that might point us in a better direction? Anything or anyone? Any suspicions at all?"

"No, nothing. Sorry."

It's only a very small lie.

SEVENTEEN

I FIND MYSELF THESE days thinking of Zillah. Running into her on that outing with Judy and Ralph has shaken me up. I had been keeping her safely in the past, but you know what Faulkner said about the past not being dead—it ain't even past. Or something like that. Well, it's true. My parents have been dead for thirty years and they can break into my mind in ways that bring tears even today. I'll do an update on Faulkner: the past is the genetic code of the future. (Okay, so Faulkner's line is better—and Wordsworth beat us both.)

Anyway, I keep mulling over Judy saying that Zee and I should go on a date and Zee responding, "Perhaps we should." Was that ironic? Sarcastic? A convenient conversation ender? Or was there a hint of interest in it? (She even said it twice, and my poetry teachers all said that if something is repeated in a poem it *means something*.) What all was residing in that "perhaps"? What, for that matter, is residing in all our perhapses and maybes in life? Maybe go to school here. Maybe take that job there. Maybe marry this person, maybe that one. Maybe God, maybe not. Maybe buy stock, maybe bonds. Maybe say I love you, maybe just smile.

I find myself asking questions with no encouraging answers. Why didn't it work out with Zillah? (Why is there not peace in the Middle East?) What *did* work for us? (Nothing.) What could I have done differently? (Everything.) What kind of husband should I have been? (Any kind but the kind you were.) Could I have changed enough to make it work? (Only by starting your life tabula rasa.)

If I had been more perceptive, I might have seen how incompatible we were from her attitude toward Judy. Judy is my older sister—and my childhood playmate, protector, and mentor of sorts. I learned early on that she is a Special, but I thought that just made her, well, special. It never occurred to me growing up that her life presented any kind of problem—either for her or for me or for anyone else. It took others to teach me that.

Like the kid in grammar school who yelled when the two of us walked into the building when I was just starting first grade, Judy holding my hand and leading me to my classroom, as she did every day that first year.

"Hey, Mote. Why are you holding hands with your gooney sister? Aren't you afraid you'll get tardo germs?"

I looked over at him, confused, but Judy just kept us moving.

"Don't pay . . . pay him attention, Jon. He is a . . . a stupid, stupid boy."

Zillah wouldn't have called a Special "gooney" to save her life, but she also had never been all that comfortable around Judy. In the years we were married, we had Judy over for all the major holidays and here and there in between. But Zillah would never go with me to visit her at Good Shepherd or accompany us on random outings. She always had a reason, but I started to think it was for reasons a few layers underneath mere reason.

Zillah was always polite to Judy—and vice versa—but she never appeared relaxed around her and seemed relieved when any visit was over. I think maybe Zillah's diluted feminism played a role. Zee was like a lot of young women coming of age at the end of the last century. She shied away from industrial-strength feminism, but she lived in the world activists had helped change and she embraced the benefits of the change without thinking twice. Or even once.

And one of those changes was the default understanding that women were supposed to be strong. And independent. And accomplished—able to compete in the world, taking no crap from anybody, doing what they wanted to do and doing it well. Normal, you might say.

By which standards, Judy looks more than a little forlorn. What with her halting speech, her elaborate deference to everyone and everything, her narrow band of gifts, and vanishingly small career options, Judy was not anyone's model of a successful, modern woman. Not that Zee would have ever said that, or even thought it, but I think it was working on her somewhere down there near the basement of her brain.

Zillah also was not a big fan of Judy's Sunday School outlook on life, as Zee called it.

"I can put up with a little God talk here and there," she said, "but, really, Judy is on friendlier terms with God than I am with my own mother." (I'm not in touch with either one.)

Religion was sort of like perfume for Zee. A little bit produced a pleasant effect, but pour it on and you just made a spectacle of yourself. I was raised Baptist and fled; she was raised Episcopalian and didn't have much to flee from. (It reminds me of a favorite conviction of mine about adolescent rebellion: parents not giving their children enough limits to rebel against are committing a subtle form of child abuse. How can you fulfill your duty to shock your parents if their own behavior has already shocked *you*? Maybe by becoming a missionary.)

Actually, Zee took the references to God more or less in stride. It was Judy's metronomic invocation of Jesus that she found more irritating. After all, God is sufficiently vague and distant. Most all religions believe in God in one form or another—no longer the Big Man Upstairs of course (no body parts for God)—but the Big Something Out There Somewhere Who Somehow Approves of Being Good (make that "Fair," "Good" being a little too preachy). Or maybe just something inside here in the brain, what's the difference?

Jesus was entirely too specific—in time and space and demands on your life. And Christ was even worse—Jesus the carpenter on steroids. Another (doomed) holy man turned by the institutional PR department into the Son of God. Like those makeovers in women's magazines: once plain, now supermodel; once itinerant wise man, now Creator of the Universe! Those dashboard Jesuses ("I don't care if it rains or freezes, long as I got my plastic Jesus . . .") are merely the descendants of two thousand years of icons, statuary, crucifixes, stained glass images, and God knows what. They've been replaced in the West today by movie tie-in action figures, but Jesus got to market first and has staying power that any Madison Avenue-type would envy.

And Judy, good Bapto-Catholic that she is, thinks that Christ is simply Jesus' last name, as in "Jesus to his friends and Mr. Christ to the rest of the world." She also suffers under the delusion that they are one and the same: man (Jesus) and God (Christ). She can recite no creed to justify it, but she doesn't need one, being as she is a simple woman with simple needs.

I was that simple once.

EIGHTEEN

TIME IS PASSING. YET again. If the police are close to charging anyone, they aren't saying. Bo is taking his role as head of security with newfound seriousness, seeing no doubt a chance to elevate his status in the New Directions universe. He now wears a small canister of mace on his belt and decides we need to do another search, particularly of the area where Abby's body was found. That area consists of maybe a hundred acres or so of high reeds—a wetland in the spring when the snow melts, but damp mud by the end of June.

Bo picks a morning when I'm not working, but he makes it clear he thinks I should be there. He also enlists Sam the groundskeeper, a couple of maintenance guys, some kitchen staff, and a volunteer parent or two. All men. This clearly is to be a testosterone-laden operation. I am wondering whether I should wear camo and face paint.

Bo has maps for everyone, with the wetland area zoned into numbered sectors. He addresses us in a voice straight out of the movies—George C. Scott addressing his tank crews before the Battle of the Bulge (or wherever it was).

"You will note that I have marked with an x the spot in sector D where the body was found. The police searched that area, of course, but the reeds are very thick and they could easily have missed something. Stu and Jackson, I'm assigning you sector D."

He puts all of us in teams of two and assigns us sectors. I am with Sam Raven again, like right after Abby was discovered missing.

"I will not be on a search team myself as I am coordinating the operation. If you find something, do not touch it. I repeat, do not touch it. Call out and I will come to where you are. Here's one flag for each search team. Wave the flag and call out if you find something."

He hands out small white flags on short sticks. I've been waving white flags all my life, so I feel right at home.

Sam and I are assigned sectors G and H, well beyond where the body was found and therefore very unlikely to contain any clues. But maybe the killer hiked out that way after dumping the body, so I'm prepared to be all eyes—a bruised reed, a slight indentation in the earth, a signed confession.

Sam and I decide to walk through the reeds together. He tells me about the good time he had with Detective Strauss.

"He went after me pretty hard. It was an easy call. Black man with a past and an opportunity is how he saw it."

I'm wondering what kind of "past" he's talking about, but as a man with a past myself, I don't ask. He tells me anyway.

"I say black man because that's what I am to him and to most people. But actually I'm as much Indian as black, with a touch of Irish."

I'm thinking Faulkner and another Sam.

"I'll say this for the detective—he did his homework. He knew about my record, but he was cagey. He didn't say nothin' about it at first. Then he asks me if I ever been in trouble with the law, and I know exactly what he's doing. Because I *have* been in trouble with the law and I know how cops work. So I say 'Yeah, a long time ago.' And he says, 'Yes, it was a long time ago, but it was serious wasn't it, Sam.'

"And I say, 'Yeah, it was serious, but like I say, it was a long time ago.'

"I can tell he's disappointed that I haven't lied to him. He figured if he could catch me lying about my past, then he could accuse me of lying about the girl. Once they got you admitting you a liar, they can go anywhere they want. Know what I mean?"

Actually, I do. I was married once. Technically, I still am.

"But I was never worried. I had a good alibi. I was a long way away from here that night and can prove it."

Ah, the old ali baba. Wish I could say the same.

He keeps talking.

"Yeah, I have a past. A serious past, but not a violent one. I stole stuff. A lot of stuff. I was young. It made me feel important. It was stupid. Of course they caught me, more than once, and eventually I went to prison. When I got out, I couldn't find work. Nobody wants a black Indian with no diploma and a past."

Sam has stopped walking and is looking back toward the campus.

"Sister Brigit was the only one. She cared about my past but she also didn't care. I remember what she said like it was yesterday. I tell her about my problems with the law, because I don't want to get no job and then get fired two months later when somebody finds out about me. She says, 'Mr. Raven, are you a thief or are you someone who stole?' I say I don't know what she means. She just repeats the question, 'Are you a thief or are you someone who stole?' I'm starting to think I know what she's getting at, so I say, 'I'm someone who stole, Sister.' And she says, 'Are you done stealing?' And I say, 'I *am* done stealing. I want a job.' And she says, 'Then you have a job.' And I been here ever since."

Sam pauses for a moment.

"She's a straight woman."

We traipse around in the reeds for maybe thirty minutes, making a lot of tracks but finding nothing except a couple of deer bedding places. I'm wondering how long Field Marshall Bo expects us to keep this up when I hear a shout. I look back toward the campus and see a white flag waving like crazy. Jackson is shouting.

"Over here! Over here! I found something."

Sam and I walk toward the spot and arrive at the same time as Bo and some of the others. It's only about fifty feet from where Abby's body had been found. Jackson is excited and breathing heavily. He points to something in the reeds.

"This could be important, right Bo?"

"Sure could be, Jackson. Good job."

It's a red tennis shoe, wedged between three reeds, about two feet off the ground.

When I see it up close, I feel a familiar pain in my stomach, one I haven't felt since that night on the bridge.

Bo produces a clear plastic bag. He breaks off a reed and sticks it inside the shoe, lifting it into the bag. I'm pretty sure he should be leaving it where it is, but he's excited too. I reach into my rich trove of detection experience and offer one bit of advice.

"Don't you think you should mark the spot?"

"Good call, Mote."

Bo sticks one of the flags into the ground at the point where the shoe was found. Then he holds up the clear bag with the shoe.

"Anyone recognize it?"

Everyone else shakes their head. I don't say anything. I need a little time to think. But Bo has been studying the shoe through the bag.

"Wait a second. There are some initials written in black marker on the heel. Can you see it, Jackson?

Jackson looks closely as Bo holds the bag up in front of his face.

"Yeah. I can see. It says, 'J.P.M.'"

Bo puts his fingertips to his forehead.

"J.P.M.? Who's that? Do any of the clients have the initials J.P.M.?"

I still don't say anything, but I know where this is going.

Jackson sings out. "J.P.! He's the guy in your place, Mote!"

I don't respond.

"What's his last name? J.P. what?"

He answers his own question.

"McCloskey, isn't it? My God! J.P. McCloskey. J.P.M.!"

Jackson is smiling like a lottery winner.

"And I found it. I was the one who found it. I was just walking along and there it was, big as life. Bang! I say to myself, 'Jackson, what have we here?' And what do you know, it's the killer's shoe. And I'm the one who found it."

Bo tries to calm him down.

"Let's not get ahead of ourselves here. We don't want to accuse anyone of something they didn't do. But we do need to check this out."

He is already on the move.

"Come on. We've got to check James's room to see if there's a match. I'll call Strauss on my cell on the way over. He can meet us there. The rest of you can go if you want. Thanks for your help."

But of course no one is going anywhere except to J.P.'s room. It's not every day you get in on solving a murder, and they all want to see the other shoe. It's the last thing I want to see, but there's no avoiding being one of the Sanhedrin. My stomach is doing flip-flops.

The whole lot stomp up the steps to J.P.'s room. Bo opens the door to the closet. There, as predictable as the sunrise, sits the other red shoe—trying unsuccessfully to look innocent. Bo is fully in charge.

"Okay, that settles it. Don't touch anything in the room. Everybody out. The police are going to want to go over this place with a fine-tooth comb. We need to wait for Detective Strauss. Mote, you stay with me. The rest of you outside."

Detective Strauss shows up within the hour. He is not happy about being called on a Saturday, but his attitude changes when Bo shows him the two shoes and explains what has happened. Strauss reprimands Bo mildly but is clearly pleased.

"You should have left the shoe where you found it. But at least no one touched it. The lab boys will want to go over everything in the marsh and in this room, but I'll do a preliminary search as long as I'm here. You and Mr. Mote just step back into the hall."

We move to the doorway but watch Strauss looking through drawers and in the closet. I'm sick to my stomach and Bo is smiling. This will give him something to tell his mates about over brewskis for years to come.

Then Strauss drops to one knee for a peek under the bed. It's a peek that seals J.P.'s fate. (Substitute random chance for fate if you like—anything but Providence.)

"What's this?"

Strauss drags out J.P.'s friends album, the one, alas, with all the photos of young girls. I start to explain, but Strauss makes another discovery.

"And what's this?"

Within the album, like a bookmark, is a large silk scarf. I've never seen it before.

Bo asks, "What is it?"

Strauss lays the scarf gently on the bed. He opens a file folder he has with him and rustles through it. He pulls out a photograph. Bo can't hold back. He steps into the room and looks over Strauss's shoulder. I can see it from the doorway, but can't tell what it is.

Strauss must figure it's all going to come out soon anyway, so he shows us the photo.

"This was taken at the victim's house the evening she was murdered, about an hour before, in fact. You can see for yourself."

What I see is Abby standing with her father, both smiling. She is wearing a scarf. I don't need to see any more.

But there is more.

Strauss leafs through the album.

"A lot of pictures of young girls here. How old did you say this James fellow is?"

I try to defuse the question.

"His mental age is a lot different than his physical age."

111

But Strauss is not hearing me. He has turned to the last page of the album and is staring at the single photo on that page. It's a picture of Abby Wagner.

NINETEEN

THE RED SHOE HAS depressed me. I feel myself sliding, a familiar zag in my zigzag life. In the past I would have reached out and touched it—Diana Ross-style—but I've been trying to level out the steep sine waves of my life to something closer to a gentle swell. Working at New Directions has helped. Somehow being with people who are mostly at ease with their plethora of problems has put me more at ease with my own.

I mean, take Ralph. On the level of basic intelligence, he's neck and neck with a cabbage. (Thank you, Flannery, for the metaphor.) His great life achievements are washing dishes, playing the bones, and killing gophers. And yet he's 100% accepting of himself and the universe. (Like Judy's favorite gorilla at the Como Zoo.)

Or Jimmy, who goes beyond self-acceptance to self-promotion. If self-esteem is the key to a successful life, as many seem to think, he is supplied for three lifetimes, with enough left over for export. And it's not tied to actual accomplishments. He's exceedingly pleased with the contribution he's making to the world simply by being one of us.

Or Bonita. Bonita is giving me backbone (even though I'm not proud of the comment I made to the lady at the funeral). She says what she thinks and it doesn't seem either to hurt her or to cause a tremor in the universe.

And J.P.? Blessed are the meek, I used to hear. Zillah thought that was just counsel of submission for the benefit of the "not meek," but there's something to it. Something to not fighting fire with fire, assertion with counter assertion, belligerence with belligerence. It's the strategy of the reed during the storm. It's Ali rope-a-doping big, bad George. J.P. *is* blessed, though none would want to share his blessing.

Even Billy, a man who appears *all* problem, whose problem, some think, is that he exists at all—even Billy whispers peace to me. Learn to hum, Jon, he seems to say. Learn to look up. Watch for the shooting star. It's come before. It will come again.

So, like I say, working here has helped. But it's not been long and I've gone longer in the past doing fine only to feel the furnace go out in mid-winter. So even a little garden-variety depression now is enough to make me edgy.

Judy, as usual, knows where I'm heading before I do. We're sitting on the back steps of the group home looking toward the playing field. I'm smoking, a habit I took up again after Zillah left. It's a pipe, so I con myself with the thought that I'm not hurting my lungs. (Ever heard of throat cancer, Mr. Mote?)

"Well, Jon, my . . . my brother of mine. How . . . how do you do?"

I know this is not merely a polite conversation starter. It's therapist Judy, and I'm on her couch. No, not therapist. Sister. Spiritual counselor. Soul friend.

"I do not well, Jude. I do not very well at all."

I expect a dose of Jesus. Judy loves Jesus the way dolphins love the sea. Jesus is the great ship plowing through the water and Judy is the dolphin playing in the bow wave—joyously, effortlessly, letting the power of the wave propel her forward, flashing that permanent smile. There are endless questions in life, but for Judy there is only one answer: Jesus.

But she surprises me.

"I think . . . I should say . . . I think you need to give a call to Z . . . Z . . . Zillah."

I laugh.

"Zillah, huh. Why Zillah?"

"She is . . . your friend, Jon."

My friend. What an idea. Zillah was my wife, legally still *is* my wife. My estranged wife, as they say. Once wife, now stranger. But a stranger who knows me, who once found me worth taking a chance on, worth loving even.

"Well, Judy. She used to be my friend. But she has other friends now."

"No, Jon. A friend is . . . is always a friend. She would be very, very pleased to . . . I should say . . . to see you."

Judy has her solemn "Listen-to-Your-Big-Sister" face on. Then she suddenly smiles.

"Silly boy."

I try resisting Judy but don't put up much of a fight. Her words are actually an echo of my own thoughts. Ever since Zee's "Perhaps we should" response to Judy's movie suggestion, I have had her on the brain. Perhaps it was a polite, filler response, but perhaps it was more. Perhaps it was . . . well . . . friendly.

What's to lose anyway? Why not call? Why not squeeze the universe into a ball and roll it toward an overwhelming question: "Wanna hang out?"

And so I do. And she is open to it. Or rather, she cracks the door but keeps the little chain lock attached. I suggest picking her up but she prefers to meet me somewhere instead. Getting picked up apparently strikes her as too committal and makes more difficult a quick escape should things go badly. I can see her point.

So I say, as nonchalantly as I can muster, "How about Stillwater?"

There's a pause on her end. I haven't been quite nonchalant enough. Stillwater, thirty minutes northeast of St Paul, was a favorite place of ours in the early days, when we thought it was summertime and the living easy. She's wondering if she's being set up. But she accepts it.

"Okay, Jon. Let's meet on the walk by the river just south of the bridge."

The Stillwater bridge, an old-fashioned erector-set lift bridge across the St. Croix River. Two towers, but with none of Tolkien's aura. All metal sticks stuck together with metal rivets, rising creakily in the middle when needed, but ready at any moment to collapse into the river. And yet increasingly beloved. Not because beautiful but because familiar. Has been there so long, it only seems natural that it stay. Like many a marriage I suppose.

We do meet in Stillwater. Zillah is, let's say, pleasant but not warm.

"Good to see you again, Zillah."

"Yes, how are you doing, Jon."

A nicely ambiguous response on her part. Does her "Yes" mean, "Also good to see you, Jon" or "Yes, it is good for you to see me"? To tell the truth, the ambiguity in meaning is kind of comforting. Because, like the bridge, familiar. Ambiguity was actually a defining quality of our marriage. But meaning? Not so much.

We shoot down the expected topics of conversation like clay pigeons. Pull.

"How is Judy?"

"Fine, etc."

Pull.

"Where are you working these day, Zillah?"

"Same place, etc."

Pull.

"What are doing to keep busy?"

"The usual things, etc."

In the past, I would have been content to keep this up until doomsday. And would have considered the conversation a success if no one was mad or crying at the end. But this time I feel a sense of urgency. I feel like it's maybe the last boat off the beach at Dunkirk and the Nazis are closing in. So I invoke Bonita and just say it.

"What about us, Zillah?"

She seems taken aback.

"What *about* us, Jon? What are you asking?"

"I'm asking how we feel about each other."

"Well, isn't that a bit strange to ask after so many months of having no contact other than exchanging legal papers?"

"Maybe. But it's still my question. How do we feel about each other?"

"Well, since it's your question, why don't you go first?"

She says this without hostility, but also without showing any cards.

"Fair enough. I miss being with you."

I shock myself. An open, direct, unambiguous declaration of—what?—affection? longing? I go on.

"I know things ended badly between us, but I'm better now. It was my fault—all the . . . the . . ."

I feel like Judy.

". . . the stuff."

Even Judy would have done better than "stuff." But Zillah knows exactly what stuff I mean.

"Well, Jon. I'd like to reciprocate, but I can't. I haven't missed being with *you*. In fact it's been a great relief. Life feels almost normal for me again, and I like the feeling. I wouldn't go back."

"No, you shouldn't want to. Neither would I. I'm not proposing anything."

Where did the word "proposing" come from?

"I'm just saying I miss being with you, that's all. Just stating what I feel."

"That's good. That's nice. I appreciate that."

I'm pretty sure she's also thinking, "that's unprecedented." I was never one to state simply and plainly what I felt, not least because it was never simple and plain, not even to me.

Then it's her turn to be direct.

"Why did you never send back the divorce papers, Jon?"

I wait for my flight instinct to kick in, but nothing happens. I actually feel quite calm.

"Well, I guess I didn't want to see it end. Our marriage. It couldn't go on, of course. I could see that. But I also didn't want it to end. So I guess I was just waiting to see what developed. Looking for a via media you might say."

"Via media? Is that Latin for paralysis?"

Ouch. Zillah has seen "waiting to see what develops" from me many times and she has never been a fan.

"Sorry, Jon. That was mean."

"No, not mean. Accurate. I *was* paralyzed. But I'm not any more. Or at least less so. At least I hope so."

Not impressive. My common three-step declination: "not any more" (assertive), "at least less so" (affirmative), "hope so" (wishful). The next step, as Zillah knows, is "not so after all," which is the step I have been trying to avoid in many areas of my life in recent months.

I want to turn her question about the divorce papers back on her. It's true I never returned them to her attorney, but then she never proceeded to divorce me without my cooperation, which she could easily have done. Why not? If I was paralyzed—or wanting to stay married—what was she? Why did she leave things unresolved and yet without any contact?

Before I can ask this—and before I have decided whether I should— Zillah responds.

"I believe you, Jon. I think maybe you *are* better. And I want you to know how glad I am about that. For you. For your own health and happiness."

She pauses.

"But for you, Jon, not for us. I haven't missed you. I haven't missed being together. I have thought about you. I have even worried about you. I really do wish you well. But I don't wish *us* well. I don't wish *us* back together."

"No, I understand that. I wasn't necessarily suggesting that."

("Necessarily"—a weasel word. Why do I always insert a weasel word?)

I continue.

"But I would enjoy being with you from time to time, Zillah. Like friends. It's very common these days. Exes as friends. Do you think we could do that? See each other here and there, like friends?"

I can't read her look. It seems a prototype for attraction-avoidance. Pain mixed with desire, with a pinch of mercy.

"I think that's possible, Jon. I guess anything is *possible*."

TWENTY

THE FELLOW AT THE guardhouse said the driver of the big yellow truck was smiling as he crashed through the razor wire, the wires popping like kernels in a hot skillet. The truck rumbled toward the barracks, a giant tick bloated with explosives. It burrowed into the main entrance of the building, eating sandbags and glass, then erupted into a concussive inferno of destruction and death. The entire building came down, crushing most everyone inside.

It's all replayed in my dream. The parts I witnessed, the parts I was told about, the parts my mind has manufactured. It's a dream I've had many times over the years since, but it hasn't been back for a while. I thought perhaps the dreaming was over, but of course it's never over. Nothing is.

In fact the dream is as real as the event itself. Both are lived out in the mind. Or beneath the mind, in the brain. Something happened "out there," but my only experience of it is "in here." It's all chemical reactions, they tell us. Peptides and amino acids and monoamines, vesicles and axon terminals, all kicking in for that big leap across the synaptic cleft to the receptors on the other side. Or something like that. Of course, I don't know what I'm talking about. But the people who do know claim that's what "reality" is—at least the bit of it in which we participate. It happens, apparently, trillions of time a day for each of us, adding up to happy, sad, alert, lethargic, addicted, confused, reflective, in love.

(I apologize for this unscheduled departure—I guess my peptides took over.)

Anyway, it was near the end of my time in the army. I was in Beirut on a not very important assignment during a very important time. I wasn't staying in the building, that was mostly Marines, but I was billeted nearby and at the scene in less than fifteen minutes.

The dust of pulverized concrete was still in the air. The building was now a stack of concrete pancakes. The floors sat on top of each other, having crushed the life out of hundreds of young men, leaving a pocket here and a pocket there to mock the rescuers, but actually allowing some to die more slowly and painfully than the rest. It happened early on a Sunday morning. I guess God was sleeping in.

The most disturbing thing in the dreams—as at the time—are the voices from the rubble. There are guys in there calling out for help and there is nothing—absolutely nothing—that you can do but call back to them. Some of them kept calling out until the next day. Then silence. It makes me cry even now.

At first we just picked at the pile with our bare hands, throwing a chunk of concrete a few feet away, as though that was helping. Maybe that was when I realized how futile is so much of what we do. How pointless. How comprehensively and incorrigibly pointless. It set me up nicely for Dr. Pratt. It lingers still.

What do you do when someone is eager to kill you and hopes to die himself in the process? Someone who doesn't know you, has no specific grudge against you personally, but against your civilization, against which you may have more than a few grudges yourself? What synapses are firing in *his* brain? How useful is neurochemistry in dealing with *him*? He who is more than half in love with easeful death?

Beirut was an early introduction to this guy—though he's had a quiver full of offspring. He distracted us for a moment from our favorite television programs. Since then the fellow has hit us at the African embassies and now blown a deadly hole in the destroyer in Yemen. In retaliation, the President bombed a pharmaceutical factory—or was it powdered milk? (That'll show 'em.) All at a distance so far. Disturbing but not life-changing. Let's hope it stays that way.

It's not hard to figure out why the dream is back. You know what the most common emotion is when we dream? Anxiety. We spend around six years dreaming, all told, in a normal life. Six years! And the most common emotion is anxiety—about being naked in public, trying to run away from something, showing up for class and not realizing there's a test today. Or holding hands with a guy reaching out from under a twelve-inch-thick concrete slab.

That's always part of my dream. I'm not even sure it actually happened, but I know it's part of my dream of what happened. I can see only his hand. He keeps asking me to help him, and I keep saying, "I *will* help you. I'm here. Just hold on. You're going to be okay." But I know I'm not helping him, and I won't be able to help him, and I know he won't be okay. That's the one thing I know for certain, in a world where so little is certain: I know I won't be able to help him.

Just like J.P.

I'm no village explainer but I know the Beirut dream is back because of J.P. The building has collapsed on him. They won't send him to jail, but they will send him to St. Peter. He will, for the rest of his life, be listed—officially and with all the proper nomenclature—as dangerous. A predator, in fact. One who hunts for victims. Hence isolated. Watched. When deemed appropriate, restrained. He won't be okay. It will kill him.

I came back from Beirut not long after the bombing. Some of those killed came back in pieces, and, in my own way, I came back in pieces too. I've sort of been a Humpty Dumpty all my life. I fell off the wall when I opened that door and found Uncle Lester among the petticoats. (Or maybe I'm just playing Junior Psychotherapist and picking the easiest trigger for something much further down.) And Judy has always tried to do what all the king's horses and all the king's men couldn't. Which is to say, put me together again.

I remember the first time I saw her after getting back. I was still in the army and on leave and spent some time in the Twin Cities. I took Judy out from Good Shepherd for a day, and she spent a lot of time studying my face. It was disconcerting. I'm making ping-pong small talk the best I can, and she's not hitting the ball back, something she's quite good at. She's studying my face like I've developed a third eye in my forehead. Finally, she makes a pronouncement.

"You . . . you are not . . . not well, Jon. What . . . I should say . . . what is the matter?"

The matter. What is the matter? The matter—as in the subject, the issue, the mater-ial under consideration. I'll tell you, Judy, what is the matter, I wanted to say. What is the matter is that I don't know the meaning of anything. I can describe. I can report. I can testify. I can even speculate. But, in point of fact, when it comes down to it, I don't know what anything means. Or what it's worth. How to rank or prioritize it. What it leads to or what action it calls for. I'm a descriptive genius but a metaphysical dunce. Worse yet, I suspect we all are.

So when Judy asks, "What is the matter?" I say . . .

"Nothing. I'm fine."

Which is to say, I'll take a pass. I'd rather not deal with it. I'd rather play ping-pong.

But she's not buying what I'm selling. She shakes her head. Just one shake. And then puts on her big sister voice.

"No, Jon. You . . . you are not fine. I . . . I am your sister of yours, and . . . and . . . I should say . . . you are not fine. You are your own self, but . . . but something is . . . is hurting you."

I don't respond. She moves over closer to me and takes my hand. With her other hand she starts to rub my back, like she used to do when we were kids and I was upset. I start to cry. It's a deep, deep in the heart, Benjy-like cry. About the loss of innocence, the loss of love, the loss of loved ones, the failure of the world to be what we need it to be, a world instead where children are betrayed, and parents disappear without a goodbye, and buildings fall down on people and squeeze the life out of them, sometimes slowly. Who can bear such a world? Who wouldn't pick instead the dark icy water on a winter's night?

But that was later. At the time, just back from Beirut, all I could do was cry, with Judy holding my hand and rubbing my back. For once I wasn't embarrassed to be falling apart. After all, it was only me and Judy. Brother and sister. Alone in a Big Bang world. But then again not alone, because we had each other.

Judy was forever trying to fix me. She's trying to fix me still. I would tell her that it's no use. There is no fix. Not for me. Not for anybody. But she wouldn't understand. And if she did, she would just reply with her one-word fix for everything—"Jesus."

TWENTY-ONE

IN THE DAYS SINCE Bo put the finger on J.P., the social organs that regulate public justice and mental health have been pumping secretions of judgments and rulings, the consequence of which is that J.P. is to be put away. (Quite literally.)

Detective Strauss has confirmed that the scarf belonged to Abby. And that she was wearing it the night she was murdered. A hastily arranged hearing has taken place to confirm that J.P. is not competent to stand trial. It has also decided that he is too dangerous to be allowed to remain at New Directions. He will instead be transferred to the high security hospital at St. Peter where he will be housed in the section for the criminally insane, though I doubt they use that terminology any longer. There will be a second hearing to confirm his guilt, but it will be a formality. J.P. will spend the rest of his life at St. Peter in small spaces under suspicious eyes.

Cassandra has informed the staff that the transfer to St. Peter will happen sometime late this afternoon. I am to spend the day with J.P., packing his things. (He's in a different bedroom, having found yellow crime scene tape across his door when he came home from work the day they found his shoe.) Cassandra has made it clear that New Directions is responsible for J.P.'s actions until he's picked up by the people from St. Peter, which means that *she* is responsible, which means that *I* am responsible, which means I had better not take an eye off him all day long.

J.P.—a risk to society. Who knew?

I help him collect his things. It doesn't take long. St. Peter (the institution, not the disciple) says he can only have seventy-five pounds of total possessions—clothes, books, memorabilia. I want to ask, "How about his bars of gold and other precious metals?" His photo album will not be going with him. That's now state's evidence. J.P.'s friends officially belong to the state.

A life condensed to seventy-five pounds of detritus. It's all so absurd: J.P. as rapist. J.P. as killer. Can't they just hang around him for ten minutes and know he couldn't have done it? I don't think Abby's picture being in his photo album is a big deal. Lots of people had pictures of John F. Kennedy on their walls, too, but that doesn't mean they shot him.

But there's that scarf. If he just had a scarf of hers, it wouldn't prove anything. He knew her and saw her often. Maybe she gave it to him because he thought it was pretty. But she was wearing that scarf the night she was murdered. How did the scarf end up in his room if he didn't take it off her body?

And the shoe. Your life brought to an end by a red tennis shoe. Absurd isn't strong enough. Life isn't just absurd, it's malevolent.

I try to engage J.P. as we pack. I'm feeling a lot worse than he is. He doesn't seem to understand the implications, and I'm asking myself if it would be doing him a favor to make the implications clearer.

"What is St. Peter, Jon?"

"It's another place like here, J.P."

"Um, why am I going there?"

"I'm not sure."

"Is it just for a visit?"

"Well, sort of like a visit."

"Mm, what about my job at the Dairy Queen? Who's going to wash the dishes?"

"They'll take care of that. Don't worry about the dishes."

"When do I get to come back home, Jon?"

"I'm not sure, J.P."

By the time the residents get home from their various places, we are packed and just waiting for the phone call from Cassandra.

Everyone gathers in the living room. The mood is somber. They were told the day before that J.P. was leaving. I had tried to finesse the question of *why* he was leaving, but there's no finessing when Bonita is around.

"They're saying that J.P. killed Abby, the bastards."

How does she know this? Can she have figured this out for herself from all the skulking going on and the fact that J.P. is being sent off? Or does Cassandra's front office have as many leaks as the Nixon White House? (Cue the plumbers, erase the tape.)

So everyone knows that J.P. is leaving today and that things are serious. This creates the perfect conditions for Bonita and Jimmy to perform a pas de deux. The ballerina goes first.

"I say it's not fair. J.P. is our friend. Abby is our friend. Abby is J.P.'s friend. Friends are nice to each other. If they are not nice, they don't get pop. J.P. is always nice to Abby. It's not J.P.'s fault that Abby is down the drain." She finishes this Solomonic analysis by jerking her thumb earthward.

Jimmy, the danseur, performs a leap.

"That's right, Bonita. You said a mouthful there, sister. It's definitely not fair for them to say that J.P. caused the deceasing of one Miss Abby Wagner. She was a fine girl. I respected her a lot and I'm sure the rest of you join me in that."

Jimmy is flying toward the mountaintop, with fragments of eloquence as his wings.

"And J.P. is a fine young man. Without J.P. I don't know where we'd be. And neither does he, I might add."

Bonita flashes Jimmy a thumbs-up as he continues.

"If they haul J.P. off to jail, if they tie him up with ropes and chains, if they poke him with hot pokers, if they lock him up and throw away the key . . ."

Everyone looks frightened. I tell Jimmy that's enough, but he's on a roll.

". . . we will not be moved. No sir, we shall overcome. We will not rest. Did Lincoln rest at Valley Forge? Did Martin Luther rest when he marched on Washington?"

Jimmy likes to watch The History Channel.

"Did Peter Pan rest when he ate Captain Hook's hand?"

Fright is replaced by puzzlement. Judy tries to say something.

"Now Jim . . . Jimmy . . . it was not Peter . . ."

But Jimmy will have no competitors.

"No, they did not rest. And neither will we. We will take it to the highest court in the land. We will keep fighting for truth, justice, and the American way."

Bonita likes it.

"Damn straight, Jimmy. Damn straight."

I look to see how J.P. is taking all this and suddenly realize that J.P. is not in the room. I ask, "Where's J.P.?" No one seems to know—or isn't saying. For that matter, Billy is missing as well.

My God, this is terrible. Cassandra could be calling at any moment to tell me they are on their way over to pick up Dillinger and I don't know where Dillinger is.

Finally Judy speaks up.

"Well, Jon. I think . . . that is, I think that perhaps J.P. is . . . is watching for his brother of his."

"What do you mean, 'watching for his brother'? Does J.P. have a brother?"

"Oh yes."

Jimmy chimes in.

"Judy's right. J.P. definitely has a brother. He drives a truck. One of those big ones. Lots of wheels. Vroom. Vroom."

Nods from everyone. Even Ralph.

"Has anyone ever met J.P.'s brother? Have you ever seen him?"

This makes them all thoughtful. Jimmy strikes a pose, arms crossed, hand pinching his chin, eyes upward, like the scarecrow in Oz when he's trying to think. No one can come up with a memory of having met J.P.'s putative brother, but that doesn't seem to concern them much. As Bonita makes clear.

"No one's seen him, Mote. So what?"

She has a point. The vast majority of the people in the universe haven't seen me either, and I'm more or less real.

"Well *where* is he 'watching for his brother'? Where *is* J.P.?"

Ralph points out the picture window toward the freeway that lies just beyond the frontage road that leads into the New Directions campus.

"Out by the highway. Da dooey."

I check his room first but it's empty. So I walk outside the group home and toward the highway not far away. And sure enough, there's J.P. sitting under a tree on a bank overlooking the frontage road, watching the highway just beyond. He's hugging his knees, his gaze fixed on the passing traffic.

Billy is standing beside him, eyes fixed on the clouds, a kind of Tonto to J.P.'s Lone Ranger. It makes sense. If you're going to be watching for something that may not exist, bring along a man who's an expert.

"What you doing, J.P."

He doesn't say anything. I ask again and he answers.

"Um, oh, um. Just sitting here watching the world go by."

He cuts me a look to see if that phrase works.

"Watching for anyone in particular?"

"Um, well maybe. But maybe just watching."

Very cryptic, J.P., you sly devil. I don't know how secret this brother is. The residents all know about him, but do the staff? Is it in a file somewhere? "James has delusions about a brother who supposedly drives a truck. James has no known brother. He should not be encouraged in this delusion. If it persists, he should be subject to an appropriate behavior modification regimen." Or has the staff over the years been as unaware of this so-called brother as I've been? I bet Sister Brigit would know.

I decide to pretend I'm in on the secret.

"How is he going to get here?"

"Oh, um, in his truck. It's a Peterbilt narrow-nose 281 with a Cummins engine and a R170 Rockwell rear axle. You know, Jon, the one with two transmissions."

I'm flattered by the "you know." As a guy pretty famous for how little he knows, I will accept any imputed knowledge with gratitude.

"Yeah, that's a nice one."

"Yes. My brother got it when he started hauling lumber."

J.P. catches himself and looks anxious. He's mentioned his brother. Maybe he's afraid of another rubber band. I keep a casual look on my face to reassure him and continue on.

"Tell me about this brother of yours, J.P."

He searches my face, shrugs, and then answers.

"Um, well Jon, my brother's name is Charles. I call him Chuck. He is older than me. We slept together when I was little. We have one bed in our room. I sleep next to the wall and he sleeps next to the lamp and when I get scared in the dark he says, 'It's all right, Jimbo.' He calls me Jimbo. 'It's all right, Jimbo, I'm right here.' That's what he says."

"How much older is Chuck than you?"

My bad again. I've asked a duration question.

"Um, well, he's older than me. Maybe this much." J.P. holds his hands about six inches apart and looks at me with hopeful eyes.

"How long since you've seen your brother J.P.?" I quickly adjust the question. "Have you seen your brother recently?"

"Well, um, it's been a while."

His face darkens a bit.

"He's on the road a lot. All the way to California sometimes."

I try to help him out.

"Yeah, those truckers have to stay on the road if they're going to make any money."

"But he'll come. When he dropped me off here in the truck to stay with Sister Brigit, he said he'd come see me. I watch the highway for a Peterbilt 281, the one with a narrow nose. He'll come see me."

Billy is starting to hum, maybe to give J.P. some reassurance. (I'm imagining this of course.)

Oh, J.P. of Diminished Capacity, your brother will never come see you. The world is not arranged that way. But someone has come, alas, to see you. Someone in a black van has pulled up to the group home. Two someones in fact. Not men in white coats—nothing so clichéd in our progressive time— but taking you away nonetheless. Taking you far away.

TWENTY-TWO

IN THE DAYS AFTER J.P.'s exile, the group home feels like a locker room after losing the big game. Less talking, less laughing, more pushing the food around on the plate.

I need to talk to someone. I need help thinking about J.P. I consider Zillah but decide it would be too complicated. We'd start by talking about J.P. and end up talking about x and y chromosomes and why homogametic folks (like her) have trouble getting along with heterogametic folks (like me). I've lived that already and it's not the help I'm looking for.

So I decide to go see Sister Brigit. She knows J.P. better than anyone I know of. Besides, it's a chance to talk to a Myth.

Sister Brigit, along with the surviving members of the nuns who ran Good Shepherd, lives in deep cloister at a convent on the way to Stillwater. They do not interact a lot with the rest of humanity, mostly spending their time in prayer and contemplation. They'd get more pats on the back if they ran a food shelf or otherwise made themselves useful, but who can figure out nuns?

It takes a bit of doing to arrange a visit. We settle on thirty minutes on a Tuesday afternoon. (Cue The Moody Blues.) As I park my car, I experience my usual "What was I thinking?" regrets. But there's something calming about the reception area of the convent. A small desk just inside the door sits empty. The decor is spare but not sterile. The obligatory crucifix hangs on the wall. Yes, my Baptist Sunday School teacher was right. For Catholics, always on the cross.

Strange when you think about it. I mean, what other religion puts the humiliation of its god at the center of its story? The Jews don't. The Hindus don't. The Muslims sure as hell don't. They believe in a kick-butt, always-in-command Allah. Where did Christians get this low self-esteem complex? I mean, turning the other cheek. Really! And the emphasis on humility, self-denial, the first shall be last, foot washing, and on and on. Nietzsche was on to something. Weakness masquerading as goodness. The submission of the slave race to the masters.

Of course the Christians got over it soon enough. Constantine, Crusades, Inquisitions and all that. Not really much different than the rest. Just a different strategy. Just a different rhetorical gambit, Dr. Pratt would say, a different discourse (from the Latin for "running to and fro").

A young woman in street clothes breaks my profound theological reflections. She knows who I'm here to see and leads me through the building to a small patio out the back. It is shaded and thick with plants and flowers. Sister Brigit is sitting on one of two wrought iron chairs, waiting for me. Unlike the evening of the public meeting, she is fully habited—black and white all over.

She nods to me.

"Please sit down, Mr. Mote."

"Thank you, Sister. Thank you for seeing me."

A strange expression—"seeing me." Denoting "visually sensing my presence," but meaning "allowing your life to intersect, however briefly, with mine."

She doesn't inquire initially about why I've asked to see her. She begins with an interrogative.

"Well, what have our friends been teaching you?"

This seems like a trick question. I'm pretty sure I've been hired to teach *them* things: how to tell time, count change, understand a pedestrian traffic signal, get on a bus and know when to get off (for the high flyers), how to load a dishwasher, how to floss (a disaster), how to talk to strangers, ad infinitum. Asking what they've taught me is a curve ball. When I'm stumped in a personal exchange, I generally smile, pretending either that the answer is self-evident or that I haven't heard the question. And so I smile.

"I see. You haven't gotten that far."

That far toward what? I don't like the implication that somehow I am, I don't know, lagging behind. What's she really suggesting? I've never been very good at cryptology. Ask Zillah. She'd be sending out these coded signals, "You've hurt my feelings. Come comfort me." And I was decoding them as, "You're a jerk. I want to be alone."

"So why have you come to see this old nun, Mr. Mote?"

There's the question I expected and thought I was ready for. Turns out I'm not.

"Well, I guess I'm looking for, I don't know, insight let's say, about the ... the ...."

I don't know how to finish the sentence. If it were Cassandra, I would say "clients." If it were Doctor Kirkoven I would say "retarded." If it were an academic or activist, I'd maybe say "cognitively challenged." If I were talking to myself, of course, I'd say "Specials." But I sense none of those work with Sister Brigit. So I come up with a lame question.

"What did you use to call them anyway?"

Sister Brigit replies quietly.

"We called them by their names."

She waits for a moment.

"And we still do."

All I can say is, "Right."

She throws me a lifeline.

"Is it possible that you are especially interested in my thoughts about J.P. and Abby Wagner?"

"Yes. Exactly. That's why I came. I'm having trouble knowing what to think about J.P. and his being accused of killing Abby. You know about that development, I take it?"

I mean, do they watch the news at a cloistered convent? Read the papers?

"I do. And I just learned yesterday about J.P. being taken to St. Peter. The sisters have been praying about that throughout the night and morning. We will begin a fast for J.P. this weekend."

The Middle Ages, alive and well in a convent on the way to Stillwater.

She continues.

"And we have been praying for Abby's soul since her death."

Hmm. My memory is that we Baptists thought the time was past for praying for someone's soul once they'd moved on. At the point of death it was "Time's up, pencils down, pass your test to the front of the row." The exam was graded immediately and you found out real fast whether you were a sheep or a goat. Apparently Catholics believe in extra time for those who need it. I think they have a name for it. Very considerate.

Sister Brigit asks how much I know about Abby's parents.

"Well, I know Mr. Wagner is rich and important and very angry."

"Yes, he's been angry since he damaged his daughter—and before."

"Damaged his daughter?"

"It was widely reported at the time, so I'm divulging no confidences. Abby was injured while riding with her father in their car. She was a teenager. There was an accident and she suffered significant brain damage. He was drunk. He ran a red light."

That explains a lot.

"As I indicated at the public meeting, Abby came to us only a short time before we left Good Shepherd. We did not know her well, but we know that God does."

She pauses. She understands that I have really come to talk about J.P., but she waits for me to make the transition in my own time. I decide to just put the cards on the table.

"And about J.P. Do you think he is capable of murdering Abby Wagner?"

"Yes."

I'm taken aback.

"Really? Yes? You think he maybe murdered her?"

"No. You asked if I thought he was capable. And I give him the dignity of answering yes."

"How does thinking him capable of murder give him dignity, pray tell?"

I like the "pray tell." Seems fitting when talking to a nun in a convent.

"Because it grants him humanity, Mr. Mote. For better and for worse. He's adequately strong physically. He is capable of thought and planning mentally. He knows the basics of right and wrong morally—and is capable of choosing either. Therefore, yes, J.P. is capable of murder, and that gives him the dignity of being taken seriously."

Laid out like a damn college professor. Dr. Pratt would have loved to get his teeth in that little syllogism. I wish he were here, so I could watch a tractor pull between a deconstructionist and a Thomist, but alas, Professor Pratt can profess no more.

"For J.P.'s sake, I will defend him against anyone who says he *couldn't* have killed her. But also for his sake, I will defend him against anyone who says that he *did* kill her."

"On what basis the latter?"

I figure "On what basis the latter?" makes me sound highly syllogistical my own self.

"On the basis of friendship, Mr. Mote. Not friendship as a concept, but my particular friendship with J.P. We have been talking abstractly. Abstractly, I insist that J.P., while limited in measurable ways, has every one of the qualities that make someone fully human—not human-like, but fully human."

What, I'm starting to ask myself, was this woman before she was a nun?

"But if we talk not abstractly but about particulars—about J.P. and me and our particular friendship in time and space—then I can say with great confidence that J.P. did not kill Abby. I say that because I know his distant past and because I have known him over decades and because I know him intimately now, though we have been apart in recent years."

I detect Sister Brigit the Philosopher being joined by Sister Brigit the Anamchara. (I once read a book on the Celtic saints.)

"How much do you know of J.P.'s childhood, Mr. Mote?"

"Nothing."

I'm wondering if I'm going to get some Thomistic-flavored psychoanalysis. I needn't have worried.

"J.P. was born with the umbilical cord wrapped around his neck. He had serious oxygen deprivation in a tiny rural hospital not equipped to deal with it, and within a few minutes he went from being a healthy fetus to a brain-damaged newborn. Physically perfect except for cell death in a square inch or two of his brain. No less valuable for that than he was fifteen minutes prior."

A valid point perhaps. But I might counter that J.P. being equal to the rest of us doesn't guarantee his value, because maybe *none* of us is valuable—to God, man, or that indifferent bitch, Mother Nature. (Pardon the language. I've hung around Bonita too long.) You certainly don't get a hell of a lot of "valuable" out of the Big Bang. (I seem obsessed with the Big Bang for some reason—maybe because it's our real father and mother.)

Like I say, I "might counter" with this. But I don't. I've learned to keep most of my countering in life inside my own head. I just nod instead.

"There were no places like Good Shepherd—much less New Directions—in those days in that part of the country. And his problem came along too late to erase him in the womb."

Count on a nun to get in a little propaganda. But she has a point there too. It does seem strange to cure disability by getting rid of the disabled—before they can become a problem for themselves and the rest of us. And to call it compassion, no less.

But having a point and proving it are two very different things. I want to signal both that I think "erase" is a little harsh and that, of course, I grant her the right to think that way. (I'm the personification of tolerance.) So I say something that I think makes me sound agreeable, but which turns out to sound differently to her.

"Yes, I understand that, as a Catholic, you would be opposed to . . ." what? "intervening in the case of . . ." what? "fetal issues."

Very smooth and reasonable sounding, I'm thinking.

She looks at me as Michelangelo might look at Andy Warhol. And speaks with Mount Sinai authority.

"There is nothing exclusively Catholic or even religious in my view of these things, Mr. Mote. It is simply humane. A created being is valuable whether made by God or blind nature. That is not negated by disability or needing assistance. My faith only gives me a way of explaining an understanding I have arrived at simply by watching and thinking and living. I could give up God tomorrow and it wouldn't change a scintilla of what I believe about the Judys and Billys and J.P.s of the world. We're all going to be disabled at some point in our lives—I'm only a handful of years away from it myself. And we are all disabled in spirit and moral judgment right now. And if we don't learn to value the overtly disabled among us—for who they are, not for what we can coax them to become—we put us all at risk."

This is not your Bing Crosby sister.

"I don't rely on God to convince me to value the disabled, but God does understand disability, because God has experienced it. He allowed himself to become disabled—first by becoming one with us, then by accepting his death on the cross. Incarnation and crucifixion, Mr. Mote."

Can resurrection be far behind? This is more theology than a simple ex-Baptist should be expected to digest.

"And Christ was resurrected with his wounds intact, or at least the evidence of his wounds. He was not ashamed of his wounds and neither are your so-called clients—until they are taught to be. Their biggest disability is not their limitations, it is our refusal to find a place for them among us just as they are. We are the ones who decide who can live and who must die, what is acceptable and what is not. You could say we ourselves create disability—not God, not nature—by our definitions and our attitudes and our hard hearts.

"I do not romanticize disability, Mr. Mote. I have emptied too many bedpans and massaged too many contorted limbs. I know brokenness when I see it and I do not wish to call it soft names. But you can describe brokenness and respond to it without giving it the power to define someone. No one *is* their brokenness. And no one approaches this world—broken or whole—who is not supposed to be. Not everyone can be cured, Jon, but everyone can be healed. And we all have a part to play in that healing."

We sit in silence for a long time. It feels as though a violent thunderstorm has passed through and we are waiting in the quiet aftermath, listening to the rain dripping from the surrounding plants.

Then she speaks again.

"I am sorry for the lecture, Jon. It's not what you came for. These are things I feel deeply about. I sometimes say too much or say it too fiercely."

I just nod my head. She goes on.

"We were talking about J.P.'s childhood. As I said, he suffered brain damage during his delivery. He was raised at home, on a ranch, a long way from anywhere, in a large family. And it wasn't a happy family. J.P.'s father was a big man and an even bigger drunk."

I nod again.

"Have you noticed that J.P. barely opens his mouth when he speaks?"

"Yes, I've noticed that."

"And that he takes very small bites when he eats."

"Yes."

"That's because his father broke J.P.'s jaw when he was a boy. And it didn't heal right because he wasn't taken to a doctor. His father beat him regularly. The other kids too, but especially J.P. Said he saw J.P. as 'God's judgment' and somehow related to his own failures. I think when he wanted to take a swing at God, he took a swing instead at God's household representative."

This news is painful to me. It makes me ashamed of my own impatience with him. J.P., if you think the clock reads "twelve-one o'clock," I'm not going to say different.

"When his jaw got broken—and was left untreated—J.P. came to us. He was seven years old. I've known J.P. since he was seven and I was young. I will not rob his mother by claiming we were his mothers, but we raised him and, in time, we became his friends."

I find this moving but I'm still not making connections. How does J.P.'s childhood, and her friendship with him, give her confidence that J.P. didn't kill Abby? I'm thinking brain damage plus parental alcoholism plus beatings plus early institutionalization equals (what else?) rage. Rage, violence, lashing out—the whole ball of wax (to use the scientific term). Even if it's been suppressed for years, I don't see any lawyer, scientist, therapist, cop, or jurist having the slightest difficulty in thinking not only that J.P. is capable of killing but is actually primed to kill. (Though they all would also immediately absolve him of responsibility—"he's not like the rest of us"—thereby "saving" him.)

This is what I'm thinking and Sister Brigit seems to know it.

"A childhood like J.P.'s can lead many ways. Any childhood can. His could have led to explosive anger or to catatonia or to sainthood. It didn't lead to any of these. It led to a man whose dominant instinct is to please those around him."

This is starting to sound unsettlingly close to home.

"At first, of course, in order to avoid punishment and pain. But eventually—I'm quite sure of this—to give pleasure. Pleasure for himself and pleasure for others."

J.P. as a pan hedonist—pleasure for all. Not a bad life calling.

"I watched J.P. transforming as he grew. That little smile he flashes when he thinks he's pleased you? That's a real smile and genuine pleasure. And it's shared pleasure. He is happy because he thinks you're happy. And that's enough for that moment—the two of you are content together. He became, I don't know, a kind of brain-damaged Francis. Not a saint the church could ever recognize, but the kind of practical, quotidian saint that we are all supposed to become.

"That's why I say I'm confident—I'd even say that I know—that J.P. didn't kill Abby. It would have been as out of character for him as for the moon to change places with the sun. I know it not because of friendship in the abstract. I know it because J.P. and I are friends. We know each other."

I'm shocked to see tears coming down Sister Brigit's cheeks. Maybe she's shocked too, because she tries to flick them discreetly away, hoping I won't see.

"Well, you can see, Mr. Mote, that I speak out of emotion as well as out of reason."

She quits trying to hide the tears and reaches up her habit sleeve and produces a handkerchief. (Just like my grandmother used to do.)

"I am aware of my persona, Mr. Mote. The stage sister, you could say. I don't mind playing that role when it's useful."

My flight instincts are rising. Woman in extremis—not an environment in which I thrive. But the tears have stopped and she continues calmly. Calm but confessional.

"That persona began quite early in my life, in response to events and relationships which I will not recount. I learned over time that I was smarter than most people, and more disciplined, and more capable of mastering my emotions and exercising my will in order to get what I needed. And I found that it worked just as well with God, or seemed to, as with people, and so I became a sort of force—first in the academy and then in the convent. And, in time, at Good Shepherd."

Why don't people stay in the boxes to which we assign them? It would make things so much simpler.

"To be honest, I thought the appointment to work at Good Shepherd a spiteful act on the part of my superior because of her jealousy of my gifts. I had more academic honors than she had fingers and I was half her age. I calculated that she sent me to Good Shepherd as a kind of ironic joke— 'Let's see how Sister Cerebral likes working with people whose lives are defined by their low IQs. She can contemplate how many angels can dance on the rim of a bedpan.'"

That's a good one. Everyone loves a witty twist on medieval theology.

"I was disappointed at first, but I decided, unconsciously, that I would simply compete in a new area. I would empty bedpans better than anyone else and I would show my organizational skills and seriousness in ways that would be noticed and would eventually lead me out of the dormitories and back into the conference rooms. And God would see all this and be very pleased. No, not just pleased—impressed.

"And that's exactly what I did. And that's exactly how it worked out— except for the 'impressed' part. But what I learned in the process was that, in matters that counted, I was not more accomplished than most, I was less so. In fact, I was impaired, more impaired than most of the people I was assigned to care for. They already knew what I didn't. They knew that they were not impressive. That had been made very clear to them. In fact, some knew that society saw them as a burden, maybe even a waste, a lamentable liability in a world that insisted on productivity. Creatures who should not have been and should not be."

Emotion is returning to Sister Brigit's voice.

"Others, like your sister Judy, are protected from this realization. It seems not to occur to them that they are anything but likeable—and valuable—just as they assume, unless proven otherwise, that everyone is as likeable and valuable as they are."

Sister Brigit smiles—the first time I have ever seen her smile.

"And I think that is how God wants all of us to think about ourselves and about others. 'Hello, I am a child of my Father, the King. I see that you are too. What's up?'"

I want both to laugh and to cry. "Child of the King" is a cliché from my churchy youth that has been empty of anything attractive until just this moment. And Zillah would give you an earful if she caught you referring to God as Father or King. And yet, coming from Sister Brigit—a woman untainted by sentimentality and too smart to easily dismiss—these words call up a longing from the deepest recesses of my heart.

I find myself wishing I had a handkerchief up my own sleeve.

"Don't just *take* care of them, Jon. Care for them. Love them. And let them love you back."

I nod.

"The exemplum is all in the Trinity, you know. It's all there—fellowship, friendship, intimate community, interdependent love. The still point of the turning world. Still and yet a dance. What a mystery! What a profound and life-giving mystery!"

She is smiling again, looking away. A bit like Billy.

I haven't the faintest idea what she's talking about.

TWENTY-THREE

I GO AWAY FROM the meeting with Sister Brigit feeling like I've just taken a master class from Mozart. One-on-one. She was conducting a symphony. I was playing a triangle. Tinkle. Tinkle.

My world feels so thin and vaporous compared to hers. I'm not saying that what she believes is actually true to the facts, but it gives her something maybe more valuable than mere facts—it gives her a story. One she can live and die in, that tells her who she is, what she is to do, and what will happen to her when she dies. I haven't had a story like that myself for a long time.

I have to think about these things.

Why, for instance, when she talked about the Judys of the world not being ashamed of their neediness, did I have the feeling that she was talking about me? I have been a walking neon sign flashing "Needy! Needy! Needy!" for as long as I can remember. I've always been embarrassed that I wasn't as independent and competent and, well, successful as I knew I was supposed to be.

Let's face it. I found myself shameful. I couldn't even be as happy as my retarded sister! There, I used the R word. About someone I love. And I don't think I'm ashamed of it.

The joke is that *I* was the one who was retarded. I'm the one lagging behind. I have a moderately higher IQ than Judy. I don't have any extra chromosomes. I can tell time. But she knows how to live and I don't. She knows how to treat people and I don't. She knows how to be happy and I don't. She knows how to give and receive love and I sure don't.

So which of us needs help? Which of us needs nurture? Which of us needs compassion and mercy?

Well, I guess we both do. But she's wise enough—not smart, but wise—she's wise enough to accept it. Without feeling like a loser.

She accepts it, but does the world accept her? And if not, if her extra chromosome is reason enough to extinguish her at the beginning, then how am *I* safe—with a lot of extras of my own, including, perhaps, extra versions of myself? How are any of us safe? Each of us is one traffic accident or aneurysm or mental crisis away from being a burden, from no longer being Normal. Like Sister Brigit said, if we have no value for just being—for being created—we have no dependable value at all.

The Judys of the world simply need what we all need. But we don't give them what they need. We give them a program. At one time we just locked them up—at home or in an institution. Custodial care at best. Then we medicalized the whole damn thing—sterilization, eugenics, IQ, prenatal testing, genetic mapping, surgical interventions. Then we added assessments of the Judys in Western, capitalistic terms—productivity, cost-benefit analysis, individual rights, independence, actualization (and called it all "normal"—as in "norm," the standard by which to judge). And now we're going all postmodern on them and think we're doing them a favor—disability as social construct, not disabled just different, "nothing about us without us." Screw it, let's drop the euphemisms and the slogans and the measurements and just admit that we're all as dependent as hell and ought to be.

(Listen to *me*—suddenly the know-it-all.)

I also go away from Sister Brigit sharing her confidence—her knowing—that J.P. didn't kill Abby Wagner. Capable—yes. Culpable—no. It's possible in theory for me to win the Nobel Peace Prize. In actuality: zero chance. Same with J.P. and murder.

And, last, I go away from the meeting with Sister Brigit thinking about God. And about ways of seeing the world, and about the possibilities for there being something bigger than the physical, and about what's it all about, Alfie. And how our chances of figuring it out—least of all through reason alone—feel like the score of a typical English football match: nil-nil.

I mean, how do two equally intelligent, equally reasonable, equally sincere, equally well-meaning people end up with wildly different understandings of what is real? Or, like I said before, true, or good, or beautiful? Or even useful, for God's sakes? (Does it count in their favor as "useful" if Specials teach us something about how to live and how to care for each other—or is that just sentimental slush?)

And it's not just two people, it's more than six billion (at a time), billions more if you count up everybody who's ever lived. Okay, so throw out the billions who never give a thought to what life means—the majority maybe—and you still have billions of us left scratching our little pin heads (sorry Bonita) and trying to decide what it all adds up to. And coming, it seems, to billions of different conclusions.

And what counts as Evidence? And who to trust as Explainers? We hear from the artists, the writers, the scientists, the priests and preachers, the rulers, the entertainers, the school teachers, the parents, the business leaders, the intellectuals, the advertisers, the government bureaucrats. And that's before we've even had breakfast.

And we don't hear just one thing from each group. The artists aren't united against the bankers and the priests. The artists and writers don't even begin to agree with each other (except about how sensitive they are). Even the scientists—the people most attached to a single method that is supposed to result in demonstrable truths—even these folks, especially at the highest levels, think each other woefully obtuse on the questions that most concern them.

And how much of life is measurable anyway? How much of the most important stuff? What do kilos, kilometers, angstroms, and curies have to do with compassion, sacrifice, suspicion, and honor? (If you are confident that you know, then you don't.)

I've been confident about God both ways. Confident that he was, then confident that he wasn't. (Sorry about the *he*. God got gendered when I was too little to know better and I still haven't been quite able to neuter him, mythic or not.) I've run the gamut from God is everything to nothing is God (or is that Nothing?). People I loved told me God was real and I believed it. People I was impressed by told me later that God was bogus (and that *I* wasn't even *really* real) and I believed that too. At one time I had more Sunday school attendance pins hanging from my chest than a Russian general has medals. At another I avoided church like it was an Ebola dispensary.

And here and there I've stopped for a bit at stations in between the extremes—God as useful symbol, God as necessary fiction (thank you, Mr. Stevens, you who capitulated on your deathbed), God as just one god among a multitude (many paths up that crowded mountain), God as real but unknowable, God as brain buzz, God as dog spelled backwards.

For the last few years, I've had too many problems to think much about God. (If God made me, I want a refund.) If pressed, I would say, out loud, "No, I don't believe in God." But inside a still, small voice would add,

"But I hope God believes in me." Why can't I just face the facts? No grand-daddy in the sky—never was, never will be. Anytime we think we've experienced something bigger than the physical, we've made it up: the physical (our brain) inventing the nonphysical (God) to meet some psychological need (the psychological, of course, being just another manifestation of the physical). Why can't I invert Peter Pan's song? "I *will* grow up, I *will* grow up. I won't stay a little boy."

Because just when I feel confident in my faith in no faith, I run across someone like Sister Brigit. Smart, tough, experienced, wise in the ways of the world. How does a woman like that end up in a nun's habit? How does she end up in an organization that says she can't be the CEO? (Hell, can't even bless the bread and wine.) How can she make herself believe that Billy Skywatcher is a valuable child of God rather than a regrettable genetic accident? That potty-mouth Bonita testifies to God's love of the creation?

I know what the academics and intellectuals would say—that she's the product of a subculture that clings to the premodern world out of fear and the desire to maintain power. (And a lot more.) But why do I find more to like in her story than in theirs? Why does their analysis seem plausible and yet thin? Why does it seem a product of their own fear and desire to maintain power?

And then there's Judy and her dogged devotion to all things Jesus. I remember her once asking me when we lived together on the boat, "Will I be this way when I'm in heaven?"

"What way?" I said, buying time.

"You . . . you know, Jon. The way . . . the way I am."

"No, I don't think so. I think you'll be all fixed."

"Then how . . . how will you know me?"

It knocked me for a loop. How do I know how you'll be in heaven, Jude? I don't even believe in heaven anymore. If I did, I guess I would correct myself and say that heaven isn't about getting fixed, it's about being with God. Maybe that's what Sister Brigit would say. Fully loved and fully loving. I don't know. Hell, the gap between us Normals and God is so immeasurable that it makes the gap between us and the Specials seem insignificant. It's like Specials know the multiplication tables up to three times three and the rest of us know them up to four times four and the geniuses among us can do, at best, short division. And God is beyond all the numbers and all the calculations.

I could almost get back to believing in God if he would just keep his distance. Like I said about Zillah and religion, it's this Christ stuff that's bothersome. God as transcendent is actually a lot easier for us moderns than God among us. He can be kept as a mental category, a concept. But have him running around getting himself crucified and then, oh my God, rising from the dead and you've ruined everything. You've made him something we have to deal with personally, like an annoying neighbor—or a spouse.

Oh Sister Brigit. Oh Judy. Oh Jesus. Please leave me alone.

TWENTY-FOUR

THE ETERNAL PROBLEM WHEN working with Specials is binding time. Binding time is a technical term for "what the heck should we do now?" And the problem is not unique to Specials. I've been trying to bind time my whole life, with limited success. I think that's why sports are so popular in the Western world. They're a hell of a time binder. They say people like baseball because the pace is so pastoral—a reminder of the slow agricultural rhythms of times past. I say it's appealing because it gets us from 7 p.m. to 10 p.m. without having to think or do—and we get to drink beer besides. Time is bound 162 times a year for a baseball fan, plus the playoffs. Hard to beat.

But you can't take Specials to a baseball game every night (though some of them wouldn't mind). And you can't have them just endlessly stare at the drip, drip, drip of television. And, unlike in the past, you can't simply tie them in a chair to pass the day humming "She'll be coming 'round the mountain when she comes." So we invent a lot of quasi-Normalizing settings: activity centers, workshops (sheltered and unsheltered), craft times, recreation opportunities, trips to movies, skills development times, and on and on.

And therefore we also get a party on my houseboat.

We're into August now. I'm scheduled for working a Saturday to Sunday shift, the toughest time for binding. The staff is forever inventing things for them to do (*something* has to go in the daily log), and I decide to invent a party on my boat. I don't have to get permission for these things—just sign out a van, collect receipts, and write a report or ten.

I figure we need numbers. If I just take my Carlson Group Home residents, we six will feel a "we're-on-an-adventure" buzz for fifteen minutes and then start staring at the river. No binding. So I talk to Larry, who oversees the independent living apartment crowd, and talk him into bringing a second vanload of his charges along. And then I do something questionable. I call up Zillah and ask her to join us.

I've talked to her a couple of times on the phone since our date in Stillwater. She seems okay with me calling, and she has even expressed some curiosity about what my houseboat must be like, so I figure this is a low-risk way for her to see where I live—and that I *do* live, do actually have a life of sorts.

Still, I'm surprised when she says yes. Like I said before, Zee has never been all that comfortable around Specials. But I think her interest in checking out the boat outweighs other considerations and she agrees to come along. I offer to pick her up in the van with the residents, but she says she'll just meet us there. So I give her directions.

When I hang up the phone, I find Judy standing behind me. She has her solemn face on, but then reaches up her hand for a high-five. Matchmaker, matchmaker, make me a match. Or a rematch.

You have to turn off at Water Street and then double back on the east bank of the Mississippi to get to the small cluster of houseboats under the shadow of the Wabasha Bridge. Downtown St. Paul greets you on the other side of the river, but all its assumptions of significance seem light years away when you're sitting on the back deck of a rusty boat all by your rusty self.

Larry has followed us with his vanload. Zillah is waiting in the parking lot. Everyone gathers by the locked gate leading to the gangplank that drops down to the docks. I buzz us through and they troop down single file, some with smiles, others with a careful shuffle and foreboding looks at the water. I squelch the impulse to start whistling "Heigh-ho, heigh-ho, it's off to work we go."

"Stop there at the bottom," I yell. And they do, more or less, waiting for the sheepdog.

My boat is to the right. As we pilgrimage toward it, I notice a few faces appearing in the windows and out the doors of neighboring boats. The Space Invaders have arrived and it's worth a look.

I've rigged up another small gangplank from the dock to my boat. No way in the world you're going to get some of these people to step over water from a dock to a deck. (They've tempted fate enough by getting themselves born; there's no need to overdo it.) Everyone does much better than we did with the escalator at the mall.

Jimmy is the first to express an opinion about my place.

"Nice digs, Jon. I like it. I like it. And I bet the ladies like it, too."

He shoots me a conspiratorial grin, an exaggerated wink, and two thumbs up. Yeah, us ladies men understand each other. Zillah rolls her eyes and looks at me with a bemused smile.

Fifteen people staring at the water is worse than six people staring at the water, and so I have planned for us to have a dance on the houseboat. Many of the Specials love to dance, and some of them actually can (a similar percentage as the rest of us). I think it's the same reason they generally like watching golf—they can easily understand the rules. In golf it's "little ball in little hole," piece of cake. In dancing it's "move repetitively as long as the music is playing, usually alongside someone else; stop when the music stops." It includes two things that Specials crave—repetition and buddies. What's not to like?

I drag out my big boom box. "What time is it?" I shout as I put in a disc. (I immediately think of our exiled friend.)

Silence. Jimmy stares at his watch, which hasn't run since the battery went dead two weeks ago. (It's my job to replace it, but I never remember—everyone has their limitations, you know—and Jimmy doesn't seem to care.) The Normals and the Specials in the room are equally confused by my question, so I answer it myself, with as much heartiness as I can muster.

"It's dance party time!"

Bingo. The place lights up. People give each other big smiles. There's even a hug or two. Judy, turning to Ralph, pronounces her blessing.

"I . . . I should say . . . I like to . . . to dance my own self. How about you, Ralphie?"

Ralph is contemplative for a moment, then replies.

"Da dooey."

"I've got sunshine on a cloudy day / When it's cold outside, I've got the month of May."

Larry helps everyone who wants to dance pair off as The Temptations warm us up. There's not enough space in the tiny living room, so some people go outside to the decks at each end of the boat. I crank up the music.

I look over at Zee across the room and see that she's smiling at me. It hits me then that this is not just any song. It is, in the timeless treacle of young love, "our song." We used to sing it together before we were married.

When the lyrics came to "my girl" I would point at her, and she would say "my guy" and point at me. It was sweet enough to give you cavities. It didn't last.

I study her smile from a distance. Is she pleased or does she think the choice of song a cheap trick? I decide to smile back. She walks over and we begin to dance. It's the best time binding I've experienced in a long stretch.

I play a bunch of Motown—The Miracles, Smokey, Gladys, and Marvin. I discovered these guys when Judy and I were living with Uncle Lester. It was a forbidden love because Uncle Lester thought it "devil music" of the worst kind. (It was a mercy that God protected him from the knowledge of Black Sabbath.) I could only listen to Motown when the house was empty or I was out on my bike with my prized transistor radio. Something attracted me to its confidence—about life, about love, about the possibility for joy in a painful world.

Everyone is having a good time, but I start to worry that maybe the music is too loud. I look out to see if any of the neighbors might be shutting their windows or seem upset. Instead I see Steve from three boats down. He's dancing by himself a few steps from two young women from independent living. In fact, one of them motions him over and, all smiles, the three of them dance together. Then from the other direction comes Marsha from the big yellow boat and pretty soon she and Larry start dancing together. My God, it's the Summer of Love breaking out again on the Mississippi.

"Hey, Mote. If this is a party, where's the treats?"

Bonita brings me quickly back to reality. And this time I am more prepared for reality than usual.

"Coming right up, Bonita. I have a cornucopia of good stuff for our pleasure."

"You can keep the corn, Mote. I want a real treat. And there better be pop."

Oh, Bonita, I think. Is there not pop a plenty? The world may be short of peace and love and justice, but does it not have oceans of pop? Does life not fill every shallow desire even if it frustrates our deepest ones?

"I've got cases of pop, Bonita. And chips and dip and chocolate drops and banana chewies and every other food blasphemy that a consumer economy can produce."

I drag out the grocery bags from under the counter and the cartons of soft drinks from the refrigerator and lay them out on the counter like a Middle Eastern merchant spreading his wares.

Things go on like this. Eventually, I leave my job as chip and pop supplier to the stars and look for a place to rest a minute. I spot Zillah and Judy sitting on a padded bench against the far wall. I go sit next to Zillah who smiles at me briefly but doesn't interrupt their conversation. I am turned toward the center of the room, while she is turned the opposite way toward Judy. I pretend to be intent on the dancing, but actually strain to hear every word they're saying. The more I can get inside Zillah's head, the better chance I have of getting back inside her heart.

At first I can't make out what they're talking about, but then realize with more than a little alarm that they're talking about me.

"Well, Jon is . . . I should say . . . is my brother of mine, and I love him very, very much."

"That's good."

"But of course, he . . . he has his problems."

"What would you say his problems are, Judy?"

Great. I'm being psychoanalyzed by my almost ex-wife and my not-firing-on-all-cylinders sister.

"Well, that . . . I think that is a very . . . a very good question, Zi . . . Zillah."

"Thank you. I think so too."

"I would say . . . I would say that Jon's problem is that he does not know who his own self . . . who his own self is. He is sometimes his own self and he is . . . is sometimes not."

"Interesting. I've seen that as well. Who do you think Jon really is?"

I find myself nervous about Judy's impending answer. This is crazy. Why am I worried about what a . . . well, a woman with, shall we say, pronounced limitations, is going to say about who I really am—even if she is my sister? And yet I feel like my life is swinging in the balance.

"Well, I would say that Jon is . . . that is, Jon really is . . . a child of Jesus. That's what Sister Brigit says. She says everyone is a child of . . . of Jesus. Jesus loves . . . I should say . . . Jesus loves the little children. And so Jesus loves Jon his own self."

What a disappointment. I'm hanging on her words like she's a cross between the Oracle of Delphi and Dr. Phil and she delivers a worn-out religious cliché. Judy is a good big sister, but her understanding of the world matches her IQ, not that either is her fault.

"You think Jesus has something to do with it, do you Judy?"

I'm afraid Zillah is going to get sarcastic and squash Judy's default explanation of all things. I remember Zee going off on television preachers and pro-life activists and even the obligatory "God bless America" sign-off in presidential speeches. "Why only America?" she'd say. "And which god?" She even questioned the "bless" part. "Why wait for God to bless us when we have the power to fix this screwed up country ourselves?" So I'm relieved when she goes easy.

"I'm sure Jesus does love Jon—or would have. Tell me more about what you think Jon is like."

"Well, my Jon is very, very nice. He takes care of me. And I . . . I take care of him. And he is very funny. He tells funny . . . I should say . . . funny jokes."

This apparently sends Judy into a flashback, because she slaps her knee and bobs her head and laughs out loud.

"My, my, yes. That bro . . . bro . . . brother of mine tells very fun . . . funny jokes."

I appreciate the credit for being absolutely hilarious, but don't figure this is winning me any points with Zillah. She got a big dose of my award-winning wit when living with it, and it wore thin. But then Zee says something encouraging, sort of.

"I like your brother too, Judy. He and I also tried to take care of each other once, but we didn't do a very good job."

The encouraging part is that she sounds sad. Like maybe she wished it had turned out differently. That maybe she has some regrets. Like maybe it wasn't entirely my fault.

"Well, you know what . . . what they say, Zillah. If at first you don't sneeze, try . . . I should say . . . try, try again."

"Yes, I've heard that, Judy."

So have I.

TWENTY-FIVE

TIME, SAYS THOREAU, IS the stream he goes a-fishing in. One metaphor among many for that great maker and destroyer of all things. Another is time as currency: something saved, something spent, something wasted. I, myself, spend it profligately, as though there will always be more. I spend some of it thinking about the constellation of things raised by Sister Brigit. And I spend some of it reading T.S. Eliot, a man who understood both the waste and the redeeming of time. But I spend most of it dressing and shaving, picking up around the boat, driving to and from work, working, unwinding from working, preparing to eat, eating, cleaning up from eating, undressing, failing to sleep, then sleeping. A Beckett kind of life actually— Samuel, not Thomas (two t's).

But I also spend some of the time talking to Zillah. We've gotten far enough that I don't have to invent a reason for calling her anymore. I can just ask, "How are you doing, Zee?" and she can say, "Fine, how about you, Jon?" Which is better than we did when we were together. And it's no small thing—two people checking up on each other, wishing each other well, willing to help out if there's a need, or even just a desire. It may not qualify as love, but if we could make it universal, we wouldn't need armies.

And we've met a few more times—not dates, just walks or doing small favors. Picking up something or dropping off something or helping to change a tire on her car that had a slow leak. (She could have just driven to a repair shop, but she called me. I take it as a good sign.)

So I'm happy but not shocked when Zillah calls and proposes a picnic. And I'm even happier when she says to bring Judy. After all, we three are my family. We're it. Uncle Lester has gone on to his eternal reward—may it be a hot one—and Uncle Bruce and Aunt Wanda are far away with no real prospect of me seeing them again. So it's me and Judy as charter members and Zee as a later addition who I'm hoping will renew her membership—if only as a kind of adjunct associate.

Zillah proposes Como Park, perhaps as a kind of gift to Judy. She knows of course that Judy and I grew up around there. She doesn't know, I'm guessing, that the whole area became a haunted place for us. But that's mostly gone now. The houses are just houses again, at least for the time being. The memories are more manageable, diluted you might say, like a weakened virus that serves as a vaccine against something more virulent.

On the way over, Judy plays a tune on my residual Baptist guilt. It's about J.P.

"I . . . I should say . . . I am worried about J . . . J.P. He . . . he is not in a good place."

"No, not a good place, Judy."

Which of us is?

"Well, then . . ."

She looks like she is trying to think.

"Well then what, Jude?"

"Well then I think . . . I should say . . . I think you should think of something, Jon."

Great. I, the great thinker, am supposed to think of something. The guy who struggles over which socks to wear each morning is supposed to storm the American justice system and spirit away one of its innocent victims.

But, strangely, Judy is speaking to a part of me that has already awakened. I do feel that I have to do something for J.P. Or at least try something, even if it's pyrrhic as hell. I know J.P. He's not a statistic. He's close up. He's like me and he's helpless. I know about helpless. I know that others—Judy, for instance—have tried to help me. This has karma written all over it. It's gone around and now it's coming around.

Besides, if I can do something myself that changes things for the better for someone else, maybe that would speak to the slim possibility that there might be significance in the cosmos. Not just energy waves, but meaning. Meaning with maybe even a hint of benevolence.

I look at Judy. She's been studying me as I drive. She looks satisfied. Mission accomplished.

We meet Zillah at the miniature golf course across the road from the zoo at the yellow streetcar that once operated on the Lake Harriet to Como line. (Around the same time as the yellow boat we took to Excelsior for Judy and Ralph's date.) It's late August and Minnesota children are getting in their last desperate minutes of frenetic action before the start of school and the descent of the leaves and the stark reality of Canadian cold fronts. (Should we really blame the Canadians rather than God or Mother Nature?)

We move to a table near a large climbing mound. Little kids are scampering up and down it, enjoying the deeply human thrill of almost but not quite breaking their necks. A feeling I'm familiar with. Zillah watches them closely, with, I'm thinking, a look mixed with pleasure and sadness.

We're having a good time. I can tell that Judy is thrilled with the whole thing. She smiles continuously, like a time-share salesman at the "free" dinner for perspective buyers.

"Well . . . isn't this . . . I should say . . . isn't this nice?"

I hit the ball back.

"Very nice, Jude."

I expect Zillah to add a volley, but she is quiet. Maybe upset. She had seemed nervous when we first met for the picnic, but smiley. I figured she was a little tense about having initiated us all getting together, like she was afraid Judy and I would read more into it than she wanted. (Truth is, I am reading into like crazy.)

I ask Zillah if anything is wrong, something an angel might fear to ask but where we fools rush in. I am a man acquainted with grief—not the first. And loss. And abandoned hopes. And with my actions resulting in opposite reactions, a living confirmation of Newton's third law.

But nothing prepares me for the look on Zillah's face. It's become a mix of pain and terror and profound sadness. She looks like she is afraid to breathe, for fear the next breath will breach a dam holding back great reservoirs of regret. She speaks in whispers.

"You know, Jon, I arranged this because there's something I want to tell you. No, actually, it's the last thing I want to tell anyone, but it's something I need to tell you—both of you."

This has the feel of so many conversations that Zillah and I had over the years. And I can't remember even one that turned out well. I want to yell out to her, "Stop, Zillah! Let's just eat our egg salad sandwiches and enjoy watching the little children play in the sun. Let's not try to solve anything or fix anything or rehash anything. Let's just be together for a while and then go home."

But of course I don't say anything. And neither does Judy, who instead is staring at Zillah, with that look of concentration she gets when she is trying hard to understand something.

Zillah goes on.

"After we separated, we didn't see each other—at all."

"Yes."

"It wasn't because I didn't want to see you, because part of me did. And, of course, part of me didn't, too."

I am mute—afraid of what she might say next, though I have no idea what it might be. I have this impulse to talk about baseball.

"I want to tell you this, too, Judy. I need for you to know about this."

Judy nods.

"Then you . . . you just go ahead and . . . and say it, Zillah."

Zillah doesn't say anything. She just starts shaking. Tiny little shakes. In her head and her hands and then her shoulders. Judy and I both put our hands on her back at the same moment. Then Zillah speaks.

"Two weeks after I left you, Jon, I missed my period. I didn't think much of it until I missed my next one too. Then . . . well then I thought a lot of it. I was terrified."

Oh no. This cannot be going anywhere good.

"And so I went to this clinic. My friend told me about it. And, well, they told me what I didn't want to hear."

I don't want to hear it either. Let's not talk about it. Let's go back to fifteen minutes ago and take a different fork in the road. Or maybe go back fifteen years ago. You choose differently and I'll choose differently and our paths will never cross and this conversation will never happen.

"And the first thing they say after telling me is, 'Do you want to continue with this pregnancy?' The very first thing."

Well, it's their job, I think.

"Like they're asking, 'Do you want this on wheat bread or on rye?' I'm trying to get my mind to engage the fact that I'm pregnant at all and they want me to tell them whether I want the pregnancy to continue."

It takes a full ten count for it to hit me. I think I'm listening to Zillah's story and trying to figure out how best to help her. Only then does it flood over me that it's not her story, it's our story. She's not just talking about something that happened to her, but to us. That's when *I* start shaking. Now I'm the one filled with grief and terror. But I hear myself talking.

"It's okay, Zillah. It's okay. Whatever happened. It's over now. It's over and it's okay."

She looks at me as though she's noticed for the first time that I'm here.

"Do you think so, Jon? Do you think it's over? Do you think everything's okay?"

She says this flatly, almost mechanically, not angry, with just a touch of curiosity in her voice. And more than a touch of incredulity. Sort of like she feels sorry for me.

And then a long pause before she speaks again.

"I don't think so."

I find myself looking for escape routes. Scenarios start running through my head. I look at Judy. Does any of this have any meaning to her? Is she following what Zillah is saying? I'm struck by a great fear that Judy is going to start invoking Jesus. Instead she says something else that I equally wish she wouldn't say.

"Go . . . go on, Zillah. It will be good for you to . . . to talk about it."

What touchy-feely pop therapy television talk show did she get that from? I'm about to say it might be better to talk to a professional about this, when Zillah goes on.

"I told them, 'Let me think about it' and they said, 'Of course, it's all up to you. Whatever you decide is good.' Then they offered some free counseling, someone I could talk to."

Zillah has stopped shaking. Her voice is still tight but talking seems to be helping her.

"That line kept coming back to me over the weeks, 'It's all up to you.' I didn't want it to be all up to me. It felt like too big a decision to be all up to me. I wanted it to be up to someone else. I wanted someone to tell me what to do. What was the smart thing? What was the realistic thing? What was the right thing?"

That's the Jesus cue.

"Well, Zillah, I . . . I my own self. When I have a problem. That is, Sister Brigit . . . Sister Brigit says. Ju . . . Judy . . . you pray to Jesus."

I'm afraid this is going to push Zillah over the edge. But I'm in line for yet another shock.

"I did pray, Judy. I did. For the first time since I was a little girl, I asked God to tell me what to do. I asked God if it really was my choice, like the clinic people said, or whether it was taking away someone else's choice. You know what I mean?"

Judy doesn't know what Zillah means. I'm sure of that. But I do and I'm feeling a little sick. Why hadn't Zillah talked to me? Even if we were separated, why didn't she think it was our decision, not just her decision? Why didn't the clinic tell her that?

I feel anger and sickness growing together, like two stalks from the same root. Why don't I count here? Why do I never count? Why did I stop counting the night my parents fled into eternity?

"But you know what, Judy? God never got back to me. I listened the best I could and I never heard a word. Not a word that I could be sure wasn't just my own word, or someone else's."

She pauses. Judy doesn't say anything.

"So the weeks pass and I'm afraid I'm going to start showing and I want to come to some resolution on all this before that happens. Either I'm going to 'continue with this pregnancy' and deal with the consequences or I'm not."

A child as a "consequence." Doesn't seem an adequate word for the referent. A mismatch between figure and ground.

Her voice goes low again, as though she is speaking only to herself.

"Only one consequence really. Only one that mattered."

I find myself jumping in.

"I'll help you."

She looks at me sharply.

"I mean, I would have helped you . . ."

I'm stumbling badly.

"Well, at least I would have tried."

Then she says something unexpected. And she reaches out and touches my face.

"Thank you, Jon. Yes, I think you would have tried. And, I don't know, maybe I should have told you."

Another pause.

"But I didn't. Instead I decided to stall by asking for more information. More data, as though that was the key. So I had a test done where they took some of the fluid and they looked at it and they told me something very troubling, as though I didn't have trouble enough. They told me that there was something wrong with the baby. No wait, they never called it a baby. They said there was something wrong with the fetus. No, they didn't use the word 'wrong,' either. They said there was an 'anomaly.' That was the word, an 'anomaly.'"

Now Zillah does start to cry. But she keeps talking as the tears come.

"And I said, what kind of anomaly, and they said there might be an extra chromosome and that the fetus was possibly defective, and I said are you sure and they said we can't be completely sure but that the test is some percent accurate—they gave me a number—some percent accurate and there was a quite good chance the baby—they said fetus—that the fetus was defective and I said is there anything that can be done and they said there was no way of curing this, not now and not after birth, and that I could either end the pregnancy or start preparing to raise a special needs child, that was their term special needs child, and that it was totally up to me and that either way was good, no they said fine not good fine, and that it was totally up to me, totally up to me . . . totally . . . "

Now she is crying hard and she suddenly reaches out and hugs Judy, who returns the hug.

"I'm so sorry, Judy. I'm so sorry. I was alone and I didn't have any money and my marriage was ending. Don't you see, Judy? And it was totally up to me and they said it would be fine. Can you forgive me, Judy? Please forgive me. I didn't want to hurt anyone. I wanted to do what was best."

Why is she saying this to Judy? Why is she asking for Judy's forgiveness? Why isn't she asking mine? Or at least asking what I think about it? I don't get it. I never seem to get it.

I doubt that Judy gets it either, but she wants, as usual, to be a helper.

"Why, why Zillah. Of course . . . of course I for . . . forgive you. And so . . . so does Jesus. Jesus loves you. And . . . and, I should say, Jesus loves the lit . . . little children."

Now they are both crying. Hugging each other and crying. I don't get it. I never seem to get it.

TWENTY-SIX

I DON'T SEE ZILLAH for the next two weeks, though we talk once briefly on the phone. I am agitated about . . . what should I call it . . . her confession? She has nothing to confess because she has done nothing wrong that I can see, but she clearly feels extremely sorry for something. Maybe you can be both innocent and sorry at the same time. Or maybe, as she knows better than anyone, I am, once again, clueless.

I'm also back to square one about J.P. Mr. Wagner's private investiga-tor, Randle, has called to ask a few more questions. He's using me to get information, but he's also giving me quite a bit, without my even asking, maybe as a way of incentivizing me for further cooperation. ("Incentiv-izing." My apologies to the English language.)

"I've got one guess and two sure things about the police investigation," he says. "My guess is that they have DNA evidence from Abby's body. They aren't saying because there's a better chance of getting cooperation in the future if the killer doesn't know anything about how DNA evidence works."

I'm thinking this should let J.P. off the hook. So I ask why, if they have DNA, they don't just test J.P., see that it isn't his, and then let him go?

"Because J.P. is their bird in the hand. Having DNA evidence and matching it are two very different things. You can't test everyone within ten miles of the crime site. They may never match it, and, for that matter, the DNA might not be from the perpetrator. Maybe someone had sex with her and someone else killed her later. In the meantime, J.P.'s shoe and the scarf are hard evidence that points to him. They need a solution and J.P. will do unless something better comes along."

I'm too disappointed by his answer to ask about the "two sure things," but he moves to them on his own.

"Ms. Pettigrew and Mr. Springer were meeting at the office the evening of the murder. But they left at eight, a couple of hours before Abby was dropped off."

Then he drops a bombshell that makes the DNA speculation irrelevant.

"The other thing that you won't hear from the police: James McCloskey has confessed to the murder."

How he knows this he doesn't say, but he seems confident about it. I guess investigators like him have inside sources. Stocks, politics, religion, car repair, murder—it's all about who you know.

So Sister Brigit "knows" J.P. didn't do it. But J.P., apparently, knows that he did. It makes my stomach churn.

Cassandra is working hard to get things back to normal (that word again) at New Directions. She tells us at a staff meeting to discourage talk about the murder—and about J.P. (James to her, though she studiously avoids using his name at all)—among the clients.

"These people have enough to deal with in their everyday lives without adding the anxiety associated with recent events. The 253B commitment process is underway and being followed to the letter, including administration of both a MacCAT and a CAST-MR. There has been a preliminary hearing and the required second hearing is scheduled. The perpetrator, I should say the accused, is being professionally assessed at St. Peter to confirm that he is an SDP, and it is expected that he will remain at St. Peter for the long term."

So long J.P.—perp—it's been good to serve you. Thanks for helping fill the trough.

The one thing that most keeps things from returning to normal is Stuart Wagner. He is very rich, very angry, and demanding justice—the Holy Trinity for a carnivorous trial lawyer. Or a whole firm full of them in this case. (I can't help thinking of America's favorite law firm: Dewey, Cheetham & Howe.)

Wagner is not happy that J.P. has been sent to St. Peter. He wants him sent to the gallows. But since Minnesota has progressed beyond capital punishment, Wagner wants him at least in prison, in as small a cell as possible. He had an ugly hallway exchange with Cassandra not long after J.P.'s shoe was found in the reeds. He paid J.P. a grudging compliment: "He looks mighty normal to me. I know one thing—he's normal enough to have murdered my daughter. And he's normal enough to pay for it." (If he knew more about high security mental hospitals, he might be more content.)

Wagner filed a suit against New Directions soon after and named a lot of excessories or whatever the term is: Cassandra as the executive director, Bo as the one in charge of security, the chairman of the board as the head of those charged with oversight, and—drum roll, please—me as the person in charge at the Carlson Group Home the night J.P. is accused of committing the murder.

I hope the national New Directions corporation has deep pockets, because I have no pockets at all. Not even, as of a few months ago, a credit card. They can take my Harmon Killebrew rookie card—my single most valuable possession—but it's slim pickings after that. The New Directions lawyer tells me not to worry, being included in the suit is only a formality. But then I was once told that a marriage license was only a formality, too.

Cassandra is clearly satisfied to close the file on J.P. He's now at another institution, under a different set of program guidelines, his life, such as it is, the responsibility of a new set of professionals.

Cassandra is satisfied, but I'm not. And neither are J.P.'s friends. They ask about him every day. They even plot. Bonita and Jimmy, as you would expect, are the brains of the potential operation.

We're sitting at the dinner table one night—one disciple less. Jimmy volunteers to pray before eating, as he often does. (And this time he stands to pray, not a good sign.) This one goes the full four quarters plus overtime.

His prayer covers the food, the hands that prepared it, a blessing on the President and Congress, the Vikings football team, his own dear mother, and the weather. All as a warm-up. He includes J.P. in the prayer.

"And, dear God, help us to spring J.P. And help us to find the dirty rat who killed Abby."

I am about to invoke supervisory authority and cut the filibuster short when he wraps it up with a solemn flourish.

"And I say to my friends and fellow residents here at Good Shepherd: you better watch out, you better not shout, you better not cry, I'm telling you why . . . Santa Claus, yes Santa Claus, is coming to town. Amen."

Jimmy hangs his head, leaning with both hands on the table, as though exhausted. The other residents open their eyes, except Billy, who never had closed them. Judy offers her appreciation.

"That was . . . I should say . . . a very good prayer, Jimmy."

The rest accept the prayer at face value, moving on quickly to negotiating with the food in front of them. Their lack of appreciation does not bother Jimmy. He is full of appreciation for his own self, and he continues to stand, smiling, as though to thunderous applause.

Bonita picks up on the idea of springing J.P. from St. Peter.

"We get a van, see. Mote, you drive. We go to where they got J.P. We punch the lights out of those bastards who are holding him and we get out of there and bring him home."

What could be easier. Then pop for the liberators, J.P., and all his friends, huh, Bonita?

Jimmy sees the need for a little more sophistication.

"That's right, Bonita. But we can't just beat them up. There's too many of 'em. We got to outsmart 'em."

There's general approval around the table for being smart instead of violent.

Judy suggests praying and then watching the walls come tumbling down, but no one else picks up on it. It falls to Jimmy to fine-tune the plan.

"Here's what we do. We all come in. Jon says that we are there to pick up J.P. because we are going to a Twins game. We all act retarded because people know that people like us go to baseball games. They bring J.P. out and we get into the van. But we don't go to the Twins game. We come back here and never go back and J.P. stays with us."

I finish it off.

"And lives happily ever after. Amen."

Everyone laughs. It's unanimously agreed to be a good plan. Billy twitches and hums.

Well, we don't spring J.P. But I do go see him. It's complicated to get permission, but I bypass Cassandra entirely and contact St. Peter on my own and explain that I am a group home supervisor who previously worked with J.P. and that I would like to visit him. I know it's probably the end of working at New Directions if I'm caught—a violation of procedure, compromising the investigation and all that—but so what? J.P. is, well, a sort of friend of mine and I'm worried about him, so, damn it, I'm going to go see him. I've become a veritable John Wayne of premeditated action.

For some reason, I ask Zee if she wants to go with me and she says yes. I pitch it as a day out of the city, with the St. Peter stop as just a thirty-minute sidelight. (Sort of like telling Davey Crockett we're going to Dallas with a pit stop at the Alamo.)

It's a nice drive once you're out of town, about sixty miles southwest of Minneapolis. Follows the Minnesota River most of the way. It's flowing north while we're heading south, but we stay out of each other's way. The river is trying to get to the Big Daddy that will carry its waters down past where Johnnie Roberts still lies. I'm trying to get to the high security ward where our buddy J.P. lies. Two men with no futures.

It's farm country for the most part, places where we process the earth just like we process each other—property lines, parallel furrows (made by satellite-guided tractors), seeds precisely placed, fertilizers, weed killers— just enough of each, not too much (unless any is too much)—harvesters, trucks, and then on to the next leg in the chain of command. (We've got to eat, don't we?) All overseen by rules, guidelines, programs, officials, corporate executives, and laws (including those of the marketplace). ("Pass the poisoned sweet potatoes, please." I've seen too many left-wing documentaries on the food industry. I need to go back to game shows.)

Zillah is quiet for the first part of the drive. I would normally be happy for that. I've always been a fan of quiet, especially in relationships with women. But I'm trying to be more grown up these days, more responsible. Even willing to talk about difficult things. And so I bring up our picnic, hoping that I can say what I have to say quickly and then we can move on to pointing out how picturesque the grain silos are.

"You know, Zillah, that picnic we had a while back—you and Judy and me?"

"Yes, we did have a picnic, didn't we?"

She's not going to make this easy.

"Well, I just want to say that I'm glad you told us . . . and I think you did the right thing and I want you to feel okay about it."

She doesn't say anything for a moment. She is looking out at the river in the distance. Then she speaks.

"Well, thank you, Jon. I appreciate your concern for me. I really do."

Good, that should take care of it. I said the right thing, she appreciates it, now we can move on. That wasn't so bad.

"But I didn't *do* anything."

Go easy here. What did she say at the picnic? What did I just say? What was her reply? Where have I missed something?

"Well, no. *You* didn't do anything yourself. I mean, someone else did it . . . literally. But I'm just saying . . . "

"No, Jon. No one did anything. I made an appointment. It was on the calendar. But a couple of days before it was scheduled, I had a miscarriage. It just happened. Spontaneously, as they say."

I'm processing this like crazy.

"Then why did you apologize to Judy? Why do you think you have anything to apologize about at all?"

She smiles wanly and leans over and kisses me lightly on the cheek.

"You're a sweet guy, Jon. I find you very loveable in a lot of ways. But some things you just don't get. Some things you never seem to get."

We look at each other.

"But that's okay. Jesus . . . I should say . . . Jesus loves you."

And then she laughs.

We get to the outskirts of St. Peter. The sign welcoming us to the city reads, "Where History and Progress Meet." Sounds like the story of my life—or at least half of it. Lots of history, hoping for progress. More like, for me, where history and progress collide.

The high security hospital is on the south side of town, not far from the Lutheran college. Well, once Lutheran and Swedish, now, like most all of them, secular and progressive. A progressive college in a progressive town—the college namesake, conqueror at Breitenfeld, would no doubt be proud.

From the outside the place looks like an architecturally challenged corporate headquarters. The original nineteenth-century Dickensian "Hospital for the Insane"—eight hundred feet long and three stories high—has been replaced twice (I've done some research), the present manifestation being clusters of brick buildings of various hues growing out of each other like sequential tumors.

I debate whether to try getting Zillah into the facility with me. She settles the question.

"You go, Jon. I'm glad to walk around in the sun for a while. These kinds of places give me the creeps."

And so I go in alone.

I have to talk to three different people before they're satisfied that I can be allowed to see J.P. I'm in their system based on my previous contacts, and so the system decides that I can talk, briefly it insists, to my friend.

That's when I'm allowed, after turning out my pockets, to go through the first locked door. Then a second. Then a third. I feel like I'm going deeper and deeper into a massive, tile-floored, white-walled brain. I half expect to come to a guarded black door labeled "Id."

So far I've seen only staff people, all wearing badges, all busy—the neurons and synapses of the neocortex—but then I go deeper. Down to the reptilian brain.

Okay, that's too melodramatic, but it's how it feels, undoubtedly because it's how I expect it to feel. The truth is, it's all quite antiseptic. Sterile even.

They put me in a small empty room with only two chairs. It has a window to the hallway with wire mesh in the plate glass. The two fellows who have brought me here (a full-employment strategy? Or am I considered dangerous too?) depart with a simple "Wait here."

Ten minutes later they lead J.P. past the window and into the room. He is shuffling. I look to see if he's wearing leg irons, but, no, he is shuffling on his own. Maybe it's how others walk in his ward and so how he has decided to walk in order to fit in. Maybe not.

I stand up and smile my bravest smile.

"How you doing, J.P.?"

I put out my hand. He doesn't respond to it or to my question. The attendants leave with a last word, "Fifteen minutes."

"Sit down, J.P. Let's talk."

We both sit down. He doesn't look well. He's pale and he's looking at the floor and his hands tremor slightly. He speaks very softly.

"Are you here to take me home, Jon?"

The question breaks my heart. No, J.P. The system says *this* is your home now. And the system knows best. It is very logical. It is created and maintained by logical people.

"Well, not this time, J.P. I can't take you home this time. But maybe later. Maybe you can come home later."

I'm lying. Barring a miracle, J.P. will never come home. And who in their right mind believes in miracles? But I didn't come here to depress him further, so I decide a lie is a small act of mercy. Ethics have to be useful, don't you think?

I wrestle with whether to tell him about the other residents. I don't know if this will cheer him up or just remind him that he's no longer with them. I decide to risk it and spend ten minutes telling him everything I can think of about Judy and Bonita and Jimmy and Ralph and Billy.

He listens. He even smiles a bit. But he doesn't say anything. I'm out of ammo. Then he asks a question.

"What if my brother comes to see me and I'm not there?"

Oh J.P., brain-damaged one of the broken jaw, clockless man, man of the shy smile, why do you torment me with your artless questions? Why this constant reminder that the world is not as it should be? That it is not fair? That it has no meaning? That it does not love?

But I, lying man, deceiving and self-deceived, must answer. And so I do.

"If he comes J.P., I'll send him down here to see you. For sure."

He accepts the lie without comment.

I see that I have two minutes left, and I haven't asked the one question I most need to ask. And so I just blurt it out.

"J.P., the police say you confessed to killing Abby. Did you confess?"

"Um, what does confess mean, Jon?"

"Did you tell Detective Strauss that you killed Abby?"

"Yes."

"Did you do it, J.P.?"

"No."

"Then why did you say you did?"

"I wanted the nice police man to be happy."

TWENTY-SEVEN

IF IT WAS CLEAR to officialdom that J.P. had, somehow, killed Abby Wagner, it wasn't clear to Bonita and Jimmy. They had come of age watching *Dragnet* on television and were committed to finding out "just the facts, ma'am." Especially, like the rest of us, the facts as they preferred them to be. They preferred that the facts point to a different suspect than J.P. And they had a favorite—Bo Springer.

Turns out it was a personal vendetta on Bonita's part more than anything else. (No harpy believed in retributive justice more than Bonita.) It didn't start with any suspicions about Bo and Abby. It started with pop machines. Bo had announced recently that they were going to take all the pop out of the pop machines on campus and replace it with fruit juices and bottled electrolytes. Part of a health initiative. And no pop in the dorms and group homes either.

Actually, it wasn't Bo's idea. His own favorite pop has "all the sugar and twice the caffeine" or whatever the slogan is. He was just following orders. Cassandra said something in a memo distributed to the staff about New Directions following a "holistic" approach to "whole-person care" and that offering sugary drinks was incompatible with our "concern for the whole person—physical, psychological, and social." But Bo, as facilities manager, is in charge of pop machines, and so the announcement about the "beverage machines" —as they were to be referred to from now on—came from him. (Linguistic cleansing being an unending obligation.) And Bonita Marie was *not* happy about it. So she set out to bring him down and recruited Jimmy as her muscle.

Having no direct link to the police themselves, they bring any fruits of their ongoing investigation to me, counting on me to pass the goods up the chain of command. I have to admit, the first fruits are a revelation.

"We got something for you, Mote."

Bonita is speaking straight Sergeant Friday: clipped, rapid-fire, expressionless.

"What's that, Bonita?"

Jimmy joins in.

"Something on Mr. Springer. You know, the suspect."

"Suspected of what?"

Bonita snorts.

"Of killing Abby Wagner, of course. The shithead."

I play along.

"Ah, of course. Well, what do you have on him, guys?"

Bonita looks around the living room, shifting her eyes conspicuously left and right.

"Are we alone?"

"We're alone."

"Well, Jimmy and I did a . . . what was it Jimmy?"

"A strikeout."

"Yeah, we did a strikeout."

I know I'm not supposed to be enjoying this. I know I'm exploiting the difference between our intellectual capabilities for the sake of my own entertainment. I should be gently squashing this conversation out of respect for their, I don't know, dignity or something. But what the heck? We're buddies and we're gossiping. That's what Normals do, so I figure I'm treating them like Normals, which, after all, is the stated goal.

"And what did you find?"

Bonita is about to present the findings, but Jimmy is proud of the details and interrupts to fill me in on the nature of the stakeout.

"We hid in the bushes outside Mr. Springer's office, see? We took turns looking in through the window. We could see his desk and everything. We did it a bunch of different times."

"And what did you discover, Jimmy?"

Bonita isn't going to let Jimmy steal her thunder. She jumps in.

"We saw Springer kissing Pettigrew!"

She emphasizes the revelation with a raised index finger.

Jimmy adds a clinching detail.

"Right on the lips!"

Bonita nods and they both point to their own lips. They are highly satisfied with themselves and await my congratulations. I buy some time for a response with a question.

166

"And that proves . . . exactly what?"

Bonita answers with utter confidence.

"That Springer killed Abby Wagner!"

Jimmy nods sharply.

I placate the dynamic detecting duo with a "That's very interesting" and matching fist bumps. I then remind them that it's time to start working on dinner. But my own mind is working overtime (nothing new) on what to make of "Bo and Cassandra sitting in a tree, k-i-s-s-i-n-g." The flitting of the little nursery rhyme through my head pulls me back to the moments after Abby's body had been found when Bo told me to get all the residents back to the group home.

"We're going into lockdown mode. Cassie is upset big time. This is bad. Real bad."

There it was. He called her "Cassie." Nobody at New Directions called her Cassie, even in private conversation. It was incompatible with her self-image, her public persona, and all those letters after her name. It would be like calling the Pope "Johnny Paul II." Why hadn't I caught that then (and how in the world did my brain retrieve this tidbit now)?

Then my "on the other hand" reflex kicks in. So there's an office romance going on at New Directions. Not a big deal. Cassandra is married but childless, perhaps a bit bored with her husband, perhaps worried that life is passing her by, all the professional accomplishments notwithstanding. No, not a big deal—in fact a cliché if she were a male CEO, and increasingly a cliché in any case.

I'm still pondering these things, Mary-like, in my heart as I head to the parking lot to drive home. I'm off at five today, which is nice. The next employee has to supervise the making and consumption of dinner, the most taxing part of a shift.

As I'm passing the main building, who should come out but Bo. It startles me. I mean, have you ever been thinking about someone and then looked up and found them in front of you? Makes you feel as though your thoughts have summoned them, like the blood of the sacrificed sheep summoning the spirits of the dead for Odysseus. One of the spirits was his mother, who Odysseus did not know had died until that moment. It's a painful scene, discovering his mother in the world of the dead, three times reaching out to hold her but three times finding there is nothing physical there for him to hold. Where is my own mother? In the shadowy world of the dead? In bright heaven? In the ground in which we placed her, becoming one with the soil? What would I not give, as Odysseus would have given, to hold her in my arms? Or to be held.

Bo interrupts this melancholy and pointless speculation with an invitation.

"Hey, Mote. You heading home? How about a couple of drinks?"

It seems fated, like I don't have any real choice other than to say, as I do, "Sure Bo, why not?"

"How about Lord Fletcher's? It's a bit of a drive, but we can sit out rush hour and watch the boats go by. And what the hell, it's Friday."

("In spite of that, we call this Friday good.")

Lord Fletcher's sits at the channel connecting Crystal Bay with the next bay west, one of dozens in Rorschach-shaped Lake Minnetonka. ("I see a duckie chasing a dog, doctor. Does that mean I'm a pervert?") It's a place designed before the foundations of the world for people like Bo—a place to fend off the emptiness of your life with booze, babes, and, in this case, boats. The latter tie up beside a large outdoor wooden patio. The slips are already full when we arrive. It's August and it's Friday afternoon and we must start forgetting about Mondays—past and future—as quickly as possible.

All of which is more than a little judgmental on my part. I mean, why not just say these are people looking to relax a little after a hard week? Maybe I'm just bitter about our respective boats. Mine is corroded and leaky and I live in it because it's cheaper than an apartment. Theirs are sleek and shiny and they play in them to bind the time. They've earned their expensive boats. Life said to them, "You can have the big-screen Sony television there in the box, or you can risk the television by choosing whatever's behind door number two." "I'll take what's behind door number two, Monty," they said and, lo and behold, life presented them a pleasure craft. And, yea, they were very happy.

Who doesn't want to be happy? So why begrudge the people who achieve it? I mean, if being happy isn't the point of life, then what is? Okay, so maybe the root for happy is "hap," as in happenstance (a combination of the two words "happen" and "circumstance"), meaning "due entirely to chance—random, unpredictable," which is to say, the opposite of providential. So happy comes and happy goes and no one can foretell its coming and going. Which is why the Romans said, "Let no man count himself happy until the moment of his death"—or something like that. Because happiness is a bitch, and it will cozy up to you one minute and bite you in the rear the next. And then there's the problem that the moment you realize you're happy, you are slightly less happy than you were the moment before. Curse of consciousness and all that. (We're all little Prufrocks, after all.)

You see. These are the kinds of places my brain goes to while other people are simply sipping their Guinness, watching the boats go by. Why can't I just be mindless, a ragged claw . . . and happy?

So while I'm sitting there thinking what the taxes must be on these boats, Bo is ordering us giant margaritas.

"This first round is on me, Mote. Us bachelors got to stick together."

Bo apparently doesn't know I'm not a bachelor. Not according to the law. Legally I'm still married. But I'm not wearing a ring. I still look passably young—okay, not old. Certainly on the right side of middle-aged at least. Oh, for Christ's sake. Who cares how or what I look like? Nobody that I know of.

Bo starts off talking sports, the safest possible ground for a bro. I speak sports and so we do—beginning with the Twins. Last place the year before, but doing better this year. A little more this and a trade for that and, like Marlon Brando, the Twins could be "contendahs." Then the Vikings. Bo shakes his head.

"That thing with Korey was a tragedy. My God, one minute you're living the NFL dream and the next minute you're dead. Really tragic."

I'm thinking maybe Bo has some awareness of the dark edge of all things, but he corrects that impression.

"But what the hell. Let's have another round."

He orders a scotch and water. I tell the waitress I'm still working on my margarita (but wondering whether I'm obligated to pay for his scotch and water).

I'm starting to look for an exit line a few minutes later when Bo begins talking about Abby's murder.

"Does it feel weird having lived with a killer? Does it make you wonder about the rest of 'em?"

"What? What do you mean?"

"You know what I mean. James McCloskey. You slept right across the hall from him. He could have done you in just as easy as he did in that Wagner girl."

For some irrational reason (is that an oxymoron, pairing irrational with reason?), I try to defend J.P. to Bo. I even go so far as to call him the name by which he knows himself.

"I don't know that J.P. killed anyone. In fact, I'm pretty sure he didn't."

Bo laughs. He's finished the second drink and ordered a third.

"J.P. is it? Well, I guess we're not on the clock, so we can call the dim bulb anything you want."

Then he leans toward me and says with a twisted smile.

"But what do you mean about him not killing her, Mote? The tennis shoe, the scarf. What more evidence do you need? Cassie tells me he even confessed to the cops. Strauss as much as told her so."

This is pissing me off. I don't like the pleasure Bo is taking in all this. I like it even less because I know he could well be right, though I still can't put J.P. and murder together in my mind to save my soul.

Bo's use of "Cassie" brings back my earlier epiphany. I decide to give Bo a little of his own medicine.

"Well, evidence isn't proof. Evidence is just someone's interpretation of facts. And facts are just someone's interpretation of data. And even data are just someone's selection from the tsunami of sense impressions."

This is pure Pratt (I knew his stuff would come in handy someday) and pure bullshit and has exactly the effect that I expect. After a stunned moment, Bo responds.

"What the hell are you talking about, Mote? I'm just looking to see if James said anything interesting before they hauled him off to the funny farm—make that the funnier farm since New Directions is the minor leagues—and you give me this data and tsunami crap."

The booze has found its way to Bo's scattered brain cells. It seems he is not one of those good drunks. Alcohol stimulates his natural belligerence—and carelessness. No saint myself, I decide to exploit it.

"You mentioned me calling him J.P. instead of James. I'm wondering about your referring to Ms. Pettigrew as Cassie."

"When was that?"

"Just now. And on the athletic field, after they found Abby's body."

"Yeah, I call her Cassie. So what?"

"I don't know. I just can't think of anyone else at New Directions who would call her Cassie. Wondering if there's a reason for it."

Bo believes in hanging his scalps from his belt, especially when he's had too much to drink.

"No one else calls her Cassie because no one else at New Directions is in her pants."

He looks at me with a kind of fierce satisfaction.

"It's no big deal, Mote. She's a harmless bit of office tail. It only started a few months ago and I'm already getting bored. I thought it would be fun, maybe even a good career move. I was mistaken. It'll be over soon. Does that answer your question?"

"It does."

But it also raises some.

TWENTY-EIGHT

AFTER BO BOASTS OF conquering Cassandra with his irresistible bro charm, I watch the next time I see them together for any vibes. Nothing. It's all Mr. Springer this and Ms. Pettigrew that. Elaborately professional. Which probably is itself a sign of panky (as in hanky) to the tutored eye.

I'm still irritated by my happy hour exchange with Bo. (Happy hour—the time when we poison our brain to render it docile, a synonym, apparently, for happy.) I want desperately to find some alternate explanation for J.P.'s shoe being in the reeds and Abby's scarf being in his photo album. It's just too plain and simple to be true. Life is never that plain and simple. Mine certainly hasn't been. Plain and simple is a clear violation of Mote's Law: things are screwed up in direct proportion to their appearing fine. Or Normal.

"Normal" covers over a multitude of unacknowledged evils (called "sins" in the old days, when superstitious people actually believed in evil). But, thank God, many Specials don't know enough not to say what they think. In this case, the Specials are Bonita, Jimmy, and, out of the blue, Tiny Tim.

Tiny Tim in the Christmas play, you will remember—or won't—reminded Jimmy of Don, the kid on the boy's floor who has cerebral palsy and uses crutches. (Are you allowed to say "crutches" anymore? "Ambulatory aids," maybe?) And late one afternoon Bonita and Jimmy show up at the group home with Don in tow.

Don is maybe ten, though it's hard to say, what with the CP and all. He's very small and his legs are a mess, but he is a cute kid in his own way, with blond hair and a kind of puckish smile. I don't know to what degree he's a cognitive Special—sometimes these CPs are and sometimes not—but I figure if he's here at New Directions he must be down at least a few points.

Anyway, the three of them come into the kitchen where I'm contemplating the near infinite mealtime possibilities afforded by Hamburger Helper. Bonita, as usual, is in charge.

"We have a crack in the case, Mote."

Jimmy wants to build the excitement.

"Do we ever, Jon. Wait till you hear this. This is big. This is going to blow things wide open."

I'm my usual half step behind.

"Blow what wide open, Jimmy?"

"Why the Abby Wagner caper, of course. What else?"

What else, indeed. Although I see no reason for it, I can't fend off a little spurt of hope. Good news, perhaps, comes in Special packages.

Jimmy turns to the kid.

"Tell him what you saw, Don."

Don's CP hasn't yet strangled his speech.

"I saw him throw a shoe."

My heart bounces against my stomach.

"Who did you see throw a shoe?"

"Mr. Springer."

(Bonita inserts, "The bastard.")

"Where did you see him throw it?"

"Into the swamp."

Every bit of information I think I know about what happened that night rushes into my mind at the same time, collides, and falls to the ground stunned. Which is to say, business as usual.

"When did you see this, Don?"

"At night. I was watching him from my window up on the boy's wing. You know, my room on the second floor. I saw him walk out with a bag over to the edge of the swamp. I was supposed to be asleep, but I like to watch out my window. I like looking up at the stars and out at the swamp and just thinking about things. And I see Mr. Springer walk over to the swamp with this bag. And he pulls something out of the bag and he throws it in the swamp."

"And it was a shoe?"

"Well, Jimmy says it was a shoe. I don't know. Maybe it was a shoe. Jimmy says it was."

Jimmy is beaming.

"That right, Jon. I know about J.P.'s shoe and so I told Don about it. And so Mr. Springer was throwing J.P.'s shoe in the swamp."

I think they call that witness tampering, and it doesn't help, but I decide not to deflate Jimmy's always inflated bubble.

I've got one more really important question for Don.

"When did you see this, Don?"

"Like I said, at night."

"Which night? Do you remember which night you saw it?"

Alas, this does not compute.

"What do you mean? It was dark, like I said."

Night is night and night is dark and one night is like any other night for Don. But I'm fighting off feeling irrationally happy.

So, we've learned something extremely useful, but also extremely unusable. Don claims he saw a man in the dark throw something into the reeds. Not sure what it was. Under cross-examination, if it ever got to that, he would no doubt also have trouble establishing for certain *who* it was. And no idea *when* he saw it—except to say that it was dark.

Okay, so useless in a court of law, but absolutely revelatory in the court that's always in session in my mind. I am sure Don is right. It was Bo. And I am sure Jimmy is right. It was J.P.'s shoe. And I am sure Bonita is right. Bo is a bastard.

What I am not sure about is what to do with this information. Or how the scarf fits in. It wouldn't have been hard for him to get J.P.'s shoe. He had keys to all the buildings. He could have gotten it any number of times between Abby's disappearance and the second search when the shoe was found. The house is often empty when all the residents are away for the day.

But then there's the scarf, which undeniably belonged to Abby and undeniably was in J.P.'s photo album. And Cassandra has confirmed that Bo left New Directions by eight o'clock that night, right after their facilities meeting, two hours before Abby was dropped off at the main building.

All right, I've admitted all along that I'm slow on the uptake. I am to crime detection what Custer was to military planning. The fog is slowly lifting after the shock of Don's revelation. If Bo is a bastard, then perhaps Cassandra is a liar. She may be just a harmless piece of office tail to Bo, but maybe the relationship, hard as it is to believe, actually means a lot to her. (Specials aren't the only ones with challenges in relating to reality.) And perhaps, because of their relationship, she was willing to lie for him (and for herself).

(I love the R-word: Relationship. It's so usefully vague, so flexible, so noncommittal. "I am in a relationship." It implies intimacy and meaningfulness without requiring it. It states no more than that one person—or object—exists in association with another person or object. We both exist. We are in the same field of perception. Therefore, we are in relationship. Mercury is in relationship with the sun. So too is Pluto. Very different realities but covered by a single word. A relationship can begin in an instant and end even faster. Simply remove one of the two from the field of perception. End of relationship. It happens every day. It has happened more than once to me. A very useful word.)

I decide I have to ask Cassandra about her relationships. It's the absolutely last thing I would normally do. Relationships are filled with angst and emotions and sharing and recriminations and disappointments and hurt feelings and a hundred other things that alarm me. In short, expectations. Besides, it could easily get me fired. And I need the job.

But I think of J.P. sitting down there in St. Peter, wondering what he has done wrong, wondering why he is no longer with his friends, wondering when he gets to come home. And it gives me courage. In fact, it pisses me off, which is closely related. This is not the way things ought to be. It's not right. It's not fair. And this is one of the few times in my life when I perhaps can actually do something about right and fair and how things ought to be.

And so I determine to go to see Cassandra Pettigrew, Executive Director of New Directions, a facility for the developmentally disabled and the cognitively challenged, BSW, MSW, with a licensure in psychology emphasizing developmental pathologies.

TWENTY-NINE

I SCHEDULE MY APPOINTMENT with Cassandra for the end of the next workday. If it goes badly, we can both head for cover. Who knows, maybe me and my good buddy Bo can go out for drinks again.

Anyone could see in recent weeks that Cassandra is troubled. Like everyone else, I assumed it was from the stress of handling Abby's murder, followed hard by the lawsuit from Mr. Wagner. A lot was at stake. Of course she looked stressed.

But now I'm thinking that may not be the half of it. I'm thinking she knows more than she's saying about what happened that night. More than she's saying to the police, maybe more than she's admitting to herself. For J.P.'s sake, I've got to find out.

We meet in her office, she sitting at her specially ordered CEO-caliber desk. She is actually cordial, which I would prefer she weren't.

"What can I do for you, Jon?"

I am not capable of an Omaha Beach assault, so I start by telling her about visiting J.P. at St. Peter. She does not take it well, so I don't have to worry anymore about cordial.

"You went to see him at St. Peter? That was very inappropriate. Did you not think to ask me? Did you not consider the legal ramifications? Did you not consider that he is a former client who is the presumed murderer of another client?"

"Well, James—J.P.—is not just a client to me. He's a friend. I guess you could say we have a relationship."

"A relationship. Do you indeed. Well, that relationship is supposed to be a professional one. You are a paid member of a professional corporation providing disability services. The clients are not your friends. They are your responsibility. You have crossed a line, Mr. Mote."

It provides such a beautiful segue that I cannot resist.

"Well, I'm not the only one who has crossed a line, Ms. Pettigrew."

She is openly angry now.

"And what do you mean by that?"

"I mean I'm not the only one who has a relationship that might be considered unprofessional."

Anger immediately marries its companion—fear.

"I assume you have something more to say about that. Because if you don't, you can consider yourself terminated."

"Well, it's true that you can fire me. But then it's also true that I can get you fired as well."

I'm not sure if my threat holds water. Do people get fired anymore for something as petty as betraying a trust? Probably not. (It made the last President more popular than ever.) For most crimes against integrity these days, folks just declare themselves a victim of some illness beyond their control (the DSM is full of options), spend a month in treatment at an upscale facility, and come out to the applause of those who love a story of overcoming. An expensive but proven form of absolution. ("Treat me, Therapist, for I have been victimized.")

"Quit beating around the bush, Mote. State your claim or leave."

Sounds like Bonita.

"I'm talking about Bo."

Her face sags. But she is a strong woman and she keeps firing to the last bullet.

"What about Mr. Springer?"

"I know you're having an affair with him."

"And how do you know this—supposedly know this?"

"From multiple sources."

"And if it were true, which it isn't, so what? Why would that be any business of yours or anyone else's?"

This is where she has me dead to rights. No one in the modern world is going to worry much about an office affair at a place like New Directions. Even if I could get her fired, I would likely get fired myself—a common strategy in chess, but more problematic elsewhere. But if my hunch is right, it may push over a domino and then another and another, all the way to St. Peter.

"I think Detective Strauss should answer that 'so what?' question. I think he would be interested to know that Mr. Springer's claim to have left the office the night of the murder at 8 p.m. after your planning meeting can only be vouched for by a woman with whom he is having an affair, which might give her reason to be less than truthful about when Mr. Springer actually did leave the building."

"He left at eight, same as I did. He told me that himself."

"He told you that, but you didn't actually see him leave, did you? Because you left before he did."

I'm totally bluffing now. I even find myself sending up little prayers that I can pull this off.

"Why should I tell you anything about anything, Mr. Mote? Really, I think it's past time that you left my office."

Okay, time for the trump card, with fingers crossed that it really is a trump.

"You know who told me about your affair, Ms. Pettigrew? Bo told me about it. Over drinks after work. Said you were a little piece of office tail and that he was already bored with you and that it would be over soon."

She starts to shake.

"Does that sound like the kind of guy you want to protect? Does that sound like a guy you should lie for?"

She has her face in her hands now, elbows on her desk. She speaks in a whisper.

"Just leave, Jon. Please leave."

I suddenly feel terrible myself. My self-righteous indignation departs as quickly as it came.

"I would like to leave, Cassandra. I really would. But there's one more thing I have to tell you."

I know how dangerous saying this is for both of us.

"Someone saw Bo throwing J.P.'s shoe into the reeds. It was one of the residents, so it probably wouldn't hold up in court. But he saw it. I think Bo knows a lot more about what happened to Abby Wagner than he's saying. He set J.P. up to take the blame, and I'm starting to think we both know why. So I'm asking you to tell me—or tell the police—what happened that night between you and Bo. We need the truth, Cassandra. J.P. will die at St. Peter. J.P. needs the truth."

Silence. Then, after the longest time, she starts talking in a low, steady voice, like she's reading off a series of phone numbers.

"We actually did have a meeting scheduled for that night to talk about the budget for facilities. We often meet in the evenings, which is probably why we hooked up in the first place. He offered to buy me a drink at Lord Fletcher's one night after a meeting and the next thing I knew we were in bed together. My husband doesn't know and if he did he wouldn't care."

She stands up and starts walking around the room.

"We started drinking that night halfway through the meeting. Bo keeps scotch in a locked desk drawer. By the end of the meeting, he was feeling loose. I wasn't. He wanted to kiss and I indulged him a bit. Pretty soon he's, you could say, aroused. He wanted to have sex here in this office. Said he watches office sex on porn sites and it's a turn-on. I told him it's not a turn on for me, but he was insistent. 'Why the hell not?' he says. 'If you put out in a bedroom, why not in a boardroom?'"

That Bo, what a charmer.

"I was disgusted. I shoved him away and told him not to ever talk to me that way again. And then I left."

I don't want to seem like an interrogator, but I have one question I must ask.

"What time was that? It's important."

"It was eight o'clock. I looked at the clock in the hallway as I left."

"And Bo told you later that he left right after you did?"

"That's right."

"And he told the police the same."

"Yes."

"And you told the police that you did in fact see him leave at eight?"

"Yes. I just assumed . . ."

"But you didn't actually see him leave."

"No. I didn't."

I'd like to think that I'm really cooking now. That I'm making prog-ress. That J.P. is as good as back in his room looking over his photo album of friends, back on the bank by the highway looking for a Peterbilt 281. I've had the illusion of progress many times before in my life. But what is progress if life is repeated cycles around the same circle? If every movement forward is a move toward where you started? (Eternal return and all that.)

If I go to the police now, all I'll prove is that Cassandra lied to them, maybe. It will get her in trouble, but it won't prove that Bo isn't telling the truth about leaving at eight. It will only indicate that she can't confirm it. Bo can brazen it out, and brazen is something that comes easy to Bo.

So I decide I need to keep talking, and not just to myself. It seems simple enough, and it's very common, but I realize how new it is for me. First Sister Brigit, now Cassandra. Maybe it will become a habit. What have I got to lose?

But who should I talk to?

Why not Zillah? Why not Judy? Why not both of them?

I haven't talked to Zee since we drove to St. Peter to see J.P. a couple of weeks ago. I'd like to see her again anyway. And I'm a bit hopeful that she'd even like to see me again. And Judy. When Zee and I lived together, she sort of put up with seeing Judy. Now I think she maybe looks forward to it. They've formed a sort of Secret Society for the Rescue of the Dense, starting with the guy who once heard voices.

I call Zee and propose the three of us meet in front of the Fitzgerald Theater in St. Paul—named after a local storyteller, now the home of another storyteller of some repute. (Lake Wobegone—I sometimes find myself yearning for a corner seat at the Chatterbox Cafe.) She warms to the idea immediately.

Judy, of course, is all in.

"I would like . . . like that Jon. She is my sis . . . sister of mine, she is. And I love her very, very much."

Sister, is it? Judy is going to keep us a family in her world, no matter what the paperwork says.

We meet outside the Fitzgerald and walk together toward a Presbyterian church, then down Cedar Avenue. I'm looking for a place for coffee but we settle for ice cream instead and sit for a bit on a low wall fronting a little green space.

I decide to lay it all out for Zillah. She can't give me good advice if she hasn't got all the facts, if what I know even rises to the level of fact. (I got that "rises to the level" phrase from the President's enablers—it's a beaut.) I think maybe I shouldn't disclose everything in front of Judy, but she's so intent on keeping up with her melting ice cream cone, and so unskilled at the intricacies of linking cause and effect, that I decide her high esteem for the New Directions leadership is not threatened.

So I tell Zillah everything I think I know. I tell her what Bonita and Jimmy saw through Bo's office window, what Bo said about his and Cassandra's affair over drinks, what Cassandra said about the same in her office, what Don reported seeing from his bedroom, and about the known time-line of events on the night of the murder.

And I tell her I don't know what to do now.

And then I throw in that I've even prayed about it—a bit. Little tweets to God you might say. Asking for a little clarification, a little guidance, maybe even a little comfort.

"So what do you think, Zee?"

"If you're asking God to solve this, then I think you're more than a little desperate. On the other hand, you seem to be somewhat healthier these days, Jon. If re-inventing God is helping, I'm okay with it. Whatever works. Some people need the idea of God. I don't, but I'm less dogmatic about it than maybe I used to be."

I'm thinking, I need food and there is food. I need air and there is air. I probably need love and the word on the street (I cast a glance at my ice-cream-cone-licking sister) is that there is love. So why not let need be an argument *for* something rather than against it?

Judy pauses mid-lick.

"God is . . . I should say . . . God is good. And so is this ice . . . ice cream cone. I like . . . like them both."

Zillah laughs.

"God and ice cream. I won't speak a bad word about either one."

Judy continues.

"And, my brother of . . . of mine, J.P. did not hurt Abby. You know J.P. He would . . . would not do that, silly boy."

Yes, I know J.P. And I know that he wouldn't hurt anyone. But "know" is a slippery word, sister of mine. Sometimes know refers to things that are true and we can prove. But sometimes it refers to things that are true and that . . . well . . . we can't prove. Maybe it's okay that we can't prove the things we know when it comes to justice and love and, maybe even God . . . but it doesn't work that way in the lab or in the courtroom. It doesn't work that way for J.P. It doesn't work that way when it comes to murder.

Just as I'm disappearing inward again, Zillah calls me back.

"It's obvious, Jon. You've got to confront Bo directly. Bo is a fool. Fools hang themselves. Just give him a little rope."

THIRTY

"BO IS A FOOL. Fools hang themselves. Just give him a little rope." It's excellent advice. But like lots of excellent advice, it is much easier to give than to execute. I don't actually know much of anything for sure. It's all a stew of quasi-facts, subjective reports, conjectures, hypotheses, hunches, and more than a little hoping. There's that word again—hope. It's got to mean more than wishing. Otherwise I'm in trouble. As are we all.

But then I decide I must again show a little courage. A little heart. After all, how often does life give anyone much more than quasi-facts, subjective reports, conjectures, hypotheses, hunches, and hoping? It's the goddamn human condition. The "if you can't measure it, it's crap" fellows can live in their lab-coat bubble, but the rest of us have to go places where numbers can't take you. I say, if you *can* measure it, it's probably not all that important.

I recite all this to screw up my courage to talk to Bo. Not just talk to him—accuse him. "J'accuse, Monsieur Bo. You are a pig. No, that is an insult to pigs. You are a murderous, lying, self-pleasuring bro! And you are doing great harm to my friend, J.P.!"

Argh. I can't see this turning out well. I lack the imagination necessary for hope. Hope requires the ability to picture a desired future. I lost that in childhood. I'm trying to get it back, but it's going slowly. I have no trouble imagining things—it's getting to the desired part that gives me trouble.

But then I think of the people around me. What would Judy do? After invoking Jesus, of course, she would quote Sister Brigit and tell me you've got to do what's right. And what the hell would Bonita do? She'd kick Bo in the shins, if he was lucky, and threaten him with street justice. Consider the Specials—they neither toil nor spin, yet they show us how to live.

And so I try to be half as good as my friends and I purpose to confront Bo. Of course, I could just tell Detective Strauss everything. Let him sort it out. But Strauss has warned me to stay out of this. He would immediately raise the issue of Don's credibility, of my credibility for that matter, of anything I have to report being usable in a court of law. No, I will have to get more on Bo than Don's story. I will have to get Bo to tell the story himself . . . somehow.

It will take some planning, but it has to be soon. I don't know what Cassandra is going to do with the information I gave her yesterday about Bo. Maybe she'll go to the police. Maybe she'll warn Bo, who may figure I'm his biggest living threat, with an emphasis on living. Maybe she won't do anything. But the longer this drags out, the better the chance that J.P. fades to black in St. Peter.

Stranger as I am to planning, I'm glad when I learn that fate or coincidence or the Holy Ghost (I had mixed feelings about that name as a kid) has worked to arrange there to be a meeting of the New Directions board tomorrow night. I definitely want to confront Bo after hours. The board meetings are usually over by nine. Bo will probably go back to his office afterwards. I'll be there waiting for him, like a pussycat stalking a rhino.

I'm nervous as hell when I arrive at the group home for the evening shift. Judy picks up on it immediately.

"Are you o . . . o . . . okay, Jon?"

Ah, the great existential question, covering everything from "how do you feel at this moment?" to "is it well with your soul?" to "are you ready to meet your Maker?"

"Yes and no, Judy. Yes and no."

While she ponders that dialectical collision, I work on how to maintain my resolve for the next couple of hours until the board meeting is over. When the time finally comes, I hope to be as resolved as Caesar at the bank of the Rubicon.

I'm not too worried about leaving the residents while I do battle with Bo. They are often on their own at one time or another. But to keep them occupied, I put in a tape of, what else, *The Wizard of Oz*. It seems fitting. I'm the scarecrow (no brains), the cowardly lion (no courage), and the tin man (suspect heart) all rolled into one. Where, oh where, is the Wizard when I need him?

"I've got to go over to the main building for a few minutes, guys. You watch the movie, and when I get back I'll make some popcorn for us."

Jimmy reassures me.

"I'll keep an eye on everyone, Jon."

Bonita points a fist toward him without diverting her gaze from Auntie Em.

"Keep an eye on this, cat litter."

Judy shakes her head and sighs.

I get a jolt as I walk toward the main building. The board meeting seems to have ended early. People are getting in their cars and pulling away. I'm afraid Bo might be one of the first to go, given his fondness for refreshment after any prolonged effort. If I miss him now, I may never get back to this point again. I have a history of missing pregnant moments. (Drop that pass in the Super Bowl, Jackie, and you may never get another one like it.)

Once inside the building I come across Cassandra locking her office. I haven't seen her since I confronted her about Bo. We exchange a few words. She's not happy to see me, but she's civil.

Then I'm off around the corner to Bo's office. He's just coming out, closing the door behind him. I have no opening line, so I default to movie dialogue.

"We gotta talk, Bo. Now."

He holds up his part.

"What's this about, Mote? I got things to do."

I point toward his office door. He opens it, studying my face. We walk inside. He remains standing and doesn't invite me to sit down. I look at the door to the small conference room off his office and see that it's cracked open.

"Okay, talk."

I am fresh out of indirections, so I just say it.

"I don't think J.P. killed Abby Wagner."

Bo laughs. Not a happy laugh.

"So why are you telling me? The rest of the world knows he killed her, so it really doesn't matter what you think about it, does it? Is that all? I'm not really in the mood to play Cato to your Inspector Clouseau."

And I thought Bo was ignorant of high culture.

"I mean really, Mote. Don't you think finding James's shoe near where the body was found is maybe a clue? Huh? Or the scarf in the photo album? The cops seemed pretty impressed with that."

"Well, about that shoe. I've been thinking about it."

"Don't strain yourself, Mote."

"Abby was murdered in late June. The ground out in the reeds was still damp, even a little muddy."

"And the dish ran away with the spoon. What's your point?"

"And Abby's clothes, I'm told, were muddy."

"And?"

"And that shoe—the one we found the day we did the second search— it wasn't muddy at all. It was very clean in fact. Like new, because those shoes were new. I bought them with J.P. myself just a few weeks earlier. And the shoe was hanging in the reeds at least two feet off the ground."

Bo is getting pissed.

"Last time, Mote. Your point?"

"My point, Bo, is that whoever put Abby's body in the reeds was not wearing that shoe. It would have been dirty. It wouldn't have been hanging two feet off the ground."

"And you're telling me this instead of the cops because . . . ?"

"Because I think you know more about that shoe than you're saying."

There it is, a straight-out assertion. An unambiguous accusation. I'm surprised at how good it feels, at how calm I am. Bo is less calm.

"What the hell are you saying, Mote? Are you saying I'm covering something up? Why would I want to cover anything up? Why would I want to pin anything on J.P.?"

I'm thinking Bo is primed. Getting him pissed is almost as good as getting him drunk. Zillah is right. He *is* a fool. Now is the time to hand him some rope.

"Maybe because you're the one who put Abby's body in the reeds, Bo."

Bo's eyes narrow. He walks up close and starts punctuating my sternum with his index finger.

"Listen carefully, Mote. You are going places you do not want to go. On the night of the murder I left this place at 8 p.m., two hours before she got dropped off. Cassie confirmed that to the cops because she was here when I left. I never saw that shoe until Jackson found it. If you saw it before when you bought the shoes with J.P., then maybe you're the one who put it in the reeds. You were working at the group home that night. Maybe you're the one who needs as good an alibi as I've got."

He has a point, but I'm in too far to let facts get in the way.

"I know someone who saw you throw the shoe in the reeds, Bo. An eyewitness."

Bo stops thumping my chest and steps back. He's thinking hard, not common practice for a bro.

"Not possible. Nobody saw me throw that shoe in the marsh."

He hesitates.

"Because I didn't throw any shoe in the marsh."

We look at each other for a moment.

"Like I said, I left here at eight. Cassie verifies it. I wasn't here when that girl died. So I couldn't have thrown any shoe in the marsh."

"I didn't say you did it the night of the murder. I only said someone saw you throw the shoe in the marsh."

Bo smiles.

"It's one of the retards, isn't it. Your precious source is a retard, isn't it?"

He laughs disdainfully.

"And how impressed will the police be with that? A mental defective says he sees me throwing a shoe in the marsh in the dark and that proves I'm the killer. That's rich, Mote."

"I didn't say it was dark. How did you know it was in the dark?"

Bo deflects the question and returns to his vomit.

"Dark or no dark, mud or no mud. Who gives a shit, Mote? J.P. killed Abby Wagner. The evidence is undeniable. I wasn't here when it happened. That's a fact . . . "

I cut him short.

"Is it a fact, Bo? Is it a real, factual, no-possibility-of-being-wrong fact? Or is it just what you say?"

"Talk to Cassie."

"I did talk to her. She says *she* left here at eight that night. She says you were still here when she left. She says you were drunk and that you wanted to have sex. She says she refused and you were more than a little angry. She says she didn't actually see you leave."

"The bitch. What a bitch. What a fuckin' little bitch. I was a fool to waste my time with middle-age snatch like that."

(Zillah's a prophet.)

Bo's eyes look unfocused. I'm moving onto increasingly thin ice, but figure if I keep skating fast enough I may get to the other side.

"By the time Abby came by your office window you were angry, frustrated, and drunk. You saw her and knocked on the window and motioned her to come in. You offered her something to drink. Eventually you forced her to have sex with you. Something went wrong. You panicked. You didn't know what to do. Maybe it was an accident. But her neck got broken and she was in your office and she was dead. And the only thing you could think of to do was to put her in the marsh and figure things out later."

Bo gives no indication that he's heard any of this. He's turned his back to me and is looking out the window into the darkness.

"Wasn't it something like that, Bo?"

It's silent. My heart is pounding now. I don't know if he's going to offer a confession or produce a gun. He serves up sarcasm instead of either.

"Something like that, Mote. Since you're so close, I'll fill in a few details for you. Because it won't matter. Maybe Cassie will take back her statement that she saw me leave at eight, but she'll get fired if she does. I'll still say that I left a few minutes after she did. No one can prove I didn't.

"And maybe you do have someone who saw someone throw a shoe in the marsh, but I know your star witness was a retard and I know it was dark and I know that any lawyer would welcome the chance to tie a retard in knots on the witness stand, and the police would see to it that it never got that far. So I'm still bulletproof and you know it.

"But since you get so much pleasure out of figuring things out, Detective Boy, let me give you a little tickle. I didn't knock on the window—she did. And I didn't wave her in. She came in on her own. And, yes, we did have a few drinks."

I'm thinking I'm glad his little bro brain hasn't considered the possibility of his having left DNA.

"But that's where your story goes seriously wrong, Mote. I didn't force her to do anything. The sex was her idea. She's a slut you know. Everyone knows she's a slut."

"I think the term is 'vulnerable,' Bo. She was a vulnerable adult."

"Call her whatever you want. Maybe she was a brain-damaged slut, but she was still a slut."

I don't want to interrupt his story, so I don't reply.

"She puts her hand on my thigh and starts rubbing it. I push her hand away and tell her to stop but she doesn't stop. And then she starts unbuttoning her blouse. I don't want to arouse you too much, Mote, so I'll cut to the chase. We do have sex, right in that conference room through that door, because there aren't any windows in there."

He points at the cracked door that connects the conference room to his office.

"And while we're in the middle of it she starts laughing, and she starts singing this little ditty, 'Bo is my boyfriend, my boyfriend, my boyfriend. Bo is my boyfriend, and everyone will know.'

"I tell her to stop but she just laughs and starts singing it louder, 'Bo is my boyfriend, my boyfriend, my boyfriend. Bo is my boyfriend, and everyone will know.' I try putting my hand over her mouth but she bites me, hard. So I pushed her. Not very hard, just enough to make her stop biting me, okay? But she falls back and hits the back of her neck on the edge of the conference table."

Bo is reliving it now and he's talking louder and in an angry rush.

"And I can tell in seconds that she's dead—her eyes are open and she's staring, but she doesn't respond when I shake her. She just stares and stares."

He pauses, coming back to the present.

"So, yes, I put her body in the marsh. It was an accident. I didn't mean to hurt her. She was the one who started it. And when I came back to the office, her scarf was on the floor. So I took it home with me. And the next day, when your place was empty, I went in and got one of J.P.'s shoes. I'd figured out a plan. But before I could put the shoe near the body, they'd found her and so I had to wait. So I waited until things cooled off a bit, then I threw the shoe into the marsh near where they found the body and I put the scarf in J.P.'s photo album. And I organized a search. And things went off just like I planned."

He's quietly belligerent now, but mostly happy with himself.

"Don't expect me to feel guilty about any of this, Mote. It was a complete accident. I didn't murder anyone. I was just there when an accident happened. If it wasn't that I knew I'd get fired for having sex with that woman, Wagner, I would have told the police what happened. It's not my fault that everyone is so uptight about sex. Sex is normal, you know."

"And what about J.P.?"

He laughs again.

"J.P. is too damaged to care. Most of these people are mistakes that should have been corrected before they got here. The rest of them are unlucky."

"Like Abby."

"Yes, like Abby. Sorry about her drunk father scrambling her brain in that car wreck. But that's not my fault."

"And this confession of yours?"

"Not a confession, Mote. A description. I told you what happened just for the hell of it. I'll deny this conversation ever happened. Trot out all the retards you want to say whatever they want. Who's going to believe them?"

The door to the conference room opens.

"I'm going to believe them, Mr. Springer."

It's Cassandra. When I ran into her in the hall, I told her what I was going to do. I asked her to quietly use the hallway door into the conference room adjoining Bo's office so that she could hear what he had to say. I didn't know whether she would do it or not. But here she is.

"I'm going to believe them, Bo. But more importantly, I'm going to believe you. I am going to believe everything you've just described. I'm going to take it for the truth, because I think it is the truth. All except the part about it not being your fault. And about Abby being a slut. I don't think those things are true. But I do believe the rest, and I think the police will be much more interested in this story than you seem to think."

Bo suddenly looks like a little boy.

"Cassie. Listen. Cassie. I just made all that up for Mote here. None of it's true. I'm just bullshitting Mote."

"That's the problem with middle-aged bitches like me, Bo. We tend to believe what people tell us."

Bo turns on a dime from penitential to aggressive.

"Well, fuck you both. I'm out of here."

He gives me a shove as he heads for the door. He swings it open and there stand the residents—Bonita, Jimmy, Ralph, Judy, and, at the back, Billy. They have followed their Dorothy all the way to the fortress of the Wicked Witch.

Bo pauses briefly, then begins to push his way through them.

"Out of my way, retards."

They fall back, but as he passes, Bonita reaches out a foot. Bo trips and stumbles into the arms of Ralph, who squeezes him like a toddler squeezing a favorite rag doll. Bo exhales loudly and Ralph drops him on the floor. Then Ralph and Bonita and Jimmy all plop down on Bo's prone body, like the Three Wise Men riding on a single camel.

Judy leans down and speaks into his face.

"You are not . . . I should say . . . not a good person."

Billy is spinning slowly around, eyes upward, arms akimbo, both hissing and humming.

THIRTY-ONE

THE POLICE WERE VERY interested in what Cassandra had to say. They also want to talk to me again. Bo hasn't been back to New Directions and never will be. He hasn't been indicted yet, but if they have DNA evidence, like the private investigator said, then I think he has some splainin' to do. Stuart Wagner is confused. There's a lot, as usual, that I don't know.

What I do know is that J.P. is coming home. Today in fact. The people who sent him to St. Peter were hesitant to bring him back because they said no one else had been convicted of the crime. But the activists—God bless 'em—got involved and insisted on J.P.'s rights, such as they are in a society that gives rights and takes them away depending on the breeze.

There's an excited buzz in the group home in anticipation of J.P.'s return. The folks are still talking about "The Capture of Bo Springer, Public Enemy Number One"—to use Jimmy's line. He has told and retold the story dozens of times to anyone who will listen, to some who don't want to, and to a few, like Billy, who can't process it at all.

"When Jon went over to the main building and left us watching the Oz, I knew something was up, see. So I says, 'Something's up.' And we all followed him over to the main building. But we didn't let him see us, see. We were going 'income neat-o.' (That means invisible.) We wanted to see what was up, and I figured Jon might need our help. Bonita wanted to watch the Oz, but Judy told her, 'My brother of mine, Bonita, needs . . . I should say . . . needs our help.' That's how Judy talks. It's okay, we all have our problems, don't we? Anyway, Bonita comes along with us, which is good, because she's the one that bags the bad guy—Mr. Springer. Well, we all do it together, but she strikes first."

Jimmy goes on to explain how they heard the argument going on behind Bo's office door and how Bo came out and tried to push them out of the way, but Bonita trips him and Ralph squeezes him and everyone sits on him. Jimmy calls it a "take down," borrowed from television wrestling, of which he is a big fan. The whole event has already moved well beyond history to legend and needs only the passage of time to become myth.

We get a phone call from the main building saying that J.P. will be here in fifteen minutes and that he'll be dropped off directly at the house, apparently by the same guys who picked him up. We decide to go outside and wait so we can see J.P. coming in the distance, the return of the Prodigal Special you might say.

Actually, I've decided to stop using that term. I was convicted a bit by some reading I was doing and I've adapted it: "I no longer call you Specials—I call you friends." It's a little sappy, but true. We're all Specials, and we're all Normals. In fact, being a bit wounded here or there is about as normal as you can get. I can do some things they can't, but they sure as hell are better at plenty of other things—such as taking themselves and each other as they find themselves. And thinking that making it to bedtime makes the day a success. And cutting other people slack. (Okay, Bonita doesn't cut anyone slack, but she's one heck of a force for payback justice.)

I've even learned a few things from putting salve on Billy's butt. At first it was disgusting, but then I found myself taking satisfaction in watching the ulcer heal. It changed my attitude toward Billy. And toward myself. I realized that Billy needed someone, needed *me*. I began to think of my-self, in a small way, as a healer. It was a new thought. Someone else was better because of me, and realizing this made me better, too. It was a sort of epiphany—not a modern-times Good Samaritan, but not useless either. One Special helping another.

You can see I haven't completely moved past using the term Specials. It's a useful term and it still floats through my head. But for the most part I try to follow the nuns' lead—and my parents'—and call them by name: Billy, Ralph, Jimmy, Bonita, J.P., and Judy. I don't pretend they're just like everybody else; I just remind myself that *nobody* is like everybody else, least of all me.

Things are not the way they ought to be, that's for sure. Not with them, not with me. The gap is not closed, but maybe it has shrunk a bit.

I don't mind pointing out that I'm on something of a roll. I've gone nearly nine months now with no voices. I'm seeing Zillah again with some regularity. We've gotten to the point of enjoying each other's company, which is enough for now. I know I've got to get a better paying job of some kind, but not one that will keep me from seeing Judy and the other folks who have been helping me.

Something will turn up. Believing so feels almost like optimism, that thinner cousin of hope.

"There . . . there . . . I should say . . . there he is!"

Judy spots a van turning into our road. It's J.P.! Kill the fatted calf! Let the party begin!

We are, in fact, in our party best. Mrs. Francis from crafts has provided us pointed party hats with elastic chinstraps. Also kazoo noisemakers with streamers attached. And confetti. Billy's hat has slipped onto his forehead, making him look like a red-headed unicorn, but his humming tells me he's happy. All of us look ridiculous, which we human beings are and do well to recognize.

J.P. gets out of the car, wearing his hesitant smile. Everyone gathers around and throws confetti. Judy hugs him. Even the St. Peter delivery guys are smiling.

Jimmy calls out, "Speech, speech."

Nobody really knows what that means, including Jimmy, but it quiets the celebration for a moment. J.P. clears his throat.

"Um, um. Well, I had a nice trip. But it's good to be back with my friends."

He looks at me as though to ask whether that was the right thing to say. I give him a thumbs-up. You go, J.P. You go, brother.

I'm about to herd everyone inside for some cake that the kitchen staff has provided when I see Sam Raven walking over from the main building. He's waving his hand like he wants to get our attention, so I hold everybody up until he gets to us.

"Just a second, Jon. There's a guy just pulled into the parking lot in a big semi. An eighteen-wheeler."

"And?"

"He's asking for J.P."

—The End—

CPSIA information can be obtained
at www.ICGtesting.com
Printed in the USA
BVOW03*1824030118
504385BV00001B/3/P